DEAD ₵OIN

Novels By Sheldon Siegel

Mike Daley/Rosie Fernandez Novels
Special Circumstances
Incriminating Evidence
Criminal Intent
Final Verdict
The Confession
Judgment Day
Perfect Alibi
Felony Murder Rule
Serve and Protect
Hot Shot
The Dreamer
Final Out
Last Call
Double Jeopardy
Dead Coin

David Gold/A.C. Battle Novels
The Terrorist Next Door

DEAD
COIN

A MIKE DALEY/ROSIE FERNANDEZ THRILLER

SHELDON SIEGEL

Sheldon M. Siegel, Inc.

Cover Design by Linda Siegel

ISBN: 978-1-952612-15-2 E-Book

ISBN: 978-1-952612-16-9 Paperback

ISBN: 978-1-952612-17-6 Hardcover

"A city is where you can sign a petition, boo the chief justice, fish off a pier, gaze at a hippopotamus, buy a flower at the corner, or get a good hamburger or a bad girl at 4 a.m.

A city is where sirens make white streaks of sound in the sky and foghorns speak in dark grays. San Francisco is such a city."

— Herb Caen, *San Francisco: City on Golden Hills*

1

"BEDAZZLE YOURSELF"

The Honorable Elizabeth McDaniel took a deep breath of the heavy air in her stuffy courtroom on the second floor of San Francisco's crumbling Hall of Justice at eleven-fifty AM on Tuesday, September sixth, 2022. "Nice to finally see you in person again, Mr. Daley."

I nodded respectfully. "Thank you, Your Honor. It's nice to see you, too. It's good to be back in court. It's been a long time."

After two and a half years of handling most of her duties on Zoom during San Francisco's seemingly interminable Covid winter, Betsy McDaniel was finally back in the courtroom that she had run with the efficiency of a Swiss train for almost thirty years. She had gone on senior status a few years ago to teach criminal procedure at Hastings Law School, travel with her grandchildren, and take pre-dawn Pilates classes at an upscale gym around the corner from her refurbished Victorian in Noe Valley. She couldn't bring herself to retire completely, so she sat in for her colleagues from time to time at arraignments, preliminary hearings, and motions.

She tugged at her shoulder-length auburn hair and spoke in a voice that still bore a trace of her native Alabama. "Why are we here, Mr. Daley?"

"To discuss a motion to modify the terms of my client's probation."

"I don't understand why the co-head of the Felony Division of the Public Defender's Office believes that it is an appropriate use of this court's time to reconsider a matter that I resolved last week."

This isn't starting well. "I will explain, Your Honor."

She glanced at her watch. "I have a luncheon engagement in eight minutes."

"I'll be brief."

I scanned the empty gallery where the retirees, homeless people, courtroom junkies, and other hangers-on had already departed to get in line at the few remaining sandwich shops across Bryant Street. The Hall of Justice was finally coming back to life after Covid restrictions were lifted. The sixties-era edifice that was touted as a state-of-the-art facility when it replaced the old Hall of Justice in Chinatown had long since passed its enjoy-by date. The courtrooms were still operational, the Homicide Detail was still ensconced on the third floor, and you could still pay for your parking tickets in the lobby. However, the District Attorney, the Public Defender, the Southern Police Station, the Medical Examiner, and most of the administrative staff had moved to other buildings with functional plumbing. The old jail on the sixth and seventh floors had been mothballed and replaced by a newer building next door, and the cafeteria in the basement was a distant and not-so-pleasant memory. From time to time, the political class engages in discussions about replacing the obsolete monolith and its asbestos-laden walls, lead-based paint, and antiquated ventilation. Then again, those conversations have been happening since I first entered this building as a rookie Deputy PD almost thirty years ago. For now, plans for a new facility are on hold.

Judge McDaniel removed her reading glasses. "I don't see your client, Mr. Daley."

She isn't here. "She's on her way, Your Honor. She'll be here momentarily." *At least I hope so.*

"You've appeared in my courtroom more times than I can count. An experienced defense attorney such as yourself understands that I expect people to be on time."

"I do, and I'm sorry. Ms. Diamond's prior appointment ran late."

She tapped her watch. "It's eleven-fifty-eight, Mr. Daley. Your client has two minutes."

"Understood."

Judge McDaniel put on her reading glasses and typed away at her computer. I turned around and looked at the door, hoping that it would open. I watched the second hand on the clock wind its way around. At five seconds before noon, the door swung open, and my client marched down the aisle and took her place next to me at the defense table.

"Sorry I'm late," she whispered.

I pointed at the judge. "I need you to apologize to her—right now." I turned to Judge McDaniel. "Your Honor, Ms. Diamond is here, and she wishes to apologize."

"Yes, Ms. Diamond?"

Debra "Dazzle" Diamond spoke in a confident voice, indicating that this wasn't her first time in court. "I'm very sorry, Your Honor."

"Thank you. Please try to be more punctual next time."

"Yes, Your Honor."

I addressed the judge in a deferential voice. "May I have a quick word with my client?"

"You may."

I pulled Dazzle aside, looked at her heavy makeup, sequined top, and leopard-spotted yoga pants. "I asked you to dress professionally."

"Sorry, Mike. I have to go straight to work when we're finished."

"I've already explained to you that this is a long shot."

"Understood."

"Let me do the talking."

Her full lips transformed into a pout. "Okay."

I heard the judge's voice behind me. "Mr. Daley?"

"Yes, Your Honor." *Here goes.* "As you know, Ms. Diamond recently pled guilty to a charge of misdemeanor theft. In exchange for a suspended jail sentence, she agreed to make full restitution. Your Honor placed her on probation for a period of six months, subject to the condition that she would remain employed, forfeit her passport, stay in the Bay Area, have weekly check-ins with her probation officer, and wear an ankle monitor."

"It was only a week ago, Mr. Daley. I am well aware of the conditions regarding Ms. Diamond's plea agreement. Why are we here?"

"One of the terms of her probation is making it difficult for Ms. Diamond to perform her job. As a result, it is more challenging for her to earn a living and fulfill her obligation to make restitution."

"Which term is that?"

"The requirement that she wear an ankle bracelet."

Judge McDaniel's Alabama accent became more pronounced. "Are you serious?"

"Yes, Your Honor."

A rookie Assistant DA sitting at the prosecution table stood up and spoke. "We object, Your Honor. We resolved this matter last week."

Yes, we did.

"Thank you," the judge said to him. "I'll let you know if I need anything more from you." She turned back to me. "You're down to thirty seconds. Give me your best argument, Mr. Daley."

"As you know, Ms. Diamond is an entertainer."

"I'm well aware of that."

There's a little more to the story. Dazzle was a pole dancer at the Gold Club, an upscale strip joint down the block from Moscone Center in San Francisco's gentrifying South-of-Market tech gulch between Union Square and the ballpark. The formerly scuzzy Gold Club now caters to the tech bros who work in the adjacent office towers and live in the nearby condos that used to be skid row. Dazzle was a single mother, a Daly City native, and a San Francisco State alum who once worked as a paralegal for a big law firm. When she was laid off during the economic downturn in 2008, she started dancing and doubled her salary. From time to time, she supplemented her income by helping herself to extra gratuities from her customers' wallets while they were distracted by her dancing skills. Her most recent theft was caught by her customer, who pressed charges. In addition to cutting a deal with the prosecutors, Dazzle persuaded her boss (who also happened to be her boyfriend) to let her keep her job if she promised not to do it again.

"Your Honor," I said, "Ms. Diamond has found it difficult to perform her dance routines with an ankle monitor. It's harder for her to keep her balance, and she has almost injured herself several times."

Judge McDaniel's eyes darted to Dazzle, who responded with a solemn nod.

I kept talking. "Moreover, Ms. Diamond's tips have been lower because the audience members do not seem to be as, uh, engaged with her performance."

The judge looked at Dazzle again. "Is this true, Ms. Diamond?"

"Yes, Your Honor. The ankle monitor is distracting."

Judge McDaniel arched her right eyebrow. "I didn't realize that your customers focused on your ankle, Ms. Diamond."

Neither did I.

Dazzle didn't fluster. "You'd be surprised, Your Honor."

"Yes, I would." The judge turned back to me. "What are you requesting, Mr. Daley?"

"That Ms. Diamond be allowed to remove the ankle monitor while she is performing."

"Denied."

"But, Your Honor—,"

She stopped me with an upraised hand. "Denied."

I figured that was coming. I started packing my briefcase when I heard Dazzle's voice.

"Your Honor?" she said.

Oh crap. I leaned over and whispered, "Let it go, Dazzle. We're done."

"No, we're not." She looked at the judge. "Your Honor, my act requires me to bedazzle the audience. I can't do that with this thing on my ankle."

"I've been told that you're an exceptional dancer."

"I like to think so, but the monitor is ugly."

"Perhaps you could decorate it to match your costume."

"I don't wear a costume for most of my performance."

That's true.

Betsy McDaniel chuckled. "Bedazzle yourself, Ms. Diamond. Your motion is denied, and we are adjourned." She didn't wait for a response before she headed to her chambers.

I turned to Dazzle, who was still standing next to me. "Sorry. I tried."

"You gave it your best shot, Mike. I'll figure out a way to work around it."

"Try to stay out of trouble, okay?"

"I'll do my best." She flashed the radiant smile that a generation of horny young tech nerds found irresistible. "You should come down to the club and see the show. I can get you free passes and drink coupons. You'll like the buffet."

Not a chance, although I have it on good authority that the chicken on the lunch buffet isn't bad. "Thanks, Dazzle. I'll let you know."

I was sweating through my shirt as I walked down the sauna-like corridor of the Public Defender's Office at one-fifteen that same afternoon. Twenty years ago, we moved into a refurbished auto body shop on Seventh Street. At the time, it was a substantial upgrade from our cramped old digs a half-block north in the Hall of Justice. Nowadays, our "new" facility has unreliable plumbing, a temperamental heating system, scuffed walls, and frayed turquoise carpet held together with duct tape.

As I approached my workmanlike office, I was met by the broad smile of Terrence "The Terminator" Love, my one-time client, and current secretary, executive assistant, process server, occasional bodyguard, and friend. The six-foot-six-inch, three-hundred-pound former heavyweight boxer and retired shoplifter was sitting in his cubicle outside my office.

"Were you able to persuade Judge McDaniel to modify Dazzle's probation?" he asked.

"Afraid not, T. She's going to have to keep dancing with the ankle monitor."

"She'll adapt. Was she pissed off?"

"Not really. She knew that it was a long shot." I winked. "She offered me free passes and drink coupons at the Gold Club. Are you interested?"

"I don't do that stuff anymore."

"Neither do I."

He arched an eyebrow. "Did you ever?"

"It's been a long time."

"You didn't go to strip clubs when you were a priest, did you?"

"Absolutely not."

I was a priest for three years at St. Anne's Parish in the Sunset. I decided to go to the seminary after my older brother died in Vietnam, and I was looking for answers. I enjoyed the spiritual and intellectual nature of the job, but I never felt qualified to save souls, and I was terrible at church politics. I threw in the towel and decided to go to law school, much to the chagrin of my father, a San Francisco beat cop who liked having a priest in the family. I still go to church every Sunday, but I like being a Public Defender a lot better. I don't try to save souls anymore, but on occasion I save lives.

Terrence let out a throaty chuckle. He had just turned sixty, the same age as I am. His boxing career ended after a handful of fights because he had a soft jaw and was too good-hearted to hit anybody too hard. The recovering alcoholic was my very first client when I was a baby PD. A decade ago, I hired him as the receptionist at the two-person law firm that my ex-wife and I were running at the time. It was part of a probation agreement that I had brokered with none other than Judge McDaniel. Everything worked out pretty well. My ex-wife was now San Francisco's Public Defender and my boss. Terrence hadn't touched a drop of booze ever since. He became indispensable to our practice, and we brought him with us when we moved back to the PD's Office.

"Anything I need to know?" I asked him.

"My retirement paperwork came in. Can you help me go through it?"

"Sure." I grinned. "You aren't really going to retire at the end of the year, are you?"

"Thinking about it."

"Can I persuade you to stay another year or two?"

"I have a new granddaughter on the way. I'd like to spend some time with her. Besides, I thought you were going to retire at the end of next year."

I pointed at the closed door to the PD's Office. "Depends on whether the boss decides to run for another term. I promised to stick around if she does."

"I thought that she was leaning against it."

"She's having second thoughts. What will it take to get you to stay?"

"Let me think about it."

"Anything else I need to know?"

"The boss needs to see you."

"Did she say what it's about?"

"She needs you to pick up some cases. One of them is a murder trial."

2

"GOOD NEWS AND BAD NEWS"

I knocked on the open door of the office next to mine. "You wanted to see me?"

"Yes." The Public Defender of the City and County of San Francisco looked up from her laptop and waved me in. "I heard that you weren't able to get Dazzle's probation changed."

"You can't win them all." *If you're a Public Defender, you lose a lot more than you win.*

I took a seat in the chair opposite the mahogany desk that she had bought on her own dime. Her window was caked in dirt. The walls were covered with photos of local politicians and awards. Her bookcases held dusty case reporters that she hadn't opened in years. If she needed a citation, she looked it up online. Framed photos of our two children were displayed in a prominent spot on her credenza between stacks of files.

"How did Dazzle take the news?" she asked.

"Not bad." I grinned. "On the bright side, she offered us free passes to the Gold Club."

Rosita Carmela Fernandez flashed the magnificent smile that I still found irresistible almost three decades after we'd met in the file room of the old PD's Office and twenty-seven years after we'd gotten divorced. "Pass."

She tugged at the sleeve of her Dior blouse—an upgrade from the days when she wore faded jeans and denim work shirts to the office when we were young Deputy Public Defenders. At fifty-six, her jet-black hair no longer fell to her waist. Nowadays, it was cut into a stylish bob. A regimen of Pilates, spin classes, and aerobics kept her fit. Her voice was a little raspier, and she measured her words a little more carefully after surviving two tumultuous election campaigns in San Francisco's chaotic political system that our City Attorney once described as "like being in a knife fight in a phone booth."

"Everybody okay?" I asked. We had reached the age where every conversation began with a check-in on Rosie's eighty-seven-year-old mother and our two twenty-something children.

"Fine," she said. "Mama's arthritis is acting up, but the new pills seem to be working. Grace is wrapping up a movie. Tommy likes his classes."

So far, so good. Rosie and I had met when I was a rookie PD, and she had just been promoted to the Felony Division. She had spun out of a brief and unsatisfying marriage to a law school classmate. Our daughter, Grace, was born a year later. The demands of a baby, our jobs, and a new marriage collided, and Rosie and I called things off when Grace was two. Nowadays, Grace was a USC film school alum and a production supervisor at Pixar. She lived across the Bay in Emeryville with her fiancé, Chuck. Our son, Tommy (named after my dad), was a junior at Cal, my undergrad and law school alma mater. He came along a few years after Rosie and I split up. We refer to our relationship as "ex-spouses-with-benefits."

"Anything new on the wedding?" I asked.

"Nothing at the moment," Rosie said. "All systems are go."

Good. Grace and Chuck had been engaged for almost three years. We had postponed their wedding twice because of Covid. We're scheduled to give it another try in December.

After the divorce, I spent five years working at a big law firm at the top of the Bank of America Building to pay the bills, alimony, and child support. Rosie started her own criminal defense practice and took me in after I was fired for not bringing in enough clients. We'd been working together ever since—first at our two-person firm around the corner from the old Transbay Bus Terminal, and, more recently, back here at the PD's Office. We were co-heads of the Felony Division for a few years before Rosie ran for PD.

Time for business. "Terrence said that you wanted to see me."

Her expression turned serious. "How's your time?"

"I can tear myself away from my administrative responsibilities if you need help."

As co-head of the Felony Division, I spent most of my time working on budgets, assigning cases, supervising younger lawyers, and handling bureaucratic matters. Once or twice a year, I stepped in and worked on a trial.

"I need you to take over Rolanda's cases," she said.

Uh-oh. "Is she okay?"

"Yes." She lowered her voice. "Good news and bad news. The good news is that she's fine. The bad news is that some of her blood work is a little off and her blood pressure is up, so the doctor wants her to go on bed rest until the baby arrives."

Rolanda Fernandez shared the leadership of the Felony Division with me. She was also Rosie's niece and, I suppose, my ex-niece. Like Rosie, Rolanda graduated from Mercy High School, San Francisco State, and Hastings Law School. She and her husband, Zach, yet another lawyer, were the proud parents of Maria Sylvia Teresa Fernandez Epstein, an energetic two-year-old. Rolanda was on maternity leave when Covid hit, and she had worked primarily from home since then. She was six months pregnant with their second child, who was due in December.

"Whatever you need," I said.

"Good." Rosie eyed me. "You're going to have to take the lead on the Jones trial."

"Fine."

Our client, Reggie Jones, was a homeless man who lived under an overpass leading to the new Salesforce Transit Center. In March, he was charged with killing a crypto entrepreneur during a botched robbery in Salesforce Park, the upscale urban oasis on the fourth deck of the Transit Center. According to the cops, Reggie got into a fight with the decedent, Tyson Gore, who was walking through the park on his way to his multimillion-dollar condo across the street in the swanky Millennium Tower. Reggie allegedly pushed Gore over a railing and into a construction zone four levels below. Reggie claimed that he passed out from a night of drinking and didn't attack Gore. Gore's wallet was found in the bushes where Reggie was sleeping.

She eyed me. "Trial starts in three weeks."

"I'll request a delay."

"Reggie wants to move forward. Rolanda has everything ready to go. She's available on Zoom and will get you up to speed. Nady is second chair."

Excellent. Nadezhda "Nady" Nikonova was one of our best young attorneys. "Maybe Nady should take the lead," I said.

"She doesn't have time. She's in trial for the next two weeks."

"Who's the investigator?"

She frowned. "It was Tom Eisenmann."

Eisenmann was an experienced investigator who had died of Covid. I asked Rosie if anybody else was available.

"We're a little thin." She rattled off the names of four investigators. Two had Covid, the third had retired, and the fourth had given notice.

"I need to hire Pete," I said. "Do we have enough in the budget to pay him?"

"I'll find the money."

Good. My younger brother, Pete, was a former cop who had been a private investigator for almost thirty years. "Thanks."

"I don't want you and your brother playing cops-and-robbers, Mike."

I pretended to cross my heart. "We'll be good, Rosie. I promise."

She responded with a skeptical expression. "I've also asked Nady to step in as acting co-head of the Felony Division to help you with the admin stuff until Rolanda returns."

"Thanks. Does Rolanda's situation impact your decision about running for another term?"

"I haven't decided."

"You're going to have to decide before she returns to work."

"I know."

For three years, Rosie maintained that she would not run for a third term. Although she wouldn't admit it to anybody but me, she was discreetly setting the stage for Rolanda to succeed her. Of course, there was no guarantee that Rolanda would win the election. There would be allegations of nepotism and other political considerations to overcome. On the plus side, there was no question that Rolanda was qualified, and she had inherited her aunt's political instincts.

I smiled. "As we have discussed, I will postpone my retirement if you decide to run. On the other hand, Terrence may be a tougher sell. He seems determined to retire."

"I'll keep working on him." She grinned. "I can always find another defense lawyer. It will be harder to replace Terrence." She shooed me out of her office. "Get out of here and call Rolanda."

"I will."

"Mike?"

"Yes?"

"Thanks."

3

"HE DOESN'T REMEMBER"

"You feeling okay?" I asked. I was sitting at my desk and looking at my laptop.

Rolanda Fernandez nodded at me from the box on Zoom. "Fine, Mike."

"Tired?"

"Not really."

You'll never admit it. "How's Maria?"

Her jet-black eyes twinkled. "Two-year-olds have two speeds: full throttle or asleep."

"I'm familiar with the drill. Rosie and I will take her to the park on Saturday."

"That would be wonderful."

Rolanda could have passed for Rosie's younger sister. Her cheekbones were sculpted, and her straight black hair cascaded to her shoulders. When Rosie and I babysat her when she was in second grade, she wasn't afraid to stand up to the big kids in the playground. By the time she was in high school, she was an all-conference softball player who loved to mix it up with the boys in debate tournaments. The only hints that she was closer to forty than thirty were the flecks of gray hair and the crow's feet—souvenirs from a dozen years as a Deputy Public Defender and two years as a mom.

"Rosie told me that you're going to take a little time off," I said. "We have your cases covered. There will be plenty of criminal activity in San Francisco to keep you busy when you come back to work." I lowered my voice. "You *are* coming back, right?"

She smiled. "Eventually."

"No pressure, but your aunt has plans for you."

"I'm aware of that."

Rolanda reported that her daughter was adapting nicely to preschool two days a week. Her husband, Zach, was insanely busy at the big law firm where he was a partner. Corporate clients never stopped doing deals and suing people during the pandemic.

She grinned. "Zach's firm hit a billion dollars in revenue last year."

"That number is incomprehensible to me."

"You and Rosie never made a billion when you were running a two-person criminal defense firm in a converted martial arts studio above a Chinese restaurant on Mission Street?"

"Uh, no. I'm going to step in and take the lead on the Reggie Jones trial. How will our client react if I suggest a continuance?"

"Not well. He was adamant that he didn't want to waive time."

Under California law, a defendant has the right to a trial within sixty days after a preliminary hearing, a mini-trial where the prosecution must show just enough evidence to convince the judge that it is more likely than not that the accused committed a crime. In most cases, the defendant "waives time," which means that the trial is delayed beyond the statutorily mandated period to give the defense attorneys more time to prepare. During Covid, the judges frequently invoked the State Emergency Covid Order to extend trials beyond the sixty-day period. We were still trying to make progress on the backlog.

She added, "Not surprisingly, Judge Stumpf denied bail. Reggie has been stuck in San Bruno Jail for six months. He wants to move forward."

It's virtually impossible to get bail in a murder case. In fairness to Reggie, if I had been sitting in County Jail #3 during Covid, I would have wanted to move forward quickly, too.

"I'm going to see him in the morning," I said. "Has the DA shown any hints of negotiating this down from first-degree murder?"

"None."

"You play the cards you're dealt. Did our client kill Tyson Gore?"

"He says that he didn't."

"Do you believe him?"

"I'm not sure."

"What happened on the night that Gore died?"

"I'm not sure about that, either."

Huh? "What did Reggie tell you?"

"He doesn't remember. He went up to Salesforce Park at a quarter to eight on the night before Gore's body was discovered. He found a secluded spot in the bushes in the Redwood Forest on the north side of the park across from Millennium Tower. He brought a sandwich and a fifth of tequila and spent the night. A security guard found him the next morning. The bottle was empty, Reggie's hands and face had some dried blood, and Gore's wallet was on the ground next to him. They brought Reggie in for questioning and arrested him two days later. They think he robbed Gore and pushed him over the railing during a robbery."

"Did he admit that he killed Gore?"

"No. He told the cops that he passed out. He said that he didn't see Gore, and he doesn't remember anything."

I felt the familiar throbbing in my temples. "Let's start from the beginning. Tell me everything you know about Reggie Jones."

She took a sip of tea from a mug bearing Maria's photo. "Fifty-five. Grew up in Hunters Point. Graduated from Balboa High. Divorced. His ex-wife and daughter died in a car accident. No family in the area. Worked as a security guard and then moved packages at UPS for twenty years. Had a back injury and went on disability. Got addicted to painkillers, and an existing drinking problem got worse. When his disability ended, he ran out of money, lost his apartment, and ended up on the street. It's sad."

"How did he get into Salesforce Park?"

"Legitimately. It's open to the public until eight PM. Homeless people sleep in the park if the security guards don't see them."

"It's a new facility in an upscale neighborhood. There must be cameras everywhere."

"There are. There's video of Reggie going up an escalator at seven-forty-five PM. A security guard found him the next morning."

"Did the Medical Examiner get a time of death on Gore?"

"Between two-eleven AM and four AM. A worker found the body in the construction area next to Millennium Tower at six AM."

Medical Examiners usually give themselves more wiggle room. "That's a tight timeframe."

"Gore was seen in a security video as he left Kanzen at two-eleven AM."

Kanzen was an insanely expensive private club on the east end of Salesforce Park. Memberships ran as much as a half a million dollars.

"What was he doing at Kanzen at two in the morning?" I asked.

"Trying to raise money. He spent the weekend at Deal Con." She said that it was a three-day convention at Moscone Center for Gore's crypto company, Deal Coin. "The conference ended on Sunday evening. There was an after-party at the Four Seasons. Then there was an after-after-party at Kanzen for his biggest investors. Gore hit them up for funding."

"Was anybody mad at him?"

"Everybody. A couple of months before Gore died, Deal Coin was the hottest crypto company in the world. Gore was viewed as a visionary genius—somewhere between Steve Jobs and Elon Musk. His investors put up five billion dollars. At its peak, the company had a valuation of forty billion. When the crypto market got shaky, the investors got nervous and started demanding their money back. Gore couldn't pay them, and Deal Coin went into a death spiral. According to the *Chronicle*, at the time of his death, Gore was looking for a quick infusion of at least five billion."

"I take it that he didn't get it?"

"No, he didn't. The company filed for bankruptcy, and the investors lost everything." She smirked. "Tyson 'The Genius' Gore pissed away forty billion in less than three months. In the financial press, they started calling it 'Dead Coin.'"

"You think somebody was angry enough at Gore that they might have pushed him over the railing at Salesforce Park?"

"We don't have any evidence that somebody did, but if I had lost forty billion, I might have been tempted."

Me, too. "Any security videos from the Redwood Forest?"

"Afraid not. The area was under construction to fix a sprinkler problem. It was surrounded by a chain-link fence covered with a tarp."

"Did our client see Gore?"

"He says he didn't. He claims that he was passed out until the security guard found him the next morning."

"And the blood on his hands and face?"

"He told me that he fell down the previous day."

Right. "What's our narrative?"

"Reggie was sleeping off a drinking binge when Gore committed suicide or somebody else pushed him."

"Any evidence that Gore killed himself?"

"He was under a lot of stress from the implosion of Deal Coin. He had gone through two acrimonious divorces. He had recently broken up with his latest girlfriend. He was drinking heavily and taking antidepressants. The ME also found bath salts in his system."

"Bath salts" is the street name for high-end synthetic drugs that are the rage among certain members of the tech crowd. It's like cocaine, only ten times stronger.

"That doesn't prove that he killed himself," I said.

"We brought in a forensic psychologist to perform a psychological autopsy. She's prepared to testify that it's likely that Gore committed suicide."

That helps, although it's far from a sure bet that it will lead to an acquittal. A psychological autopsy is a systematic process where a trained investigator reviews the decedent's medical and psychological records, interviews family and friends, and renders an opinion as to whether the decedent was suicidal. The science has been around since the fifties, but questions remain about its validity.

"Who is our expert?"

"Gina Cole."

"She's very good." I had known her for years. She was a leading expert in the field.

Rolanda held up a hand. "As you might expect, the DA is going to call Gore's therapist, who is adamant that Gore was not suicidal. Gina will argue that he was. We'll present it to the jury and let them decide."

"It might be enough to get a juror or two to reasonable doubt," I said.

"Hopefully. I'd feel better if we had something stronger."

So would I. "What about the possibility that somebody else pushed him?"

"I interviewed everybody at the gathering at Kanzen. Other than the manager of the club, Gore was the last person to leave. It's possible that somebody was waiting for him in the Redwood Forest. As far as I can tell, nobody else was around."

"Evidence that anybody else was there?"

"Afraid not, Mike."

"What about the claim that it was a robbery?"

"Reggie denies it."

"What about the fact that they found Gore's wallet next to him?"

"It could have fallen out of his pocket when Gore walked by or somebody else pushed him. They didn't find Reggie's fingerprints, blood, or DNA on the wallet, which was empty. Reggie had twelve dollars in his pocket."

"The cops think Reggie killed a guy over twelve bucks?"

"So it seems." She said that she had filed pre-trial motions and submitted preliminary witness lists. "The police reports, witness statements, and security videos are in the file. I'll email you electronic versions of everything else. Text me if you need anything."

"I will. For now, I need you to do what the doctor says and make sure that my soon-to-be-great-nephew comes out happy and healthy."

"Thanks, Mike. Nady will help you get organized."

"I'm going to see her next."

4

"HERE WE GO AGAIN"

I knocked on the open door of the windowless office across the hall from mine. "Got a sec?"

Nadezhda "Nady" Nikonova took off her reading glasses, tugged at her shoulder-length blonde hair, and smiled. "I hear we're going to be working together on a murder trial."

"We are."

"Here we go again."

Nady was a brilliant, creative, and driven woman of thirty-nine. When she was a kid, she accompanied her single mother to the U.S. from Uzbekistan. They moved in with cousins in L.A. where Nady learned English on the fly. She became an excellent student and graduated at the top of her class at UCLA and, later, Berkeley Law. She began her career at a downtown firm where she pored over phonebook-length documents for real estate deals. I liberated her five years ago, and she became one of our go-to lawyers. Her husband, Max, was a partner in the antitrust group of the megafirm of Story, Short & Thompson in Embarcadero Center.

"Where's the Chief?" I asked.

Nady pointed at the corner of her cramped office with just enough room for a desk, a bookcase, a file cabinet, and a credenza, none of which matched. "She's been waiting for you."

Her fourteen-year-old Keeshond was sleeping soundly. I crossed the room, took out a treat, and held it under her nose. "How's my good girl, Luna?" I whispered.

Her nose twitched. Her left eye opened halfway. The forty-pound ball of silver and black fur wagged her tail, licked her chops, gave me her best smile, and pulled herself up into the sitting position. Without prompting, she went through her full repertoire: she extended a paw, lowered herself to the floor and then raised herself back to the sitting position, picked up her teddy bear and offered it to me, and then extended her other paw.

I held the treat in my right fist. "Have you been good today?"

Her ears perked up as she waited patiently. I handed her the treat, which she accepted enthusiastically. Her huge brown eyes opened wide as she waited for seconds.

"That's the last one," I said.

Her expression transformed into one of profound disappointment. She waited a moment to confirm that I was telling the truth, then she slunk down to the linoleum floor, curled up, and resumed her nap.

Nady grinned. "You'll make it up to her tomorrow."

When Nady came to work for us, I declared that the PD's Office would be dog-friendly, much to the chagrin of my bureaucratic masters at City Hall. As a legal matter, the pencil pushers were right—City policy prohibits bringing pets (other than service animals) to work in the interest of "public and employee safety." Rosie promised not to enforce the ban as long as I persuaded the City Attorney's Office to issue a written exception, and Luna didn't piddle on the floor. The second condition was a slam dunk: Luna was better behaved than many of the humans working for the City. The first was more difficult, but I convinced the City Attorney to approve what she dubbed the "Mike Daley Exception" after I agreed to indemnify the City if Luna ever bit somebody. Luna quickly became the most beloved creature in the PD's Office and, perhaps, San Francisco government.

"We should aspire to have a more Luna-like approach to life," I said.

Nady nodded, then her expression turned serious. "Is Rolanda okay?"

"Yes. The doctor is putting her on bed rest as a precaution. How's your trial?"

"A slog."

Nady had the unenviable task of representing a drug dealer in Hunters Point who got high on crystal meth and stabbed one of his customers during an argument about money. The encounter was caught on a security camera in front of a dry cleaners on Third Street.

She exhaled. "Our client admitted that he killed the decedent. The only question is whether our expert will be able to convince the jury that he was so high that he couldn't have formed the requisite intent to act with premeditation."

"Any chance of an acquittal?"

"Doubtful. I might be able to get one or two jurors to reasonable doubt, in which case the jury will hang, and the DA will almost certainly decide to start over." She said that her trial would continue for at least two weeks. "Rosie said that you're going to take the lead on the Reggie Jones trial."

"I am. Rolanda believes there's a chance that he didn't do it. What do you think?"

"Hard to say. There isn't much hard evidence supporting the DA's claim that Reggie killed Gore during a robbery. They found Gore's wallet on the ground, but no prints, blood, or DNA from Reggie. Reggie had only twelve dollars in his pocket when he was arrested. Gore's Rolex was still on his wrist when they found the body. Most important, if Reggie killed Gore, he wouldn't have stuck around until the security guard found him."

Her instincts were very good. So were Rolanda's. Rosie's were the best in the office.

I asked if there was any evidence of a struggle.

"Gore had a fractured skull, two broken arms, and some fractured ribs, but that can be attributed to the fact that he took a seventy-foot fall into a pile of gravel. There were no bruises on his hands, indicating a struggle. Reggie had a few scratches on his right hand and left cheek which he attributed to a fall the previous day."

"You believe him?"

"It's the only explanation that he provided."

I took a seat in the chair opposite her desk. "What do you think of him?"

"He's a reasonably intelligent guy who's had a lot of bad luck. He could be a strong witness if he remains composed." She confirmed the information that Rolanda had provided. "His life went off the rails after he lost his job and started drinking. He didn't have any family support, so he lost control."

We chatted for a few more minutes. I told her that Rolanda had emailed me the police reports, security videos, and other evidence. Nady promised to walk me through the files.

"Rolanda thinks it might have been suicide," I said.

"It may be our strongest argument, but you know as well as I do that psychological autopsies are never dispositive."

"Rolanda said the same thing." I asked about other potential suspects.

"There were five investors with Gore at the gathering at Kanzen. The police didn't find any of their prints, DNA, or blood on Gore's body, clothes, or wallet. We talked to everybody who was there. Nobody admitted to killing Gore, but all of them had lost a lot of money. Rolanda and I calculated that the people at Kanzen lost close to forty billion when Deal Coin tanked. I wouldn't have blamed them if they wanted to kill Gore, but we have no evidence that they did."

"Any favorites?"

"Matt Bosworth was Gore's co-founder of Deal Coin. Gore squeezed Bosworth's interest down shortly before Deal Coin's stock took off. If you believe the *Chronicle*, Bosworth would have been worth north of five billion at that time if Gore hadn't squeezed him. At the end of the day, it didn't matter. Like Gore, Bosworth lost his entire investment."

"Anybody else?" I asked.

"A venture capitalist named Steve Warren lost over a billion dollars of his fund's money. Most of his investors were friends of his father, who started the fund."

"Sounds like Thanksgiving dinner at the Warren household may be a bit awkward."

"So it seems." She filled me in on our witness list. "I've also been working on a preliminary draft of the questionnaire for potential jurors.

"Do we have budget for a jury selection consultant?"

"No."

As is usually the case, Nady and I would have to go with our instincts. "Were you and Rolanda planning to put Reggie on the stand?"

"Only if we're desperate. I think he'd hold up okay, but a smart prosecutor will rip him to shreds on cross." She gave me a knowing look. "Have you met our client?"

"I'm going to see him in the morning."

5

"I DIDN'T KILL HIM"

Reggie Jones fidgeted with the sleeve of his orange jumpsuit. "You're my lawyer now?"

"Yes."

"I liked Rolanda."

"She has to stay home until the baby arrives. Doctor's orders."

At ten-forty-five the following morning, a Wednesday, my new client and I were sitting in plastic chairs on opposite sides of a metal table in an airless consultation room in the bowels of County Jail #3, the Costco-like edifice about ten miles south of the Hall of Justice near the top of San Bruno Mountain. The boxy gray building seemed out of place in a quiet suburban community. It opened to great fanfare in 2005 and was a substantial upgrade over the Depression-era jail a couple of miles away. A few dozen guards in high-tech pods monitor about eight hundred prisoners. It is the nicest facility in the San Francisco jail system, with a reputation for progressive programming and functional plumbing.

He eyed me. "What about Nady?"

"She's in trial for a couple of weeks. There isn't enough time for her to finish her trial and prepare to take the lead on yours."

"Do I have any choice?"

"I can ask the judge for an extension."

"How long would that take?"

"At least six months. Possibly a year."

"I'm not going to sit here for another year."

Reggie was fifty-five, but he looked older. He was about five-ten with a wiry frame and muscular arms covered in tattoos. His closely-cropped hair was a dull gray. His pockmarked face was covered with stubble. His ebony skin had a yellow cast.

His modulated baritone was tinged with resignation. "Are you any good?"

"I've been doing this for almost thirty years. I trained Rolanda and Nady."

"It doesn't mean that you're a good trial lawyer."

Fair enough. "The State Bar once said that I was one of the best PDs in California."

"This isn't a popularity contest."

True. "Ask around."

"I will."

It's the best that I can do for now. "How are you feeling?"

His tone turned sarcastic. "Great."

"Are you staying healthy?"

"For the most part. I've had Covid twice."

"Are you eating?"

"Some. The food is terrible. My stomach feels like it's been through a meat grinder. And I haven't had a drink in six months."

"You sleeping?"

"Not much."

"I need you to be strong for trial." I leaned back in the plastic chair. "I trust that Rolanda explained that we have only one hard-and-fast rule: you have to tell us the absolute unvarnished truth, and you can't leave anything important out."

"She did."

"Everything you told Rolanda and Nady was true?"

"Yes."

"Anything you'd like to reconsider?"

"No."

So far, so good. "Rolanda told me a lot about you, but I'd like to know more." *And I want to get you talking so that maybe you'll start to trust me. More importantly, I want to know if I can trust you.* "Tell me a little more about yourself."

"I didn't kill Tyson Gore."

"We'll get to that shortly."

His tone became more adamant. "I didn't kill him."

*Good to hear, but it's a mixed bag from a legal standpoint.
The Rules of Professional Conduct prohibit attorneys from
letting our clients lie on the stand. If I find out that you
did, in fact, kill Gore, I can't let you testify to the contrary.
Defense lawyers go through all sorts of intellectual contortions
to dance around this rule, but I prefer to avoid it altogether if
I can.*

"We'll talk about what happened in a minute," I said.
"Rolanda told me that you're from Hunters Point."

"I am." He confirmed the basic info that Rolanda had
provided.

"What were you doing in Salesforce Park?"

"Sleeping." He admitted that he had been drinking most of
the day. "I brought a bottle of tequila with me and found a spot
in the bushes when nobody was looking." He confirmed that
he arrived at a quarter to eight on Sunday night, about fifteen
minutes before the park closed.

"How did you get in?"

"Same as everybody—I took the escalator. Nobody stopped
me."

"There are security cameras everywhere. How is it possible
that they don't have video of you entering the Redwood
Forest?"

"The area was being renovated. There were fences and tarps
around it."

"Was this the first time you were in the park?"

"No. I've stayed there a couple of times. It's quiet. I got
caught there a few weeks earlier. The security guard was a
decent guy who asked me to leave. I appreciated that he didn't
just throw me out."

"What happened on the night that Gore died?"

"I don't know. I drank my tequila and went to sleep." He
said that he woke up at six-fifteen AM when a security guard
jostled him. "A cop showed up a few minutes later."

"Did you see anybody or hear anything during the night?"

"No."

"You're a sound sleeper."

"I drank a fifth of tequila and passed out, okay? Do you really think I would have stayed there if I had killed somebody?"

Seems unlikely. "Did you ever meet Tyson Gore?"

"No."

"Did you know who he was?"

"I read about him in the paper. He was a rich asshole who made billions in crypto."

And lost it. "The DA says that you tried to rob him."

"I didn't even see him."

"They found his wallet on the ground next to you."

"I didn't take it."

"You're saying somebody planted it to frame you?"

"I don't know. Maybe somebody else tried to rob him. Or maybe Gore dropped it."

"Any chance he committed suicide? Or somebody else pushed him over the railing?"

"How would I know if I never saw him?"

I pushed him for a few more minutes. His denials became more adamant, and he didn't modify his story. I took this as a good sign. Guilty people change their stories on the fly. Innocent people get mad.

6

"THERE'S NOTHING TO TALK ABOUT"

"Congratulations on your appointment," I said.

"Thank you." The mayor's hand-picked District Attorney forced a phony smile as she sat behind her government-issue desk in her office in a refurbished industrial building about a mile south of the Hall of Justice. "It's always nice to see you, Mike," she lied.

Right back at you. "It's always nice to see you, too, Vanessa."

Vanessa Turner was thirty-five, whip-smart, intensely political, and profoundly ambitious. The Oakland native was a UC Davis and Hastings Law School alum and a law-and-order zealot with a reputation for tenacity in court and sharp elbows around the office. When her former boss and mentor, DeSean Harper, announced his retirement, she threw her hat into the ring to succeed him. After a vitriol-filled campaign among a dozen candidates, one of my former colleagues from the PD's Office somehow emerged with the most votes. He was too liberal even for San Francisco, and he was recalled a year later in a campaign with even greater vitriol. When the dust settled, the mayor had the legal authority to appoint an interim DA, and she picked her political crony, Turner. Our new DA's back-room maneuvering might not lead to a long tenure. Under the San Francisco Code, the mayor is required to call a special election to fill the DA slot for a full term. A half-dozen of Turner's former opponents have already filed papers to run against her.

I glanced around her office. The DA's new digs aren't as spacious as the old suite on the third floor of the Hall of Justice, but the furniture is new, the plumbing works, and the building has Wi-Fi. The ADAs could no longer walk to court, but it's a short drive to the Hall, and Turner had found money to pay for a shuttle van service.

She tugged at her Ralph Lauren blazer. "You're here about the Reggie Jones case?"

"Yes."

"There's nothing to talk about."

Yes, there is. "Rolanda's doctor wants her to go on bed rest, so I'm taking the case to trial. I wanted to discuss timing, motions, and other housekeeping items." *And to see if I can get you to reveal anything about your strategy.*

"Please give Rolanda my best."

"Thank you. I will."

Her concern seemed sincere, which was pretty typical among those of us who work in the criminal justice system. San Francisco is a small town where everybody knows everybody. While we have our share of jerks, most of us understand that everybody has families, health issues, aging parents, and day-to-day concerns. If you treat people badly, it will catch up with you.

She gestured at her subordinate, Andy Erickson, who was sitting in the chair next to mine. "As I'm sure you're aware, Andy is handling the Jones case."

"I am." I nodded at Erickson. "Looking forward to working with you again."

"Same here."

Erickson was a competent career prosecutor who had diligently worked his way up through the ranks at the DA's Office for fifteen years. He was a by-the-numbers lawyer and a reasonably straight shooter. He made it to Chief Assistant and was in line to succeed his former boss until he got caught in the middle of the political buzz saw and came in sixth in the special election that resulted in my former colleague's surprise election. After Turner became our new DA, she demoted Andy to Assistant Chief of the Felony Division. He found himself in the unenviable position of having to suck up to his former subordinate.

"Trial starts on September twenty-sixth," he said. "We've submitted motions and exchanged preliminary witness lists. We won't object if you decide to ask for a delay."

"My client wants to go to trial right away."

"Fine." Erickson started to stand. "I think we're finished."

Not so fast. "Are you planning to stick with a first-degree murder charge?"

He glanced at Turner, then he turned back to me. "Yes."

"Any flexibility?"

"Not at this time."

Andy was in a tight spot. Turner had already started cleaning house, and his name was undoubtedly at the top of her list. She knew that he was a solid prosecutor, but this had nothing to do with competence. Andy was likely to run against her in the spring—an unforgivable act of disloyalty. You might think that Turner would have fired Andy immediately, but that would have given him carte blanche to rip her in the press. By letting him stay, she was able to keep an eye on him. Moreover, it enhanced her odds of getting a conviction in Reggie's trial, for which she could claim victory. Conversely, if Reggie was acquitted, Turner could blame Andy.

I spoke to Erickson. "At the very least, the judge will need to instruct on second-degree."

"I'm well aware of that, Mike."

Under California law, in a first-degree murder trial, the judge is legally obligated to instruct the jury that it may find the defendant guilty of the lesser charge of second-degree. The implications are significant. The minimum sentence for first-degree is twenty-five years. The minimum for second-degree is fifteen.

"There is no evidence of premeditation," I said.

"Robbery. The decedent's wallet was on the ground next to your client."

"Reggie had only twelve bucks in his pocket. Obviously, he didn't take any money. You found no prints or DNA on the wallet. Gore's Rolex was still on his wrist when he died."

"Doesn't matter."

"Yes, it does. There was no premeditation."

"He saw a bunch of people go inside Kanzen. He knew that he would have an opportunity to rob somebody when they came out. There's your premeditation."

"He was asleep."

"Says your client. The jury will put the pieces together."

"Not beyond a reasonable doubt to convict for first-degree."

"We'll see."

We went back and forth, but Turner and Erickson didn't budge. Nor did they provide any additional information.

Turner stood up and extended a hand. "Thank you for coming in, Mike." She might have added, "Dismissed."

"Thank you for seeing me, Vanessa." I looked over at Erickson. "I understand that Ken Lee is the homicide inspector on Reggie's case. I trust you have no objection if I talk to him?"

"Fine with me, but he has no obligation to talk to you."

7

"YOU KNOW THE DRILL"

At two-forty-five on Thursday afternoon, I was sitting on the wooden bench in the almost-empty corridor outside the Department Thirteen courtroom, the professional home of my longtime friend, Judge Stephen Murphy. I was waiting for Steve to recess the murder trial over which he was presiding so that I could talk to one of the witnesses.

A burly sheriff's deputy opened the door, and a few stragglers made their way into the cavernous hallway. Next came the lawyers. Finally, Inspector Kenneth Lee exited the courtroom. He saw me, rolled his eyes, and continued without stopping.

"Ken?" I said.

He kept walking. He was wearing his standard going-to-court ensemble: a charcoal Men's Wearhouse suit, a white dress shirt, and a polka dot tie. At fifty, his hair was mostly gray. The scar running across his left cheek was bright red. The limp from an injury sustained when he was an undercover cop in Chinatown had gotten worse.

I tagged along and tried again. "Ken?"

"Late for a meeting. Can't talk."

You mean you won't talk. "I left a message with your assistant to set up an appointment, but he didn't call me back."

"Try again."

He entered the stairwell, and I followed him up one flight and into the corridor.

I tried once more as he was about to enter Homicide. "Please, Ken? Rolanda had to go on bed rest, so I picked up the Reggie Jones case. I need just a few minutes. I promise that I won't bug you again."

He flashed a caustic grin. "Yes, you will."

Yes, I will. I was reduced to groveling. "Five minutes."

He exhaled heavily and motioned me to follow him. "Five minutes."

I accompanied him through the labyrinth of hallways with yellowed linoleum floors and walls covered with chipped gray paint. File cabinets and boxes were strewn haphazardly among the windowless offices and cubicles. We made our way into the bullpen area where San Francisco's two dozen homicide inspectors worked. Most of the metal desks were grouped in twos so that the teams could face each other. Lee had worked alone after his partner, the legendary Roosevelt Johnson, retired. Coincidentally, Roosevelt had walked the beat in the Tenderloin with my dad before he was promoted to Homicide.

Lee and I were the only people in the room. His colleagues were on the street or in court. He removed his suit jacket and draped it on the back of his swivel chair. He took a seat and motioned me to a folding chair on the opposite side of his desk.

"You still planning to take early retirement at the end of the year?" I asked.

"Yes. I'm getting my hip replaced."

"Any chance I can persuade you to change your mind?"

"You *want* me to stay?"

"Yes."

"I didn't expect to hear that from a Public Defender."

It would be an overstatement to say that I liked him, but I respected him, and he played by the rules most of the time. "You've always been straight with me. We aren't going to agree on everything, but the system works better when we have guys like you."

"Are you flattering me to see if I'll give you information about the Reggie Jones case?"

Well, maybe a little. "I mean it, Ken."

"Go figure."

I pointed at the framed photos of his two daughters. The elder had graduated from Cal. The younger was a senior at Cal Poly in San Luis Obispo. "Everybody okay?"

"Fine. Leah is working for a mobile gaming start-up that's printing money. Justine is thinking about law school. With my luck, she'll become a Public Defender."

"Happy to talk to her."

"Thanks. I'll let you know."

"You will recall that my father walked the beat with your former partner. My dad wasn't happy when I decided to become a PD."

"Maybe Justine will become a prosecutor."

"I will look forward to trying cases against her. If you stick around, you can be the star witness in her first murder trial."

"Right." He changed the subject. "Is Rolanda okay?"

"Fine. Her doctor is being cautious."

"Give her my best. Are you going to ask for an extension for the Jones trial?"

"No. My client wants to proceed right away."

"You ought to cut a deal."

"Our new DA isn't in a dealing frame of mind."

"Andy Erickson is usually pretty reasonable."

"Andy isn't calling the shots." I waited a beat. "I think Vanessa is testing him."

"No comment. You've used up four of your five minutes. Why did you want to see me?"

"My client says that he didn't kill Tyson Gore."

"He robbed Gore and pushed him over the railing into the construction site."

"Reggie had only twelve dollars in his pocket when you arrested him."

"He wasn't a very successful robber."

"Reggie drank a fifth of tequila and passed out. He was unconscious when Gore walked by."

"So he says."

"Do you have any evidence proving that my client pushed Gore?"

"You know the drill, Mike. This is where I tell you to read my report."

"I did. I was hoping that you might provide some context."

"The context is in my report."

No, it isn't. "You didn't list any witnesses who saw Reggie attack Gore."

"There weren't any."

"And you have no video of my client attacking Gore."

"There isn't any." His eyes shifted to his desk and back to me. "The area where the attack took place was being refurbished. It was surrounded by a fence and tarps."

"You didn't find my client's fingerprints, blood, or DNA on Gore's wallet."

"The jury will put the pieces together."

"Or on his body or his clothing," I added.

"It would have been impossible to find usable samples. Gore fell seventy feet into a construction zone and died instantly from head trauma. His body was covered with dust."

"You have no evidence that Reggie made any contact with Gore."

"There was evidence of a struggle. Your client's face and hands were bloodied."

"He fell down the previous day."

"You're free to argue it to a jury."

I will. I probed further, but Lee wasn't forthcoming. The default response of every experienced homicide inspector is to refer to his report.

He stood up and put on his jacket. "Your five minutes ended five minutes ago. I'll show you out."

"I know the way. Did you consider the possibility that it was a suicide?"

"We considered all possibilities. We didn't find a note or other evidence of suicide."

"Gore was under a lot of stress. Deal Coin was imploding."

"He was a big boy."

"Who lost billions. Maybe he freaked out."

"We found no evidence that he did. His therapist is prepared to testify that she saw no signs that Gore was suicidal."

"He was drinking heavily, taking antidepressants, and using bath salts."

"If you want details about the toxicology report, you'll need to talk to the Medical Examiner." He gave me a knowing smile. "She'll tell you to read her report, too."

8

"THEY'RE VERY POTENT"

"Thank you for seeing me on short notice," I said.

The Chief Medical Examiner of the City and County of San Francisco nodded. "You're welcome, Mr. Daley."

For the last decade, I have tried to convince Dr. Joy Siu to call me by my first name, but she isn't a first-name person. We were sitting on opposite sides of a glass-topped table in a windowless conference room of the ME's new facility in India Basin, about halfway between the ballpark and Candlestick Point. The location isn't as convenient as her old office in the bowels of the Hall, but the state-of-the-art examination rooms and expanded morgue are a substantial upgrade.

I adjusted the face covering that I was asked to put on when I entered the building, even though San Francisco had eliminated masking requirements. "How much longer do you think we'll need these?"

"Hard to say." She touched the white N95 mask that made it impossible to read her expressions. "I will re-evaluate in a few weeks. We have several employees who are immunocompromised, and my assistant is pregnant, so we are taking additional precautions."

"Very prudent," I said.

"I think so." She smoothed the sleeve of her white lab coat. "I understand that your colleague, Ms. Fernandez, is on bed rest. Please give her my best. I hope that the rest of her pregnancy is uneventful, and she delivers a healthy baby."

"Thank you, Dr. Siu. I will let her know."

She folded her hands and placed them on the table in front of her. From her precisely cut black hair to her meticulously applied makeup, Dr. Siu embodied exactness. She had been our ME for ten years and was a worthy successor to the legendary Dr. Roderick Beckert, who had held the job for three decades. The Princeton and Johns Hopkins Medical School alum and former researcher at UCSF was a world-class academic and an internationally recognized expert in anatomic pathology. In addition to her full caseload in San Francisco, the one-time Olympic figure skating hopeful consulted on complex autopsies around the world.

Her voice turned clinical. "I provided my autopsy report on Tyson Gore to the police, the DA, and your office. I presume that you've read it?"

"I have."

"Then you know everything that I do."

Not quite. "Cause of death was a head injury?"

"Massive brain trauma. The decedent was pushed over the railing of Salesforce Park and landed in the construction zone in front of Millennium Tower. He died upon impact."

"What makes you think he was pushed?"

"There was dried blood on your client's hands and face indicating a struggle."

"I understand that you didn't find my client's fingerprints, blood, or DNA on the decedent's person or clothing."

"Mr. Gore landed on a pile of gravel. His body was covered with dust. It was impossible to obtain usable samples."

"Time of death?" I asked.

"Between two-eleven AM and four AM." She said that Gore was spotted in security video footage leaving Kanzen at two-eleven. "I based my determination on the usual metrics: state of digested food in his stomach, rigor mortis, etc."

"The toxicology report says that Mr. Gore had alcohol in his system."

"He was below the legal limit."

"He was also on a blood pressure medication called hydrochlorothiazide."

"So am I."

So am I. "The side effects can include headaches, dizziness, muscle spasms, and erectile dysfunction."

"Mr. Gore died of massive head injuries, Mr. Daley."

"Did you consider the possibility that the blood pressure meds may have caused him to become lightheaded or even suicidal?"

"I saw no evidence that it had any impact on his physical well-being or state of mind. Furthermore, I have found no peer-reviewed research studies indicating that hydrochlorothiazide leads to suicide."

Neither have I. "The toxicology report also says that he was taking an antidepressant called Zoloft."

"He was."

"His personal life was a disaster. He had gone through two acrimonious divorces. His company was on the brink of insolvency. He had lost billions. His investors were irate. He was desperately trying to raise money to keep Deal Coin afloat. Did you consider the possibility that he committed suicide?"

"I consulted at length with the decedent's therapist who had recommended Zoloft. She had worked with Mr. Gore for many years. She saw no signs that he was suicidal and is prepared to testify to that effect if necessary."

Our expert will come to a different conclusion. "I understand that he was also taking bath salts."

"He was."

I eyed her. "The side effects include hallucinations, agitation, violent behavior, paranoia, and suicidal thoughts. Did you consider the possibility that the bath salts may have led him to attack my client or even attempt suicide?"

"The amount of bath salts in Mr. Gore's bloodstream was very small, Mr. Daley. I found no evidence that he was suffering from hallucinations or acting erratically."

"They're very potent, Dr. Siu. Bath salts are like cocaine, only ten times stronger."

"I'm well aware of that, Mr. Daley. It sounds as if we will have a few things to talk about in court."

9

"LUCKY HAD A SOUL"

The gregarious bartender flashed a broad smile and spoke to me in a practiced but fake Irish brogue. "What'll it be, lad?"

"Guinness, Joey," I said.

"Coming right up, Mike."

At ten-thirty on Thursday night, the aroma of fish and chips wafted through the half-filled Irish pub at Twenty-third and Irving, around the corner from the house where I grew up. My uncle, Big John Dunleavy, had run Dunleavy's Bar and Grill for sixty years. Except for the flat-screen TVs and the Wi-Fi password on the blackboard, the wood-paneled watering hole looked the same as it did when I drank my first beer at fourteen and tended bar on weekends when I was in college. Fifteen years ago, Big John handed over the day-to-day operations to his grandson, Joey, but he kept coming to his beloved saloon to make his fish and chips and visit with his regulars. He died of a heart attack two years ago as he was counting the day's receipts and sipping Glendalough, a twenty-five-year-old single-malt Irish whiskey.

"How's business?" I asked.

"Getting better." Joey dropped the brogue. "The regulars are coming back."

When Covid hit, Joey transitioned to take-out only. He reopened for indoor drinking and dining in early 2021, but many of his customers stayed away or sat on the makeshift patio in the back. Things were starting to look normal again.

I glanced at the framed photo of Big John above the bar, Guinness in his hand, towel over his shoulder. The consummate barkeep was also a savvy businessman.

Dunleavy's had put his children and grandchildren through college.

"He would have been proud that you stayed open during the pandemic," I said.

"He always said that Dunleavy's never closes."

Joey had just turned forty, and he was single. He almost got married to his high school sweetheart, but it didn't work out. He got a business degree from State and went to work for Big John. At six-four and two-forty, he had continued our family tradition of playing football at St. Ignatius. The former offensive lineman was still imposing, although he was getting a little soft in the middle. His bright red hair had turned gray, and his jowls had expanded along with his girth.

Joey set his mug on the bar, checked the score of the Giants game, and gave me his best bartender's smile. "Did you really tell Big John that he could open an Irish pub in heaven?"

"Uh, yes." I winked. "How can it be heaven without an Irish bar? People need a place to watch the Giants and the Niners."

"They have sports up there?"

"Eternity is a long time. People need stuff to do."

"If they're dead, why do they need to eat and drink?"

"Because it's fun."

"Is everybody up there with him?"

"The whole crew: Grandma Kate, your dad, my parents, my older brother. I'll bet that my dad comes over for a beer every night after his shift."

My father, Thomas Daley Sr., was a San Francisco cop who had died of lung cancer twenty-five years earlier. He and his partner used to sit in the back room by the pool table and wind down after their shifts in the Tenderloin. It annoyed my mom that Pop spent so much time at Dunleavy's, but she knew that Big John would make sure that he got home safely.

"Why do they need cops if only good people go to heaven?" Joey asked.

Good question. "Crowd control. They direct traffic. There are a lot of people up there."

"If everybody has wings, can't they just fly everywhere?"

Good point. "It's probably not a very demanding job."

He took another draw of his beer. "Is Lucky in heaven?"

"Of course."

Lucky was Big John's German Shepherd who came to the bar every day until his heart gave out on his fourteenth birthday. His photo was mounted on the wall by the door where he stood guard and greeted the regulars. Big John never had a doorman.

Joey's tone turned serious. "When I was a kid, Father Pat told me that dogs can't get into heaven because only humans have souls."

"Lucky had a soul."

"Father Pat was a priest a lot longer than you were, Mike."

That's true. "It doesn't mean that he was right." I invoked my best priest-voice. "We talked about this at the seminary. For centuries, the popes have disagreed about whether animals go to heaven. For what my two cents are worth, I believe that they're God's creatures, too. I know that you were just a kid when Lucky was here, but he wasn't just a dog. He knew where the regulars lived. If they had too much to drink, he used to walk them home."

My cousin eyed me. "Seriously?"

"Swear to God, Joey. I was tending bar on St. Patrick's Day when a dozen people got pretty hammered. It was pouring rain, and Lucky made sure that every one of them made it home." I took a draw of my Guinness. "I don't care what Father Pat told you. Lucky is up in heaven sitting by the door at Big John's saloon."

His round face transformed into a wide grin as he hoisted his mug. "To Lucky."

I touched my mug against his. "To Lucky."

We gossiped for a few minutes as the few remaining customers left. Joey poured himself a club soda. I declined his offer of another beer in favor of coffee.

He eyed me. "You still planning to retire next year?"

"Depends on Rosie. I promised to stick around if she runs for another term."

"Two terms aren't enough?"

"Grace is a grown-up. Tommy is in college. I have nothing else to do."

He grinned. "You could tend bar for me."

Sounds pretty good. "You serious?"

"Yes. Big John always said that the customers loved you. You can come full circle and end your career the way it began—pouring beers at Dunleavy's."

Best job I ever had. "I can't lug kegs up from the basement anymore."

"I'll do the heavy lifting. Will you think about it?"

"I will."

"Good. Let me know when you want to start." He tossed his dishtowel over his shoulder. "Pete said that you're taking the Reggie Jones case to trial in a couple of weeks. Did he do it?"

"He says that he didn't."

"I read that Tyson Gore was a world-class asshole who lost forty billion. His investors must have been pissed off."

"They were."

Joey arched an eyebrow. "Maybe he had it coming."

"Unfortunately, the fact that the decedent was a jerk isn't a legal defense to murder."

"Maybe it should be. Can you get Reggie off?"

"Not sure."

"You're a good lawyer, Mike. You'll figure out a way."

The back door opened, and my younger brother, Pete, let himself inside. He was stockier than I was. His full head of silver hair and matching mustache were once a half-shade darker than mine. His leathery face was unshaven. He hung his bomber jacket on the hook next to the door, walked past the pool table, and took a seat at the long wooden bar on the stool next to mine. Without being asked, Joey poured him a cup of black coffee.

"Thanks, Joey," he said. They exchanged pleasantries for a moment, then he turned to me. "Rosie and the kids okay?"

"Fine. Donna and Margaret good?"

"Fine."

His wife, Donna Andrews, was the chief financial officer of a big law firm downtown. Margaret was Pete's eighteen-year-old daughter. She was a freshman at UC Santa Barbara. She was named after our mother, who had passed away a decade earlier.

"You got anything on Tyson Gore?" I asked.

"Working on it." He glanced at the TV. "I made a few calls. Gore was a dick who made a lot of money for himself and his investors—until Deal Coin collapsed. He had some very unhappy investors." Pete confirmed the basics that I had gleaned from Rolanda. Gore was thirty-eight. Divorced twice. His parents had died in an auto accident five years ago. His father was a venture capitalist. His mother was an artist. Gore graduated from Princeton and Stanford Business School. His father gave him twenty-five million to make investments. Microsoft bought his first start-up, which subsequently failed. Google bought his second start-up, which failed, too. His first crypto venture also failed. His second was Deal Coin. "He had a knack for making money for himself while losing money for everybody around him."

Nice work if you can get it. I asked about the ex-wives.

"He cheated his way out of two marriages." He explained that the first ex was an executive at Google. "She lives with their three kids in a co-op on Central Park West. The second was the former HR Director at Deal Coin. She lives with their son in a condo two floors below Gore's at Millennium Tower. Gore had visitation privileges for the kids, but the ex-wives had custody. There are rumors that he had several other kids, but I haven't been able to verify."

"Did either of the ex-wives have financial incentive to want Gore dead?"

"Unlikely. There was no life insurance. He had a prenup with each one. Each ex was getting six figures in monthly alimony and child support. The bulk of Gore's estate—now worthless—was going to endow a chair in his name at Stanford."

"Any chance that one of them got mad and pushed him off Salesforce Park?"

"Not likely, Mick. Both were out of town when Gore died. I checked their bank accounts and investment portfolios, and they're both worth eight figures, although it may be lower since their investments in Deal Coin vaporized. I didn't see any suspicious transactions or evidence that one of them paid a hired killer. You can try foisting the blame on one or both of the ex-wives, but it's going to be a tough sell to the jury."

"I understand that Gore was in a relationship when he died."

"His latest squeeze was a woman named Amanda Blair, but she broke up with him. Twenty-five. Single. Supermodel beautiful. Grew up in South City. Her father was a mechanic. Her mother cleaned houses. Graduated from State with a degree in communications. Did some freelance marketing work and made ends meet by waiting tables and working for a caterer. Then she started putting dance videos on TikTok and YouTube. Evidently, she has a big following. She's done well enough to move into a high-rise a few blocks from Salesforce Park."

Nice work if you can get it. "Where did she meet Gore?"

"At a fundraiser for the symphony at the Four Seasons."

"She had the money to attend a charity dinner?"

"She was working for the caterer."

Got it. "Did the ex-wives know about the ex-girlfriend?"

"Hard to imagine that they didn't."

True. "You think she had anything to do with Gore's death?"

"There's no evidence that she was in Salesforce Park that night."

"Maybe she hired somebody."

He scrunched his face. "There's no evidence."

"I want to talk to her. Can you have somebody keep an eye on her?"

"I will." He glanced at Joey, who filled his empty coffee cup. "I've been going through the security videos. As far as I can tell, the only people in the vicinity on the morning that Gore died were the people who attended the gathering at Kanzen."

"You ever been inside Kanzen?"

"I managed to talk my way inside once for a look." He smirked. "The half-million-dollar entry fee is a little rich for me. It's an upscale Hooters for billionaire tech bros. It always comes down to rich frat boys looking to get laid."

Some things never change. He listened attentively as I told him about my conversations with Vanessa Turner, Andy Erickson, Ken Lee, and Dr. Siu. "We're going to argue that Gore may have committed suicide. Rolanda hired Gina Cole to do a psychological autopsy."

"Good luck convincing the jury."

"If that doesn't work, I'll try to foist the blame on somebody who was at Kanzen that night." I told him about Gore's connections to his college buddy, Matt Bosworth, and the venture capitalist, Steve Warren.

Pete responded with his usual clear-eyed practicality. "In my experience, billionaires don't kill other billionaires."

"Maybe one of them paid somebody."

"You're going to need some hard evidence connecting them to Gore's death."

True. "That's where you come in."

"I'll see what I can do, Mick." He read a new text and smiled. "Meet me at Salesforce Park at seven o'clock tomorrow morning. I may have something for you."

10

"HE WAS DISORIENTED"

At seven AM, Pete emerged from the escalator leading from the street to Salesforce Park. He pulled up the collar of his bomber jacket to protect himself from the gusting wind and heavy fog. I handed him a medium Peet's coffee, black.

"Thanks, Mick." He turned to Sergeant David Dito, who was also holding a cup of Peet's that I had brought for him. "Good to see you. Family okay?"

"Fine, thanks. Yours?"

"All good."

Dito was a solid cop who worked out of Southern Station, which had relocated from the Hall of Justice to the new Headquarters south of the ballpark. The thirty-eight-year-old was a member of a multigenerational SFPD family scattered in the bungalows in St. Anne's Parish in the Sunset. His uncle, Phil Dito, was my classmate at St. Ignatius and a fellow back-up on the football team who had worked with Pete at Mission Station. David, his wife, five-year-old daughter, and infant son lived around the corner from Dunleavy's.

Pete drank a bit of coffee. "You and your family make it through Covid okay?"

Dito shrugged. "Everybody's had it except the baby. Thankfully, our cases were mild."

I always enjoy watching Pete work. More important, I like to have a non-lawyer with me when I interview witnesses. If necessary, Pete could corroborate (or rebut) Dito's account of our conversation in court. It's also helpful to have an ex-cop present when I talk to law enforcement.

We were standing in the northeast corner of Salesforce Park, four levels above the unfinished subterranean space that may be transformed into a new CalTrain Station provided the powers-that-be raise billions to extend the line from the current station at Fourth and Townsend. If all goes exceptionally well and the state raises even more billions, it will someday also house the terminal for a bullet train connecting San Francisco and L.A. The chances that it will be completed in my lifetime are slim. We were three levels above the street, two levels above the mostly empty retail space, and one level above the underutilized bus station.

The architecturally bold new transit hub is four blocks long and a block wide. It replaced the crumbling old Transbay Bus Terminal, a hulking slab of gray concrete constructed during the Great Depression which was damaged by the Loma Prieta Earthquake in 1989. The exterior of the new facility is boldly decorated in rippling white metal. It sits smack-dab in the middle of what used to be a light industrial area that's now San Francisco's South of Market tech hub. It took the City and various local and state agencies two decades to plan it and another ten years to build it at a cost of more than two billion dollars.

"You spend much time up here?" I asked Dito.

"Not really." He warmed his hands on his coffee cup. "Things were quiet during Covid. Salesforce Park has a big security force, and many people are still working from home."

The park is patrolled by a small army of private security guards dubbed "ambassadors" who monitor the area twenty-four/seven. Its flowing lawns are encircled by a walking path bordered by landscaped areas. It's an inviting space where workers from the nearby office towers sip coffee, check messages, work on their laptops, and do yoga. It's surrounded by gleaming high-rises, the tallest of which is the phallic-looking Salesforce Tower, the world headquarters of San Francisco's biggest private employer. The most notorious building in the area is Millennium Tower, a high-end condo building that garnered national attention because it wasn't anchored to bedrock, and it had tilted fifteen inches northwest. After years of litigation among its millionaire residents, architects, construction firms, and the City, the parties grudgingly agreed to a hundred-million-dollar settlement to shore up the leaning tower of Mission Street. For the last couple of years, it's been surrounded by cranes, fencing, tarps, and cement trucks. A pile driver was pounding one of dozens of new columns into the bedrock a hundred feet below ground.

Pete spoke to Dito. "Mike is taking over the Reggie Jones case, and I'm helping out. I understand that you were the first officer to talk to our client."

"I was." Dito pointed at the area between the walking path and the railing, which was planted with a strip of redwood trees and indigenous bushes, all of which were overshadowed by Millennium Tower. "A foreman for the contractor found Gore's body in the construction area below us at six AM. He called security at Millennium Tower, Salesforce Park, and 9-1-1. My partner and I were among the first officers at the scene. The EMTs arrived a couple of minutes later. While we were securing the scene, Salesforce Security reported that one of their guards found your client sleeping in the bushes. I came up here and met the guard, the head of Salesforce Security, and your client."

Pete asked whether Reggie was cooperative.

"He was disoriented."

"He told us that he had passed out after a drinking binge."

"Wouldn't surprise me. The guard found an empty tequila bottle next to his backpack."

"You questioned him?"

"Yes. He wasn't cooperative at first. Then he answered some of my questions grudgingly. He claimed that he spent the night in the bushes and didn't see anybody or anything."

"Did he try to run?"

"No."

"Evidence of a struggle?"

"Some dried blood on his hands and face."

"He told us that he had fallen down the night before."

"He told me the same thing."

"You had reason to disbelieve him?"

"I just gathered information, Pete. I offered him medical attention and a trip to the emergency room, which he declined. I took him to Southern Station to take his preliminary statement. Ken Lee followed up a few hours later."

"Was he a suspect?" I asked.

"Everybody in the vicinity was a potential suspect until ruled out. He wasn't in custody when I talked to him, so I didn't Mirandize him. I understand that Ken did, in fact, Mirandize him and offered to call a lawyer. Your client declined."

"Where did the guard find Gore's wallet?"

He pointed at the bushes. "The guard found it on the ground next to your client. There was no money inside, and the credit cards were still there." He confirmed that Reggie had only twelve dollars in his pocket.

"You think he killed Gore over twelve bucks?"

"That's a question for Ken."

"You believe that Reggie robbed Gore and pushed him over the railing?"

"That's another question for Ken."

"Did you consider the possibility that Gore dropped his wallet on his way to committing suicide, or that somebody other than Reggie was involved?"

"I'm sorry, Mike. You'll have to ask Ken."

"The connection between my client and Gore's death seems pretty tenuous to me."

"That's for you lawyers to argue about."

Pete spoke up again. "You canvassed the area?"

"Of course." Dito confirmed that there was nobody else in the vicinity when he arrived.

Pete pointed at the private club behind us. "Gore was at a gathering at Kanzen with some of his investors that broke up around two AM."

"I understand that Ken provided Rolanda with security videos from Kanzen and a list of people who were there."

"Did you find any witnesses who saw Reggie push Gore over the railing?"

"No."

"Do you know if anybody at Kanzen was especially angry at Gore?"

He shrugged. "Everybody had lost money on Deal Coin. I would guess that they were all unhappy about it."

11

"IT IS OUR POLICY TO COOPERATE WITH LAW ENFORCEMENT"

Pete flashed a perfunctory smile. "Good to see you again, Dave."

The imposing man with the no-nonsense demeanor sat ramrod straight behind his immaculate desk. "Same here, Pete."

I extended a hand. "Mike Daley. PD's Office. I'm representing Reggie Jones."

His grip was firm. "Dave Evans. Director of Security. Salesforce Park."

"How long have you been working here?"

"Since the park opened in 2018."

Evans was about my age. He said that prior to taking the job at Salesforce Park, he was the head of security at the Fairmont Hotel. Before that, he was a Supervisory Special Agent with the FBI. Thirty years earlier, Pete was one of a dozen cops who assisted Evans and his team to shut down a heroin distribution network in the Mission. The ex-Fed's shaved head looked as if it was sitting directly upon his muscular shoulders. He wore a charcoal suit, a white shirt, a polka dot tie, an earpiece, and an ID badge. The only thing missing was a pair of mirrored sunglasses.

We were sitting in his windowless office in the bowels of Salesforce Transit Center and next to a high-tech control center where a dozen of his subordinates hunched over laptops and monitored images from the security cameras scattered throughout the complex.

Pete feigned admiration for the flat-screen monitors mounted on the walls. "How many cameras do you have?"

"More than a hundred." Evans pointed at a young man with a cherubic face sporting a navy windbreaker with the word "Ambassador" stitched above his name. "This is Kevin Sanders."

"Nice to meet you," Pete said. "How long have you been working here?"

"Two and a half years." He said that he lived in Daly City and was working on a marketing degree at State. "I drive for Uber and Lyft. I work here at night for additional income."

The poster child for Gen Z.

"Very industrious," Pete said.

"Pays the bills. My fiancée and I are planning to get married next year."

"Congratulations." Pete turned back to Evans. "We appreciate the fact that you and Kevin were kind enough to speak to us."

"It is our policy to cooperate with law enforcement."

The PD's Office isn't exactly law enforcement, but I'm not going to quibble.

Pete's eyes were locked onto Evans. "I understand that you were in the office the morning that Tyson Gore's body was found."

"I was." He arrived at work by four AM. "First to arrive, last to leave."

Pete turned to Sanders. "You were also working that morning?"

Evans answered on his behalf. "He was." He said that Sanders worked the overnight shift. "Kevin arrived at eleven PM. His shift was scheduled to end at seven AM."

Pete spoke directly to Sanders. "What are your responsibilities?"

He glanced at Evans, who nodded. "My partner and I walk around the circumference of the park and look for anything out of the ordinary. If we do, we report it."

"Must be kind of boring."

"Most of the time." He cracked a half-smile. "Boring is good."

Evans interjected again. "We try to create a positive environment where our guests feel safe and secure."

Pete kept talking to Sanders. "The park closes at eight PM?"

"Yes."

"What do you do if you see somebody walking around after hours?"

"We politely ask them to leave and escort them out. Most people do what we ask."

"And if they don't?"

"I call my supervisor, who comes up to assist. If that doesn't work, we call the police. It doesn't happen very often."

"I understand that there was a gathering at Kanzen on the morning that Tyson Gore died."

Evans spoke up again. "There was. Mr. Gore's people and the management at Kanzen had informed us about it."

"You provided security?"

"Yes." He pointed at Sanders. "We instructed Kevin and his partner to keep an eye on Kanzen during their rounds. Obviously, he walked by several times during the late night and early morning. He didn't see anything out of the ordinary."

Perhaps he wasn't paying close attention.

Pete asked whether Gore provided his own security.

"No."

"Did Kanzen have its own security in the building?"

"No. They rely on us. They've never had any trouble."

"What time did the last guests leave?"

"Two-eleven AM. We have a security camera showing the entrance to Kanzen. In addition, there is a security camera inside the door of Kanzen. We provided our video to the police. So did Kanzen. We worked with the management of Kanzen to provide a guest list to the police." Evans's leathery face crinkled as he spoke to me. "I presume the police provided copies to your office."

"They did."

Pete asked Sanders whether he saw anybody else in the vicinity that morning.

"Other than the people who went inside Kanzen, no."

Pete turned back to Evans. "What happened on the morning that Mr. Gore died?"

"I got a call from the head of security at Millennium Tower at six-fifteen AM. He said that a body had been found in the construction zone. I offered assistance and remained here to monitor the situation. At six-twenty, Kevin reported that he had found your client in the Redwood Forest."

Pete shifted his gaze to Sanders. "You didn't see him on your earlier rounds?"

"No."

Evans spoke up again. "The area was under repair and cordoned off by a fence covered by a tarp, so it would have been difficult for Kevin to have seen anybody, especially at night."

I admired the fact that Evans stood up for his employee.

Pete was still talking to Sanders. "You saw Reggie in the redwood trees at approximately six-twenty AM?"

"Yes. I saw movement in the bushes, so I radioed for assistance and approached Mr. Jones. I politely informed him that the park was closed. Per our policy, I took his name and offered to escort him downstairs."

"Did you have any reason to believe that he was involved with Mr. Gore's death?"

"At the time, I didn't know that Mr. Gore was dead."

"How was his demeanor?"

"He looked like he had just woken up, and he was a little confused. There was an empty tequila bottle next to his backpack. I thought he might have been hungover."

"Did you detain him?"

Evans spoke up again. "I called my counterpart at Millennium Tower to inform him that we had identified a potential witness. He informed Sergeant David Dito, who said that he was going to meet with Kevin and question your client. At the time, I had no idea whether Mr. Jones had anything to do with Mr. Gore's untimely death. I told Kevin to remain with your client until Sergeant Dito arrived."

Pete looked at Sanders. "Reggie stayed and spoke to the police?"

"Yes."

"He was cooperative?"

"He wasn't uncooperative."

"Was he hurt?"

"There was dried blood on his face and hands. He said that he took a fall the night before."

"Did he make any effort to run?"

"No."

I spoke up again. "Kevin, my client didn't confess to killing Mr. Gore, did he?"

He glanced at Evans for an instant. "No."

"You didn't see him fight with Mr. Gore or push him over the railing, did you?"

"No."

"So you found no evidence that he had anything to do with Mr. Gore's death?"

"I found a wallet on the ground next to his backpack. I thought it was his. I pointed at it and offered to hand it to him, but he said that it didn't belong to him. Later the same day, I gave my statement to Inspector Lee."

Evans cleared his throat. "You now know everything that we do, Mr. Daley."

Pete spoke up again. "Did you ever meet Gore?"

Evans nodded. "A couple of times."

"Good guy?"

"Hard to say." The ex-Fed's voice filled with the skepticism of a man who had witnessed a lot over the course of his career. "He struck me as a young guy who made an insane amount of money in a short period of time. In my experience, sometimes they're smart, and sometimes they're lucky."

"Was Gore smart or lucky?"

"I don't pretend to know much about crypto, but my friends who understand that space think it was more of the latter than the former."

"Was Gore smart or lucky?" I asked Pete.

"Lucky." He grinned. "And I never even met him. What do you think?"

"Lucky. And I never met him, either."

A gust of wind hit my face as we walked along the path between Kanzen and the Redwood Forest. The park was quiet at ten-fifteen AM.

I looked at my brother. "Evans seems like a straight shooter."

"He is."

"You think Sanders was telling the truth?"

"The kid has no incentive to lie."

True. I looked over at the refurbished Redwood Forest between the path and the railing where Gore jumped, fell, or was pushed. The repairs had been completed, and the temporary fencing was gone. I inched closer to the railing and looked down at the construction area where Gore's body was found. A pile driver was hammering another support beam into the ground.

What the hell really happened here?

I pointed at the three-story redwood and brick structure with an expansive deck overlooking the park. "You know anybody with connections at Kanzen?"

"I know people everywhere, Mick. Let me make a couple of calls."

12

"IT'S NEVER TOO LATE"

Sylvia Fernandez sat at her usual spot at the head of the table in her cramped dining room at eleven-thirty on Sunday morning. Rosie's mother took a sip of coffee, placed the porcelain cup in its saucer, and looked my way. "Father Lopez gave a lovely sermon this morning."

"He did." I took a bite of the chicken enchilada that Sylvia made for our post-Mass brunch. "He's very good."

"Yes, he is."

The sweet aroma of Sylvia's enchiladas wafted in from the tiny kitchen in the two-bedroom, one-bath post-Earthquake bungalow where the plaster walls were covered with photos of four generations of the Fernandez family. On most Sundays, Rosie and I joined Sylvia after church in the stucco house in the heart of the Mission.

Sylvia was born eighty-seven years earlier in Monterrey, Mexico. She was an older, stockier, and equally intense version of Rosie. At twenty-four, she and her late husband, Eduardo, a carpenter, made their way to San Francisco's Mission District along with Rosie's older brother, Tony, who was a baby. Sylvia and Eduardo worked long hours and saved for a down payment on the little house that cost twenty-four thousand dollars. Today, Sylvia could sell it to a tech entrepreneur for almost two million, but she has no intention of ever doing so.

Sylvia was still razor-sharp and pretty spry for someone with two artificial knees and an artificial hip. She lived around the corner from the apartments on Garfield Square where my parents had grown up. When I was little, my mom and dad, two brothers, baby sister, and I squeezed into a two-bedroom apartment a block from where we were sitting before we moved into a larger house in the Sunset.

Sylvia adjusted the white apron that she wore over her going-to-church dress. "Do you ever miss being a priest, Michael?"

"Sometimes. I still like going to church. I don't like being the star of the show."

"Yet you like performing in court?"

"I like being a lawyer."

"Suit yourself." She turned to Rosie, who was checking messages on her phone. "Have you heard from Tony?"

"He's fine, Mama. He's in Marin with Rolanda and the baby."

"Is Rolanda staying in bed?"

"Yes, Mama. She's very conscientious."

"Good. I'll FaceTime her later today." She turned back to me. "Have you reassigned all of her cases?"

"Yes."

"I don't want her to feel any pressure to go back to work. I understand that you are handling the Reggie Jones trial. The *Chronicle* said that your client tried to rob Tyson Gore and pushed him over the railing at Salesforce Park."

"He told me that he was sleeping in the park on the night that Gore died. I'm not convinced that Reggie pushed him over the railing."

"Then who did?"

Good question. "Gore may have committed suicide. There were other people in the area. Gore lost forty billion dollars of his investors' money. A lot of people were mad at him."

"I'd be mad at him, too. I think crypto is a hustle."

Her instincts were excellent.

Rosie touched her mother's hand. "You wouldn't have pushed him over the railing into a construction zone, Mama."

"Of course not, dear. If he had lost forty billion of my money, I would have made his life miserable for decades."

Rosie grinned. She placed her phone on the table and drank iced tea. "You okay, Mama?"

"Of course, dear."

"You need anything?"

"I have more than I need. I think I'm getting addicted to online shopping."

Sylvia had weathered Covid at home by chatting with her family and friends on FaceTime and Zoom and ordering copious amounts of food and drink from her favorite stores in the Mission. Tony provided fresh fruit and vegetables from his produce market on Twenty-fourth, around the corner from St. Peter's Catholic Church, where we had attended Mass.

"How's your back?" Rosie asked.

"Fine." Sylvia would never admit that she was getting older. Rosie finally convinced her to get hearing aids for her FaceTime visits with her great-granddaughter.

"Are you playing tonight?" Rosie asked.

"Of course, dear. It's Sunday."

"In person?"

"Online. It's easier for everybody."

Sylvia and a rotating cast of her friends had been playing mah-jongg on Sunday nights since Rosie was a kid. When Covid hit, they started playing online. Sylvia was the second-youngest of the group. Jan Harris was the baby at eighty-six. Mercedes Crosskill was in her late eighties. Marge Gilbert and Flo Hoffenberg were in their early nineties. Char Saper and Yolanda Cesena were ninety-five. A few years ago, at the suggestion of Ann-Helen Leff, a nonagenarian hippie, great-grandmother, and lifelong rabble rouser, they switched the refreshments from sherry to marijuana. Sylvia received a weekly delivery of edibles from a young woman who ran a designer dispensary on Valencia Street and took orders after Mass at St. Peter's.

Sylvia smiled triumphantly. "I have some edibles that you should try, Rosita."

"I'm sticking with wine, Mama."

"Don't be such a prude. It'll take the edge off. Besides, it's legal now." She finished her coffee. "Have you given any more thought about running for another term?"

"Still thinking about it."

"You know that I would never interfere or offer advice, right?"

Yes, you would.

Rosie smiled. "Something on your mind, Mama?"

Sylvia spoke in a maternal tone. "I think two terms at a very stressful job might be enough."

"I like stress. And I really like my job."

"Grace is getting married in December. You'll want to make time to spend with your grandchildren."

"Grace and Chuck told us that they aren't planning on kids for at least three years."

Sylvia arched an eyebrow. "They may change their minds, dear."

Rosie squeezed her mother's hand. "They're adults, Mama. They will make the decision based on what's right for them."

"I can be very persuasive."

Yes, you can.

Rosie grinned. "I know, Mama."

"I trust that you'll make the right decision, dear." She turned back to me. "You can retire, too, Michael. You're already eligible for a generous City pension."

"I wouldn't have anything to do."

"You can go back to being a priest."

"It's too late."

"It's never too late."

"The process is complicated."

"It's like getting your driver's license renewed. Then you can pinch-hit for Father Lopez from time to time at St. Peter's. I want to see you in action, Michael."

Rosie egged her on. "So would I."

I held up a hand. "I can't be a priest again."

"Why not?" Sylvia asked.

"Rosie and I never got an annulment, so in the Church's eyes, we're still married."

"You'll get a waiver."

"That isn't how it works."

"Then you can sue them."

"The Archdiocese has good lawyers."

She chuckled. "You're a good lawyer, too."

13

"SHE NEEDS A WIN"

"Your mom was feisty this morning," I observed.

Rosie sipped Cab Franc. "Mama has never been shy about expressing her views."

At eleven-thirty on Sunday night, we were sitting on the sofa in the living room of Rosie's post-Earthquake bungalow in Larkspur, a leafy suburb about ten miles north of the Golden Gate Bridge. Rosie rented the house after we split up, and I moved into an apartment a couple of blocks away. Since the Public Defender is required to have an "official" residence in San Francisco, Rosie also leased a studio apartment a few doors from her mother's house. We became the proud owners of the Larkspur house when a grateful (and well-heeled) client bought it for us after we got his murder conviction overturned. We could sell our little piece of the American Dream for somewhere close to two million dollars, but it would cost more to buy a replacement. I spent most nights here with Rosie, but I kept the apartment for those occasions when we needed a little space. It also became our de facto quarantine location when I caught a mild case of Covid in February.

"She doesn't want you to run for another term," I said.

"She never wanted me to run for PD in the first place. I respect her opinion, but I'm going to make the call."

You always do.

Her eyes reflected the glowing embers in the fireplace. "You going to get an acquittal for Reggie?"

"It's late, Rosie. Can we talk about business in the morning?"

"It's my responsibility to monitor the cases of my subordinates." She placed her goblet on the end table. "Have you found anything that might get you to reasonable doubt?"

"Not yet. Pete and I spent the weekend going through security videos from Salesforce Park and Kanzen. We haven't found anything that would lead to a slam-dunk acquittal."

She tugged at the sleeve of her worn Cal hoodie. "What does Rolanda think?"

I didn't take it personally that Rosie was more interested in her niece's opinion than mine. "She isn't wildly optimistic, either." I filled her in on my conversations with Reggie, the DA, Inspector Lee, the ME, Sergeant Dito, and the security guys at Salesforce Park. "There were no eyewitnesses."

"Except for our client and Gore."

"Reggie doesn't remember anything. Gore is dead."

"And the real killer."

"You believe Reggie?"

"I don't know. I met him only briefly. I do know that Gore had two unsuccessful marriages and a broken relationship with his latest girlfriend, his business was imploding, he was about to lose billions, and his investors were furious."

"Rolanda thinks our strongest argument may be suicide. Gore was under an insane amount of stress, drinking heavily, and taking very strong antidepressants and bath salts. Gina Cole did a psychological autopsy. She's prepared to opine that Gore was suicidal."

"There's your answer."

"Not necessarily. Gore's therapist is going to testify that he showed no suicidal tendencies. She knew Gore. Gina didn't. Who do you think the jury will believe?"

"Gina is very good. Besides, we don't have to prove that he was suicidal. We just need to persuade one juror that he might have been. That'll get us a hung jury and our esteemed DA will have to decide whether she wants to start the process all over again."

"I'm not as confident as you are."

She grinned. "I'm not as confident as I'm pretending. By the way, how is our new DA?"

"Couldn't be better." Rosie respected Vanessa Turner's skill as an attorney, but she thought that she was more interested in TV time and politics than convicting criminals. "She spent the past year blaming all of the City's problems on her predecessor, which got him thrown out of office, and landed her the job that she always wanted. Lo and behold, there's still drug dealing and homelessness in the Tenderloin, people are still breaking into cars, and shoplifting is out of control. It's happening on her watch now, and people are starting to point fingers at her."

Her voice turned serious. "She needs a win, Mike."

"Yes, she does. She tapped Andy Erickson to get it for her. If he doesn't get a conviction, she'll blame him, and he'll probably be out of a job."

"Great. We can hire him to work for us."

"I'm not sure that he would be interested in working on our side of the street."

"He might if he thought that he could stick it to Vanessa. What's Plan B?"

There is none. "Blowing smoke and making wild and unsubstantiated accusations."

She responded with her magical smile. "Any evidence to support those wild and unsubstantiated accusations?"

"That's why we pay Pete the big bucks." I pointed at the framed engagement photo of Grace and Chuck taken two years earlier. "Anything I need to know about the wedding?"

She poured herself another glass of wine. "Chuck's mother wants to expand the invitation list again, but I'm holding firm."

I knew better than to suggest that it might be in the best interest of family harmony to add a few names. "Works for me."

"I knew that you'd see it my way." She touched her heart. "Your ticker okay?"

"Everything's working fine."

Two years ago, my doctor discovered that I had developed an extra heartbeat called a ventricular bigeminy. It's fairly common even among people like me who aren't overweight, have low cholesterol, exercise pretty regularly, and don't smoke. My cardiologist did a high-tech procedure called an ablation where she sent a little probe into my heart, did a detailed map, and zapped the spot causing the extra beat. I was in and out of the hospital the same day, and I didn't feel a thing. Thankfully, the procedure was successful, and my heart was back to normal.

Rosie's voice turned serious. "I know that I'm asking a lot from you, but I don't want you to overdo it. I need you to be at full strength for the wedding—and beyond."

"I'll be careful."

She arched an eyebrow. "What time are you going in to the office tomorrow?"

"Not too early."

"Good. I'm going to need more details on your case."

"Now?"

"In the bedroom." She grinned. "If your heart is up to it."

14

"JUST BUSINESS"

The wiry man with the buzz cut, muscular forearms, and dyed black goatee pressed his phone to his ear and pointed at the two chairs opposite his metal desk. His Patagonia vest and designer khakis were standard attire in the gentrified tech gulch which now extends from Market Street past the ballpark and the new UCSF Medical campus to the Warriors arena and all the way to Potrero Hill. He spun around in his swivel chair so that Pete and I couldn't see his face. He barked out a string of profanity-laced commands and ended the call by shouting, "Get it done!"

He turned to face us, placed his phone on the desk, extended a thin hand, and switched to an engaging tone. "Matt Bosworth. People call me 'Boz.' Welcome to Boz Coin."

"Mike Daley. I'm with the Public Defender's Office. This is my brother, Pete, who is a private investigator. We're representing Reggie Jones. Thank you for seeing us."

"You're welcome."

The "world headquarters" of Boz's crypto start-up was housed in a thirty-by-thirty-foot bullpen area on the third floor of Salesforce Tower. The single window looked out at the white latticework surrounding the Salesforce Transit Center across the alley. A dozen employees wearing noise-cancelling headphones sat shoulder-to-shoulder at metal tables and stared at their laptops. There was a coffee pot and a mini-fridge in the corner. The walls were painted off-white with holes revealing where somebody else's artwork used to hang.

"Apologies for the modest surroundings," Bosworth said. "We're trying to keep our costs down until we get our next round of funding. Salesforce is renting us this space at a substantial discount until they find a new tenant."

Given the glut of empty office space in downtown San Francisco, that may take a while.

I pointed at the people hunched over their laptops. "You have a dedicated team."

"I brought over the best people from Deal Coin. Everybody is getting 'sweat equity.'"

In other words, nobody is getting paid until you get funded. It may be challenging to find investors for a crypto start-up put together by the old management team at Deal Coin.

I asked him about his new platform.

"It's a big upgrade on the Deal Coin technology with significant enhancements. It has unlimited potential."

They said the same thing about Deal Coin until it lost forty billion in value. "The Deal Coin situation must have been very difficult for you."

"Just business."

"I'm sorry about Tyson Gore. I read that you were roommates at Princeton. You must have known him very well."

"I did. He was the best man at my wedding. I was the best man at his weddings. After Princeton, he went to Stanford Business School and started several companies. I went to Columbia Law School and worked at a Silicon Valley law firm where I represented Tyson on a couple of deals. We were already friends and we enjoyed working together, so we started doing deals. He came up with the ideas and led the technology team. I handled the business side. We hit a couple of home runs and made a lot of money."

And then you struck out a few times and lost a lot of money.

I wanted to keep him talking. "The *Chronicle* said that Tyson was ahead of his time."

"He was a visionary. Some people compared him to Steve Jobs and Elon Musk."

Others compared him to Bernie Madoff and Elizabeth Holmes.

"Deal Coin was doing great for a while," I said. "What happened?"

"Bad timing and bad luck."

What about bad management?

"You know much about crypto?" Bosworth asked.

"A little. I have friends in finance who think it'll never work in mainstream commerce."

"They're wrong. Bitcoin has been around since 2009. You can't run a company that long without proof of economic viability."

It also helps if you have investors with unlimited capital at their disposal.

Pete and I listened attentively as Bosworth launched into a ten-minute lecture sprinkled with terms like blockchain, tokens, mining, cold and hot wallets, public and private keys, NFTs, Ethereum, and stablecoins. I had heard most of the jargon, but I had a limited understanding of how everything fit together.

"When do you think crypto will be in the mainstream?" I asked.

"It already is. You got a 401(k)?"

"Yes." I said that it was managed by Fidelity. "It invests in mutual funds."

Bosworth smirked. "Many of those funds are investing a portion of their assets in crypto. When institutional investors put money into a new asset category, it's real."

Not necessarily.

Pete pretended to be impressed. "What about the reports that people are using crypto to pay for drugs and launder money?"

"Not anymore."

"You can't buy groceries with it."

"That's where Deal Coin came in, and now Boz Coin. Tyson and I developed an algorithm to make crypto usable for retail transactions in person, on your phone, and on your computer.

Deal Coin didn't get there, but we will. We're one of several start-ups trying to get our platform running at scale. Whoever gets there first will be worth more than Google and Amazon combined."

Forgive me if I'm skeptical.

Pete played along. "If Deal Coin was so close, why did its valuation drop so quickly?"

"The market isn't always rational. Rumors spread that our competitors were going to ramp up before we did. Some of our investors and customers got nervous. People started asking for their money back, and we didn't have the liquid resources to pay them. Tyson and I were trying to raise another round of capital to finish our rollout when our valuation crashed." He held his right thumb and forefinger an inch apart. "We were this close."

Pete waited a beat. "You lost a lot of money when Deal Coin cratered."

"I put up a couple of million dollars. At one point, it was worth over a billion. At the end, it was worth nothing."

"The *Chronicle* said that Tyson reduced your percentage interest in the company before things went sideways."

"We needed to free up some extra points for our new investors."

"Did he take a similar haircut?"

"No."

"That must have been frustrating for you."

"Just business."

"Why did you stay at Deal Coin?"

"I had invested a lot of time, energy, and money. I believed in what we were doing."

And you were hoping for a huge payout.

I spoke up again. "You were with Tyson on the morning before he died?"

"Yes. I was with him all weekend at Deal Con." He confirmed that he went to the after-party at the Four Seasons and the later event at Kanzen. "We invited a few of our big investors to ask them for a little more cash to tide us over."

In his world, "a little" means billions.

"Any luck?" I asked, already knowing the answer.

"We had a couple of expressions of interest."

But nobody actually ponied up. I asked him who was there, again knowing the answer.

Bosworth rattled off the names of four masters of the universe representing venture capital funds, private equity firms, investment banks, and sovereign funds. I recognized them from the list that Rolanda had provided.

"Was anybody angry at Tyson?" I asked.

"Nobody was happy about the situation at Deal Coin."

"Did anybody get into it with Tyson at Kanzen?"

"Not really."

I waited.

Bosworth kept talking. "One of our venture investors is a guy named Steve Warren. His firm put up over a billion dollars. He was really upset about writing off such a big investment."

"He must have been through the drill before."

"He's a young guy. Deal Coin was his first big investment. He took a lot of heat from the investors and the head of his VC firm, who also happens to be his father."

This was consistent with the information that Nady provided.

"Steve laid into Tyson pretty hard," Bosworth said.

I feigned surprise. "Did Mr. Warren threaten him?"

"Not really. Steve is a hothead. He was just blowing off steam."

"What did you think of Bosworth?" I asked Pete.

"A cross between a frat boy and a tech bro."

Sounds about right. "We need to talk to Warren."

"Let me see what I can do."

We were standing in the plaza at the base of Salesforce Tower. A warm breeze hit my face as I looked at the gondola from street level up to Salesforce Park. The pile drivers were once again pounding inside the construction area surrounding Millennium Tower across the street.

He added, "Is it just me, or does it seem like everybody in the crypto world has a trust fund, an Ivy League degree, and an attitude?"

"There does seem to be a pattern."

"Some of these tech guys stumble into a lot of money and think they're geniuses. They surround themselves with sycophants who keep massaging their egos."

"I prefer to refer to them as 'suck-ups.'"

Pete glanced at his phone, read a text, and looked at me. "Got a few minutes?"

"Sure. Why?"

"The manager at Kanzen is willing to talk to us."

15

"HE WAS VERY DEMANDING"

"Thank you for seeing us," I said. "I'm Mike Daley."

"My pleasure, Mr. Daley." The young woman wearing a gray blazer and black slacks flashed a practiced half-smile. "I'm Susan Gallardo."

Her smile remained frozen in place as I introduced Pete.

At ten-forty-five on Monday morning, we were sitting in a private dining room in the members-only area on the third floor of Kanzen, the private club where Tyson Gore had spent his final hours hitting up his investors in a last-ditch effort to keep Deal Coin afloat. The picture window overlooked Salesforce Park. The room was more clubby than ostentatious. The walls, table, and credenza were made of redwood veneer. It looked like a stripped-down version of the century-old Redwood Room at the elegant Clift Hotel a few blocks from Union Square.

"How long have you worked here?" I asked.

"Three years." She said that Kanzen opened a few weeks before Covid hit.

"Your timing wasn't great."

"Our owners are well capitalized and in for the long haul." She explained that Kanzen was one of a dozen private clubs operated by an investment firm in Japan. She said that "Kanzen" meant "perfect" in Japanese.

I asked her where she was from.

"Connecticut." She earned a degree in hotel management from Cornell. "I worked at hotels in New York after I got out of college. Then I was hired as assistant manager of Kanzen in

Tokyo. I helped open our locations in Tokyo and Dubai before I was asked to come to San Francisco to open this location."

"You've seen a lot of the world in a short time. You're the manager?"

"General manager."

With her creamy skin, subtle makeup, and jet-black hair worn in a severe pixie cut, I figured that she was in her mid-thirties. Her muscular shoulders suggested that she had been a competitive swimmer in high school and/or college. I noticed a few worry lines on her forehead that were mostly hidden by a talented Botox artist.

I feigned admiration for our surroundings. "Beautiful place. I understand that the entry fee is mid six-figures. Your membership must be very exclusive."

"That's our business model." She said that the Michelin-starred sushi restaurant on the first floor was open to the public. The private club on the second floor would set you back "only" fifty grand. "The bar, dining area, and private meeting rooms on this level are open only to a hundred members in our most exclusive tier."

"You're fully subscribed?"

"Yes, we are. We have a lengthy waiting list."

I looked at Pete, who picked up the cue. "You knew Tyson Gore?"

"Yes."

"How did he treat you and your staff?"

"He was very demanding, but always professional."

I'll bet you've used that line a million times.

"How well did you know him?" Pete asked.

"Not that well. Our relationship was strictly business. He was in our highest membership category, so I made sure that he had everything that he needed. He came in a couple of nights a week for private dinners. On occasion, he came for lunch by himself. He was always cordial."

"Did he ever give you any trouble?"

"He was very demanding."

Got it.

Pete kept his tone conversational. "Did he ever mention his family?"

"He told me that he was divorced with several children. I didn't ask for details."

You get paid to be discreet.

"He had two acrimonious divorces," Pete said.

"It never came up. I never met his ex-wives."

"He had an ex-girlfriend named Amanda Blair."

"I never met her." Her expression transformed into a half-smile. "I understand that she's developed a large following on TikTok. Good for her."

"Did Ms. Blair ever accompany Mr. Gore to the club?"

"No."

Pete arched an eyebrow. "Did you ever see Mr. Gore with a woman other than Ms. Blair?"

A hesitation. "No."

Pete waited a beat. "Was Mr. Gore cheating on Ms. Blair?"

Gallardo cleared her throat. "I heard rumors."

"Do you have any names?"

"I'm afraid not." She quickly added, "Like I said, it was just rumors."

Pete's expression didn't change, but I sensed that he thought there was more to the story. He decided to move on. "Mr. Gore set up the event here at the club?"

"Yes." She said that Gore arranged for a gathering in the bar next to the room where we were sitting. "He ordered light hors d'oeuvres and desserts. And, of course, the bar was open."

"How many of your staff were working?"

"Four of us: a bartender, two servers, and me."

"Security guard?"

"No. We rely on Salesforce security and our surveillance cameras. This is a safe area, and we've never had any trouble." She handed Pete a list of the employees along with their departure times. "The police interviewed everybody. You can talk to them if you'd like."

"We will. What time did you leave?"

"Right after Mr. Gore at two-twelve AM. I was the last person here."

"You went straight home?"

"Yes." She said that she walked to her condo a few blocks away at the upscale Infinity Towers.

"That's a nice building," Pete said. "How do you like it?"

"A lot. Great views. Nice neighborhood. Very convenient for work."

Pete always interspersed a few personal questions to put a potential witness at ease.

"You walked by the Redwood Forest on your way home?"

"Yes."

"Did you see or hear anything?"

"No."

"You saw Mr. Gore leave?"

"Yes." Gallardo confirmed that he left by himself.

"How was his demeanor? Frustrated? Angry? Agitated?"

"Exhausted."

"We were told that he was soliciting additional funds for Deal Coin. Do you know if he was successful?"

"We don't listen to our members' private conversations."

"Did you get the impression that he was having a good night?"

"He didn't look happy when he left."

"How many other people were here besides you, your staff, and Mr. Gore?"

"Five." She handed Pete another list, which we had also received from the DA. "We usually keep the names of our members and their guests confidential, but in the circumstances, we felt obligated to provide this information and surveillance videos to the police."

"How many cameras do you have?"

"Just one inside the front door."

Pete handed me the list, which I had already seen. I asked Gallardo if she had met any of the people on the list.

"Mr. Bosworth was Mr. Gore's business partner and is also a member of the club. He didn't come in as often as Mr. Gore.

Mr. Warren is also a member of Kanzen who attended Mr. Gore's gathering. I don't recall meeting the others."

"How well do you know Mr. Warren?"

"Not that well. His office is in Menlo Park, so he doesn't come in very often."

"I understand that you weren't privy to the details of conversations between Mr. Gore and his guests. However, did you notice whether Mr. Gore had any disagreements or heated exchanges with any of his guests?"

She paused to consider how much she wanted to tell me. "Mr. Gore and Mr. Warren had a tense conversation. They didn't raise their voices, but Mr. Warren was very upset."

16

"I WAS TRYING TO BUY HIM SOME TIME"

The young man with the tiny blue eyes, thinning blonde hair, pronounced double chin, and physique of an offensive lineman squeezed my hand and spoke in a raspy voice. "Steve Warren. Thank you for coming in so early. I like to work out before I go to the office. My days are packed with meetings."

"Not a problem," I said.

At seven-thirty AM on Wednesday, September fourteenth, Warren and I were sitting on opposite sides of his teak desk that looked as if he had purchased it at Scandinavian Design and assembled it himself. Pete was trying to track down Gore's ex-wives and Amanda Blair, so I was flying solo.

"I appreciate the fact that you were able to fit me in," I said.

"My pleasure."

Right.

Warren Capital was founded forty-five years earlier by Steve's father, Charles Warren. It was housed in a cookie-cutter two-story office park at 3000 Sand Hill Road, next door to the swanky Sharon Heights Country Club, and about a hundred yards from the entrance ramp to the 280 Freeway. Warren was one of a half-dozen well-scrubbed Gen Y venture capitalists who worked in matching ten-by-ten-foot glass-enclosed offices surrounding a bullpen where a dozen grungier Gen Z analysts crunched numbers on their laptops. There was an empty conference room at one end of the bullpen. At the other end was the huge office of Warren's father, which had a custom mahogany desk and matching bookcases and credenza, an expansive table, a full wet bar, and a private bathroom. Unlike his subordinates who had views of the fountain in the courtyard and the Teslas in the parking lot, the elder Warren had an unobstructed view of the first tee of the Sharon Heights golf course. Founder's privilege.

"How long has your firm been here?" I asked, already knowing the answer.

"Since 1978. My father started with ten million under management. Now it's ten billion."

"That's impressive." *It's also incomprehensible to me.* I looked at the empty walls and pedestrian furnishings. "I guess I was expecting something a little more, uh, lavish."

"My grandparents ran a shoe store in Hazleton, Pennsylvania. My dad didn't want to spend his life selling loafers, so he put himself through Penn State and Columbia Law School. He doesn't like to spend money on unnecessary expenses."

How refreshing. I pointed at a framed photo of two smiling toddlers—the only personal item in his office. "Cute kids. You and your wife must be very proud."

"We are." He frowned. "Actually, my wife and I got divorced a couple of years ago."

"I'm sorry." I wanted to keep him talking. "I take it that you grew up around here?"

"Atherton."

Nice. Home to tech moguls, venture capitalists, and professional athletes, the tree-lined suburb in the hills north of Menlo Park was among the most expensive zip codes in the U.S. A fixer-upper would set you back five million. A more typical house would run eight million. Stephen Curry bought his two-story mansion for a cool thirty million, and it isn't even the most expensive house on his cul-de-sac.

"Where do you live now?"

"Atherton."

It must be nice to have a trust fund.

We exchanged stilted small talk for a few minutes. He confirmed that he had attended the exclusive Menlo School, where annual tuition was sixty grand. He was a backup offensive lineman at Penn and graduated from Wharton, then got an MBA at Northwestern. He came home to work at Kleiner Perkins, one of Silicon Valley's seminal venture capital firms.

I asked him why he left Kleiner.

"My dad made me an offer that I couldn't refuse." He said that his father had always wanted him to join the family business. "I was reluctant. Everybody assumes that you got the job through nepotism."

Another nepo baby. I didn't ask whether his father had interviewed any other candidates.

"My father just turned seventy," he said. "He's implementing a succession plan. My brothers aren't interested in working for him, so I agreed. My dad needed somebody with experience in the crypto and NFT space." He feigned modesty. "It seemed like a good fit."

I'll bet that you didn't have to take a pay cut. "You seem happy with your decision."

"I am."

I asked him about his most successful deals. He seemed to relish the opportunity to talk about himself. I feigned admiration as he spent fifteen minutes expounding on the millions that he made investing in a half-dozen crypto companies whose names I didn't recognize. He characterized every investment as a "home run." He didn't mention any strikeouts.

"What percentage of your investments hit it big?" I asked.

"Five to ten percent. They pay for the ones that don't."

The names of which are never spoken aloud. "As I mentioned to you by phone, I'm representing Reggie Jones. I understand that you invested in several of Tyson Gore's businesses."

"I did." He leaned back in his chair. "The first two were grand slams." He said that his investors made more than a hundred million dollars when Gore sold the companies.

How many baseball metaphors can you recite? "They must have been pleased," I understated.

"They were."

"You and your dad must have been pleased, too."

"We were."

"Any others?"

He exhaled heavily. "The third investment was Deal Coin."

I grimaced on his behalf, but I didn't say anything.

He felt compelled to offer an explanation. "Tyson put together the most impressive business plan that I had ever seen." He wagged a finger for emphasis. "It was the most impressive business plan that *my dad* had ever seen."

Rosie says that my superpower is that I'm able to convince people that I'm genuinely interested in what they're saying. "What was so good about it?"

"What's the biggest problem with crypto?"

"You can't buy anything with it." *Except drugs, stolen goods, and other cryptocurrencies.*

His small eyes lit up. "Do you know where Elon Musk made his money?"

"PayPal."

"Exactly. The company revolutionized the way we pay for things. Deal Coin was on the verge of doing the same thing. Tyson developed a program to use crypto to pay for groceries, computers, baseball tickets—anything. It was safe, easy to use, and fast. Deal Coin had the potential to make cash, credit cards, PayPal, and Venmo obsolete."

Right. "What happened?"

"Bad timing. The war in Ukraine started. Gas prices and interest rates went up. Stock prices went down. Investors got skittish and rushed to safer investments. The crypto market crashed. Deal Coin went from a forty billion valuation to almost nothing."

"How much did your investors put up?" I asked.

"That's confidential."

"Was there anything that you could have done to keep Deal Coin afloat?"

"I spent the weekend with Tyson at Deal Con. I was trying to buy him some time. I tried to persuade some of the other investors to put up additional cash to keep Deal Coin going until the market got better. After Tyson died, we had no choice but to take the company into bankruptcy." He got a wistful look in his eyes. "It's a shame. It had so much potential."

And you would have made enough to buy a house in Atherton that's even bigger than Stephen Curry's. "You were at Kanzen that night?"

"Yes. I arrived shortly after midnight." He said that the gathering was tense. "Tyson needed money. It was his last shot to raise additional capital."

"How was his mood?"

"He was exhausted, but Tyson was always optimistic."

"The manager at Kanzen told us that you and Tyson got into an argument."

"I wouldn't characterize it that way. We had a forthright discussion about raising additional funds. I told him that I expected a premium return for putting more money into a distressed company. He wasn't happy about it, but he understood the request."

"Just business."

"Exactly."

I'm starting to get the hang of crypto speak. "Did anybody else get into it with Tyson?"

"Matt Bosworth was on his case all night. And Cynthia Mitchell laid into him."

Mitchell was the founder of a venture capital firm that made the second-largest investment in Deal Coin.

He added, "Cynthia is super-smart and very direct. She doesn't like losing money."

Nobody does. "What did she say to him?"

"If he didn't get his act together, she would take Deal Coin into bankruptcy and make sure that he never got funding on another deal."

"What time did you leave?"

"A few minutes after two." He said that Gore, Bosworth, and Gallardo were the only people left at Kanzen when he departed.

"Did you see anybody outside Kanzen when you left?"

"No."

"Did you see my client or anybody else in the Redwood Forest?"

"No."

The good news is that I can place you in that vicinity the morning that Gore died. The bad news is that I don't have a shred of evidence that you had any involvement in Gore's death.

"You must have been pretty upset about losing your investment," I said.

"I was. So were my investors."

And your father. "Who else should I talk to who was at Kanzen that night?"

"Cynthia, but she isn't likely to tell you anything more than I just did."

17

"IT WAS FOR REAL"

The woman with the intense brown eyes, severely cut black hair, and hoop-style earrings measured her words with surgical precision. "Tyson Gore was brilliant. It's a shame that he couldn't get Deal Coin to scale. It would have been a game changer in the crypto space."

At ten-thirty that same morning, a Wednesday, I had returned to the City, where I was sitting in the spacious office of Cynthia Mitchell, the founder, chair, and largest investor in Mitchell Investment Partners, the most successful female-controlled venture fund in the U.S. The forty-five-year-old was the daughter of a Greenwich hedge fund sponsor and a big-firm lawyer. After graduating from Bryn Mawr and Wharton, she worked at Goldman Sachs in New York. She moved to the Bay Area a few years later and became one of the first female partners of Andreessen Horowitz, one of the preeminent venture capital firms in Silicon Valley.

I admired her panoramic view of the Bay Bridge, Treasure Island, and the Oakland Hills from her top-floor office in the gleaming 181 Fremont Tower on the south side of Salesforce Park. When it was completed, Facebook had rented the entire building as its San Francisco headquarters.

"How did you pry this space away from Facebook?" I asked.

"Their stock has dropped more than sixty percent since January. Mark needed to cut costs, so he subleased the space to us at a fraction of what it would have cost a year ago."

"Good timing."

"For us. Not so good for Mark."

I appreciated her directness. I pointed at the framed photo of a smiling Mitchell along with her teenaged daughter. "Tahoe?"

"Vail. My ex-husband and I are very proud of our daughter." She said that she and her ex had met when she was working at Andreessen and he was at Google. Her daughter was a sophomore at University High School in Pacific Heights.

"Why did you leave Andreessen?" I asked.

"Women are not well represented in venture capital and private equity. I wanted to start a firm run by women, funded primarily by women, and which invests mostly in companies founded by women."

Admirable. "Your investors are all female?"

"My ex-husband is our token male." She chuckled to herself. "We refer to him as our 'affirmative action investor.' We also make it a priority to mentor the next generation of female investors."

I asked her about her investment criteria.

"We are very selective. We identify entrepreneurs of great integrity and vision who have a unique and compelling business plan. We invest in companies that will change the paradigm or create a new industry. That eliminates ninety percent of the companies we look at. We do an extraordinary amount of due diligence on the management team to make sure that they have the leadership and operational skills to execute the plan. That eliminates ninety percent of the companies that we haven't already ruled out."

"What percentage of your investments are winners?"

"One in twenty."

I noted that Deal Coin wasn't a female-founded business.

"We consider companies founded by men that look especially promising."

"You must have thought that Deal Coin was for real."

She lowered her voice. "It was for real."

"What made you think so?"

"Over the years, we've looked at many companies claiming to have the technology and the expertise to turn crypto into a viable platform for day-to-day transactions. Deal Coin had a compelling strategy and the technological knowledge to pull it off. The upside was infinite."

I eyed her. "Billions?"

"Trillions."

I have nothing against people making money, but it sounded obscene. "You were comfortable with Tyson Gore?"

"Yes. We met when I was at Goldman. I persuaded Andreessen to fund two of his start-ups—both successful. We did our homework. I respected his technological knowledge and leadership skills. He checked all the boxes."

"You were aware of his divorces, extramarital affairs, drinking, use of antidepressants, and drug use?"

"Of course. I put a premium on leadership, competence, and vision. We concluded that his personal issues did not interfere with his ability to operate his businesses."

"Sounds like you wouldn't have been interested in spending a week with him in Vail."

"Probably not."

"What happened with Deal Coin?"

"Mostly bad timing." She cited the Russian invasion of Ukraine, high gas prices, and inflation that caused the stock market to drop. "Investors got nervous about new technologies."

Warren said the same thing. "Was there fraud?"

"Not as far as we can tell. No criminal charges were brought against Deal Coin's management. We've been over the books. The rollout was delayed because of glitches in the company's technology. Then the crypto market crashed and took Deal Coin with it."

"Do you still believe in crypto?"

"Yes. I think somebody will accomplish what Tyson was trying to do. I don't know how long it will take, but whoever gets there first is going to be obscenely rich."

"I talked to Matt Bosworth, who is trying to do just that. Any plans to invest in his new company?"

"We're looking at it." Her eyes narrowed. "You didn't come to talk to me about my investing strategy."

True. "I understand that you were with Mr. Gore shortly before he died."

"I saw him at Deal Con. He invited me and several of his key investors to an after-hours gathering at Kanzen."

"Matt Bosworth and Steve Warren told me that Mr. Gore hit you up for more money."

"He did. I listened to his pitch, but I didn't find it persuasive. I informed him that my investors and I were not prepared to put more money into the company." She said that she left Kanzen at one-fifty AM.

"Did you see Mr. Gore after you left?"

"No."

"What about my client?"

"I didn't see anybody."

"How was Mr. Gore's mood?"

"Disappointed."

"We have reason to believe that he was suffering from severe emotional distress."

"I didn't notice anything out of the ordinary."

"Deal Coin was imploding. He had been through two divorces and a breakup with his most recent girlfriend. He was drinking heavily, taking antidepressants, and using designer drugs. Did you consider the possibility that he was suicidal?"

"It didn't appear that way to me, Mr. Daley. On the other hand, you never really know what's going on inside somebody else's head, do you?"

I guess not. "Did anybody have angry words with him at Kanzen?"

"Matt Bosworth snapped at him. Steve Warren laid into him pretty hard. Gene McAllister told him that he would never invest in another one of his projects."

Eugene McAllister was an Oakland native who came from modest beginnings and became one of the most successful real estate developers in the U.S. He invested some of his fortune in tech start-ups like Facebook, Twitter, and Square. If you believed the financial press, he was worth a cool five billion. He was working on a deal with Magic Johnson and LeBron James to redevelop a significant parcel of land next to the site of the proposed new A's ballpark at Jack London Square in Oakland.

She read my expression. "I've known Gene for years. He is one of the most astute investors in the Bay Area. If you think he had anything to do with Tyson's death, you are mistaken."

18

"NOT UNLESS YOU'RE PREPARED TO LOSE IT"

"Thank you for seeing me, Mr. McAllister," I said.

"You're welcome, Mr. Daley." The African-American man with the short gray hair, trim mustache, and paternal manner touched his gold cuff links. "Happy to help."

Eugene McAllister's immaculate office was on the thirty-fourth floor of the 555 Mission Street high-rise, three blocks west of Salesforce Tower. Coincidentally, the steel-and-glass tower was built on the former site of a crumbling brick walk-up that used to house a mediocre Chinese restaurant, a Krishna copy shop, and the original Law Office of Fernandez and Daley, where Rosie and I worked in a converted martial arts studio on the second floor. When the building was torn down to make way for the office tower, Rosie and I moved around the corner into a century-old building at 84 First Street in a suite that was formerly occupied by Madame Lena, a tarot card reader who now tells fortunes in a condo on a golf course in Palm Springs.

"Coffee?" he asked.

"Thank you," I said.

McAllister buzzed his assistant, who arrived with a bone china cup of Peet's. I took a sip and paused to admire his antique rolltop desk, rosewood table, and floor-to-ceiling bookcases filled with leather-bound volumes holding the documents for McAllister's numerous deals. His credenza was covered with Lucite cubes that law firms give to their clients as trophies to celebrate their multimillion-dollar transactions.

There was also a framed portrait of McAllister, his wife, three sons and their spouses, and seven grandchildren. The table was covered by a model of the proposed new A's ballpark complex adjacent to Jack London Square.

I pointed at the photo. "You have a lovely family."

"Thank you." He reported that his eldest son was a doctor, his second son was an engineer at Oracle, and the youngest was a struggling writer in Hollywood. "Do you have kids?"

"Two. One is in college at Cal. The other graduated from USC Film School and is working as a production supervisor at Pixar."

"Very impressive, Mr. Daley." He sounded sincere.

I gestured at the diorama of the ballpark. "Do you think it will move forward?"

"We'll see."

I pointed at a photo of McAllister standing between Buster Posey and Tim Lincecum. "When was that taken?"

"The 2014 World Series ring ceremony." He opened his drawer, took out a jewelry box, and showed me his diamond-studded ring. "I'm in the Giants' ownership group." His voice filled with pride. "I have a little piece of the Warriors, too. I have four rings from them."

I am insanely jealous. "You should buy an NFL team."

"I've tried."

In response to my inquiry about his background, he said that he had grown up in East Oakland, graduated from McClymonds High School, worked his way through Cal, and started his career with a property management firm in downtown Oakland. "I saved my money and bought a few apartment buildings near Lake Merritt when prices were depressed. Then I bought a few more. I started bringing in investors to buy bigger projects in Southern California. Then we moved into Arizona, Nevada, Texas and the East Coast."

"You've been very successful."

"I hired smart people, made some good investments, benefited from excellent timing, and had some extraordinary luck. We were able to ride out the economic downturns, the

Great Recession, and, more recently, Covid. It's been a great ride."

His modesty sounded a bit rehearsed, but it was still refreshing in San Francisco's ego-fueled billionaire class.

I turned to business. "I'm representing Reggie Jones."

"So I understand. It's a great tragedy. Did he kill Tyson?"

"He says that he didn't."

He arched an eyebrow. "You believe him?"

"Unless and until I have reason to disbelieve him. You invested in Deal Coin?"

"Yes." He glanced at an autographed photo of Stephen Curry. "A couple of my fellow investors in the Warriors introduced me to Tyson and said that Deal Coin was a good bet." He shrugged. "Turns out that it wasn't." He cited "bad timing" without elaborating.

I asked him if he had invested in other crypto deals.

"Yes. A couple of them have done well. Others haven't."

"Should I put my money into crypto?"

He responded with a knowing smile. "Not unless you're prepared to lose it."

"How well did you know Tyson Gore?"

"Not that well."

"You were comfortable with him as the CEO of Deal Coin?"

"He was a brilliant entrepreneur and a seasoned CEO."

Sounds like you're reading from a script. "You think he was honest?"

"Yes."

"Competent?"

"I wouldn't have invested if I didn't think so."

"Did you like him?"

"Yes. He was smart, well-read, sincere, and, at times, funny."

"Did you socialize with him?"

"Occasionally. He invited me to his box at the ballpark. I reciprocated by letting him use my Warriors seats."

"Did you notice any changes in his behavior when Deal Coin started going sideways?"

"Obviously, he was very concerned about the company, but I didn't notice any differences in his personality."

"Did you know that he was taking strong antidepressants?"

"Yes."

"And designer stimulants called bath salts?"

He waited a beat. "I didn't know, but I'm not entirely surprised."

"Did you notice any signs of depression or impairment?"

"No."

"Did you talk to him at Deal Con?"

"Yes. He spent the weekend reassuring the investors that Deal Coin was still on track." He shrugged. "He was wrong."

"You were at the gathering at Kanzen?"

"I was." He confirmed that Gore asked for money. "I listened to his presentation, and I told him that I couldn't justify an additional investment."

"Even to protect your original investment?"

"In my judgment, it would have been putting in good money after bad. He was disappointed, but he was an experienced entrepreneur who knew how to deal with rejection."

"What time did you arrive at Kanzen?"

"A few minutes after eleven." He noted that Gore, Bosworth, Warren, and Mitchell were already there along with Susan Gallardo and several staff members from the club. "I left at one AM." He didn't see anybody outside. He picked up his car from the garage at 555 Mission and drove straight home to his house in the Oakland hills.

"Was anybody angry at him?"

He considered his answer. "The gathering was tense. He and Matt Bosworth exchanged words. Steve Warren was pretty upset. So was Cynthia Mitchell."

"Anybody else?"

"Jack Emrich had a couple of glasses of wine and said a few things that he probably shouldn't have." He explained that Emrich was a senior investment manager for Deutsche Bank. "He is no longer working for the bank."

"Was he fired over Deal Coin?"

He gave me a cryptic smile. "I don't know who initiated his separation."

"What's he doing now?"

"Last I heard, he started a hedge fund."

19

"CHECK THIS OUT"

Pete looked up from his laptop. "You don't look happy."

"I've been meeting with venture capitalists all day," I said.

He gave me a sideways grin. "Were they nice?"

"They were rich."

"I have nothing against people trying to make a buck."

"Or a billion. It seems like gambling to me."

"It is."

He was sitting at the table in the conference room at the PD's Office at seven-forty-five the same night. Nady was across from him, staring at her laptop. The ever-present Terrence "The Terminator" was at his cubicle outside my office. The aroma of leftover pizza and Caesar salad wafted through the room.

Pete held up a hand. "Did you get anything useful from the geniuses who made the brilliant decision to invest in Deal Coin?"

"Not much." I summarized my conversations with Warren, Mitchell, and McAllister.

He grinned. "Any chance you persuaded McAllister to invite you to his luxury box for a Giants game?"

"Afraid not."

"If you were rich enough to be in the ownership groups of the Giants and the Warriors, why would you set your money on fire by investing in a crapshoot like Deal Coin?"

"Fear of missing out. His rich pals did the same thing."

"Did he acknowledge that it was a mistake?"

"Yes."

"How refreshing."

Enough. "Did you get anything on Jack Emrich?"

"He got fired by Deutsche Bank after the Deal Coin fiasco."

"I need to talk to him."

"He's in London looking for investors for a hedge fund that he's putting together. He'll be back next week." His expression turned skeptical. "You really think one of the rich guys killed Gore?"

Seems like a long shot, but you never know. "We need to consider every angle. We can prove that the Deal Coin investors were in the immediate vicinity."

"You're grasping, Mick."

Yes, I am. "I want to talk to Gore's ex-wives and his ex-girlfriend."

"The ex-wives were out of town. We have no evidence that the ex-girlfriend was at Salesforce Park that night, Mick."

"I'm not suggesting that they killed him. They knew him as well as anybody. Maybe they can shed some light on his state of mind. And I want to talk to his therapist."

"I'll track her down."

"Thanks, Pete." I turned to Nady. "Anything in the security videos that I don't already know about?"

"There might be." She pulled up a video on her laptop. "Check this out. It was taken at two-twenty AM on the ground level of the Salesforce Transit Center."

I watched the video. A clean-shaven young man wearing a Patagonia windbreaker and black pants walked back and forth several times, as if he was looking for somebody.

"Who is he?" I asked.

"I don't know."

"What is he doing there?"

"I don't know that, either. Looks like he might be waiting for somebody."

She fast-forwarded five minutes. The man continued to pace. He looked at his phone every few seconds. At two-twenty-five, he gave up and left.

"Any video of him upstairs in the park?" I asked.

"No."

"Keep looking. He was waiting in the area directly beneath the spot where Gore fell or was pushed."

"Maybe it's a coincidence," she said.

"You don't believe in coincidences. Neither do I." I looked at Pete. "Show this video to your sources at SFPD and see if they know who this guy is."

"Will do, Mick."

20

"HE WASN'T SUICIDAL"

The willowy woman with sparkling blue eyes, impossibly high cheekbones, and dyed blonde hair leaned back in her ergonomic leather chair and spoke in a soothing voice. "I'm sorry, Mr. Daley. I can't talk about Tyson Gore."

"I need to ask you just a few questions."

She gave me a practiced smile. "You know that I can't talk about my patients."

"Mr. Gore is deceased. The privilege expired upon his death."

She wrinkled her perfect brow. "We have a difference of opinion about confidentiality. It is my policy not to discuss my patients in the absence of a court order."

"I can arrange it."

The smile disappeared. "You really want to go there?"

"Only if I have to."

At eight o'clock the following morning, Dr. Madeline Swartz sat behind her immaculate oak desk in her office furnished in earth tones on the third floor of an Earthquake-era building on South Park, a two-block strip of greenery between Second and Third Streets, about midway between Salesforce Park and the ballpark. In the early 1900s, it was an exclusive residential area. After the Great Earthquake, the two- and three-story buildings fell into disrepair, and the neighborhood transitioned into boarding houses and light industrial buildings. By the fifties, it was a desolate no-man's land where it was dangerous to walk at night. Things started to change in the eighties as nearby Rincon Hill and South Beach gentrified. By the start of the twenty-first century, the little park was at the center of San Francisco's tech renaissance, and the old warehouses were converted into chic offices and trendy lofts. Nowadays, South Park is surrounded by upscale coffee shops and fashionable boutiques. The rents are among the highest in town.

I looked around her office, which was bathed in sunlight. The exposed brick walls were supported by wood beams and accented by track lighting. There were two leather chairs where I surmised that Swartz spoke to her patients. The artwork included two nondescript landscapes. The windows overlooked the park. The overall effect was appropriately calming.

"You're a medical doctor?" I asked.

"PhD from Duke. Bachelor's from Stanford. I'm a psychologist and life coach. My practice focuses on executives in the tech industry."

Impressive. "Your office is very soothing. How long have you been here?"

"Twenty-five years."

"I remember when this neighborhood was skid row."

"So do I." Her tone became pointed. "You didn't come to talk about my office. You've been around the block enough times to know that I can't talk about my patients."

"Tyson Gore's death was a great tragedy. I'm just trying to figure out what happened."

"The police believe that your client killed him."

"My client says that he didn't."

"That's why we have trials, Mr. Daley. I am under no obligation to talk to you."

"That's true. On the other hand, you're on the prosecution's witness list. I would assume that they want you to testify as to Mr. Gore's state of mind on the night that he died."

"I can't talk about it, Mr. Daley."

Yes, you can. "You've been around the block enough times to know that we can do this the easy way or the hard way. The easy way means that we have a brief and polite conversation now. The hard way will involve subpoenas, lawyers, and a not-so-brief and not-so-polite conversation at a later time. It's your call."

She pushed out an exasperated sigh. "He wasn't suicidal."

We're making progress. "Our expert came to a different conclusion."

"I talked to your expert who conducted the psychological autopsy." She made air quotes when she said "psychological autopsy." "I've met Gina Cole. She has a fine reputation. However, it is well-documented that such autopsies are inherently unreliable. Moreover, I treated Mr. Gore for seven years. Dr. Cole never met him. Tyson was a complicated and driven man who had business and personal issues that we worked through over the years. In my judgment, he wasn't suicidal. If he was, I would have recommended treatment."

"You prescribed antidepressants."

"I *suggested* that he try them. Mr. Gore persuaded his physician to prescribe them."

"How long was he taking them?"

"Two years."

"Did they work?"

"They helped." She didn't elaborate.

"Obviously he was under a lot of stress."

"There's a difference between being stressed and being suicidal. Mr. Gore was the former, not the latter."

"He was drinking heavily and taking designer drugs."

"He was working on both issues."

"He went through two acrimonious divorces and he had broken up with his latest girlfriend."

"I can't talk about that."

"His business was imploding."

"He was an experienced entrepreneur who had dealt with failed companies on several occasions."

I lowered my voice. "Deal Coin was on the brink of bankruptcy. He lost billions. He was looking at personal bankruptcy."

"He was going through a difficult time, Mr. Daley, but in my judgment, he was not suicidal. And I'm prepared to testify to that effect if the DA asks me to do so."

Nady called me as I was walking up Seventh Street. "Did you get anything useful from Gore's therapist?" she asked.

"No." I pressed my phone to my ear. "She's prepared to testify that Gore wasn't suicidal."

"Our expert will say that he was. Gina Cole is very good."

"She's going to have to be. Where are you?"

"The gym."

"Aren't you supposed to be in court?"

"We're dark today. We start closing arguments tomorrow. I ran into Amanda Blair at CrossFit. I think I can persuade her to talk to us."

Blair was Gore's last ex-girlfriend. "Tell her that we'll buy her lunch."

21

"I'M AN INFLUENCER"

"Thank you for seeing us," I said.

"Thank you for lunch." Amanda Blair's expression was serious as she picked at a chicken taco salad. "I can't stay long. I need to get back to work."

"Is your office nearby?"

"I work from home." She said that she lived in one of the high-rises a few blocks south of Salesforce Park.

Gore's last ex-girlfriend was in her late twenties. Her eyes were clear blue, skin creamy, straight blonde hair flowing to her shoulders. Her sculpted biceps and toned abs indicated that she worked out regularly. She and Nady had just finished a grueling CrossFit session at an upscale gym around the corner from the ballpark. She was wearing a pink Lululemon half-zip hoodie with matching yoga pants.

"What do you do?" I asked.

"I'm an influencer." Her voice filled with pride. "I have almost two million followers on YouTube and TikTok."

"Is that a lot?"

"It's enough to make real money."

Blair, Nady, and I were sitting at a table on the patio of Mars Bar, a watering hole a half block south of the PD's Office which was a regular hangout for my colleagues. Terrence "The Terminator" came here every week for "Taco Tuesday." The food is hearty, the drinks strong, the prices fair. It's housed in a nondescript building between a digital photo processing company and an auto repair shop. There is a long bar with a pool table inside, and a patio with umbrella-covered tables and propane heaters in the back. You still see blue-collar workers at the bar, but most of the customers work for the nearby tech firms. Zynga is around the corner. Adobe is down the block. There are a lot of Patagonia vests.

Nady set down her phone and spoke to Blair. "You have one more follower now."

Blair flashed a practiced smile. "Thank you."

"What kind of videos do you post?"

"Anything to get views. I talk about my day. I tell stories. I sing and dance. I post at least a couple times a day. You hope that other influencers will like your stuff and you'll go viral."

"How often does it happen?"

"A lot. You'd be amazed."

Nady grinned. "Do you think there might be a demand for TikTok videos of a Deputy Public Defender talking about life at the PD's Office?"

Blair returned her smile. "It might be a tough sell. Can you dance?"

"A little."

"Do you have a pet?"

"A Keeshond. She's very mediagenic."

"That might work."

Nady asked Blair about the nuances of growing a brand on social media. Blair seemed to enjoy the attention. She explained that the average person watches a TikTok video for less than two seconds before moving on, so it's critical to get their attention right away.

In response to Nady's question, Blair said that she had grown up in Fremont and attended James Logan High School and Cal State East Bay. Her parents divorced when she was two, and she was raised by her mother, a hair stylist. After college, she worked in customer service at an insurance company. "It didn't pay well, and the work was mind-numbing." She said that she shared an apartment with four people in Hayes Valley. "I quit my job and started doing TikTok. It took time before it started paying, so I worked for a caterer, waited tables, drove for Uber, and did a gig as a professional dog walker."

Notwithstanding our endless whining, we Baby Boomers had it relatively easy.

Nady glanced my way, and I turned to business. "Did you meet Tyson Gore at CrossFit?"

"No, I met him at a charity event at the Four Seasons when I was working for the caterer."

"You also had a personal relationship?"

"Yes. He was charismatic and funny. I was flattered when he asked for my number."

"He was still married at the time?"

"Yes, although he and his wife were living separately, and she had filed for divorce." She stated that she had no contact with Gore's ex-wives and children.

I asked if she moved in with Gore.

"No. I was starting to make good money on TikTok. I had just moved into my new apartment when I started seeing Tyson."

"How long were you and Mr. Gore seeing each other?"

"On and off for about a year." She swallowed. "I found out that he was seeing other women. I ended our relationship about two weeks before he died."

"I'm sorry. The breakup must have been traumatic for you."

"It was."

"How did Mr. Gore react?"

Blair drank some club soda. "He seemed more relieved than upset."

How sad. I looked over at Nady, who picked up the cue.

"How was Mr. Gore doing when you last saw him?"

Blair waited a beat. "He was under a lot of stress. He was drinking a lot and taking Zoloft."

"Did you know that he was also doing designer drugs called bath salts?"

"Yes." She said that Gore offered them to her, but she declined.

"Do you know where he got them?"

"Afraid not."

Nady's voice was empathetic. "We hired a psychologist who did a detailed analysis of Mr. Gore's personality. She believes that he might have been suicidal." Nady eyed her. "Do you think she was right?"

"I don't know. I could never figure out what was going on inside his head."

"Do you think there's a chance that he committed suicide?"

"Inspector Lee asked me the same thing, and I will tell you what I told him: I don't know."

"Best guess?"

Blair shrugged. "Unlikely. Tyson believed that he could solve any problem. He was confident that he could get Deal Coin back on track. He just needed a little time and a lot of money."

I spoke up again. "Was anybody mad at him?"

"Everybody who invested in Deal Coin. He was concerned that he would never be able to raise money to fund another start-up."

"Do you have any names?"

"We never talked about his business associates."

"Do you think any of those people might have been involved in his death?"

Blair's tone turned dismissive. "Seems doubtful. They run multibillion-dollar investment funds. They aren't the kind of people who would kill somebody over a failed business deal. If anything, they'd sue."

You're probably right. "The DA included you on his witness list."

"I know. Mr. Erickson said that he might want me to testify about Tyson's state of mind before he was killed. I told him that I wouldn't be able to offer an opinion either way if he asked me whether Tyson was suicidal."

Good to know. I placed my credit card on the check. Then I picked up my phone and showed her a photo of the man who was waiting on the street level of Salesforce Transit Center on the morning that Gore died. "Ever seen him?"

She studied the picture. "No."

"Thank you for your time, Amanda."

"Thanks for lunch. Don't forget to follow me on TikTok."

22

"WE'RE IN THE WRONG LINE OF WORK"

Rosie appeared in the doorway to my office at seven-fifteen the same night. "What are you watching?"

I looked up from my phone. "Amanda Blair's TikTok. Gore's ex-girlfriend is an influencer."

She grinned. "You don't have more important things to do?"

"Many years ago, you taught me to learn as much as I can about every potential witness."

"Right." Rosie walked around behind me and looked at my phone. "What is she doing?"

"Sitting in her apartment and talking to the camera. Sometimes she dances or sings. It looks like she's channeling Stevie Nicks. Her version of *Landslide* has over two million views."

"Come on, Mike."

I put my phone down. "She makes six figures."

"You can make a hundred grand posting homemade videos of Fleetwood Mac songs?"

"There are a billion and a half active users on TikTok."

"We're in the wrong line of work."

I looked at her. "Does it strike you as a bit, uh, exploitative?"

"Nobody's forcing her to do it, Mike. She's an adult who has made a business decision to overshare for profit. I don't think it's especially healthy, and I wouldn't do it, but it's her call. Did she tell you anything useful?"

"Not really."

"How is Reggie's case going?"

"Slowly. We've talked to everybody who was at Kanzen on the night that Gore died." I filled her in on my conversations. "We haven't been able to identify the man in the video who was waiting on the ground level of Salesforce Transit Center at two AM. It's possible that he had nothing to do with Gore's death."

"Where does that leave you?"

"Suicide may be our best argument."

"And if the jury doesn't buy it?"

"We'll try to foist the blame on somebody else."

She arched an eyebrow. "Any hard evidence?"

"Uh, no." I added, "Pete is looking."

Her lips turned down, but she didn't say anything.

"Have you talked to Rolanda?" I asked.

"She's fine, but she's bored out of her mind. You can only binge-watch so much stuff on Netflix, and she has to deal with a two-year-old."

I smiled. "I miss having little kids around the house."

"So do I." Her eyes twinkled. "How long do you think it will be before Grace and Chuck have kids?"

"At least a couple of years."

"I'll have Mama talk to them. She can be very persuasive."

Yes, she can.

We allowed ourselves a moment to talk about potential grandchildren instead of murder trials when Nady marched into my office.

"How's your trial prep going?" I asked her.

"Closing arguments tomorrow. Then jury instructions. If all goes well, deliberations will start by the end of the day."

"Good." I drank a bit of a warm Diet Dr Pepper. My doctor allowed me to drink one can of soda a week. "How are you feeling about it?"

"He's going to be convicted. The only question is whether it will be first- or second-degree murder."

"Which way do you think it will go?"

"A wise lawyer taught me that it's better not to make predictions while you're in trial."

That was me. "Any chance you might get a hung jury?"

"The same lawyer told me that there's always a chance."

"Is there anything I can do to help?"

"I have it covered. Do you have an hour to spare for Reggie's case?"

"Of course."

"Good. I just got a text from Gore's second ex-wife. She's willing to talk to us for a few minutes."

"When?"

"Now."

23

"I SHOULD HAVE KNOWN BETTER"

"We're very sorry about the death of your ex-husband, Ms. Gore," I said.

"Thank you, Mr. Daley."

"Mike."

"Wendy."

She took a sip of water from a crystal glass. She was late thirties, prim nose, slim build, shoulder-length hair pulled back into a ponytail. Her tired voice reflected the exhaustion of a single mother of a toddler.

"How long were you and Tyson married?" I asked.

"Two years. Our divorce became official a month before he died."

"My ex and I split up twenty-five years ago. It's difficult."

"Yes, it is. I'm sorry."

"Thank you." I didn't feel compelled to mention that Rosie and I had never actually stopped sleeping together.

At eight-fifteen on Thursday night, Gore's second ex-wife, Nady, and I were sitting on the black leather sofas in the living room of her expansive condo on the thirtieth floor of Millennium Tower. The furnishings were more functional than luxurious: the two sofas, a cream-colored leather chair in front of the seventy-inch flat-screen above the phony fireplace, two end tables that could have come from Wayfair. The coffee table was covered with Dr. Seuss books, drawing paper, and crayons. Wendy's three-year-old son was in the bedroom with his live-in nanny. The mantel was lined with framed photos of the smiling boy along with his mother and a couple whom I presumed were his grandparents. There were no pictures of his father.

"Your son is handsome," I said. "It must have been difficult for him—and you—when his father passed."

"It was." Wendy stared out the picture window at the Bay Bridge. "It is what it is."

One of the reasons that I left the priesthood was that I never found the right words at moments like these. Rosie found it ironic that I never seemed to have similar issues in court.

"Are you from the Bay Area?" I asked.

"San Mateo." She explained that her father was an engineer at Bechtel, and her mother was a grammar school librarian. "I graduated from San Jose State with a psychology degree and got a master's in human resources." She worked in HR at an architecture firm for two years, and then moved to a biotech company. She was recruited to Deal Coin as assistant HR director. "When my boss went on maternity leave, I moved into her slot. It was supposed to be temporary, but she and her husband decided to relocate to Reno. That's how I became the head of HR at Deal Coin."

"And you met Tyson?"

"Yes."

"It must have been an exciting time."

"It was." She said that there were fewer than twenty employees when she started. "Six months later, we had two hundred. A year later, it was five hundred. Crypto was taking off, and we thought we were in on the ground floor of something huge. Our valuation accelerated along with our growth. We couldn't hire people fast enough."

I glanced at Nady, who picked up. "I take it that at some point, your relationship with Mr. Gore became more than just business?"

Wendy responded with a world-weary smile. "I should have known better. Tyson was still married when he asked me out for a drink. I assumed that he wanted to talk about business. It became clear that he was looking for something else. In hindsight, I guess we weren't breaking any new ground."

Nady nodded but didn't say anything.

Wendy kept talking. "Tyson was brilliant, charismatic, and charming. The company was doing well. He was on TV all the time. We traveled around the world. When his divorce from his first wife became final, we got married on Kauai and bought the penthouse upstairs. Then I got pregnant with Jared. Everything was going great."

Nady's tone was empathetic. "And then?"

Wendy's voice turned melancholy. "You know the old saying: if they cheat with you, eventually, they'll cheat on you."

"When did you find out?"

"I had suspicions when I was pregnant. After Jared was born, Tyson started coming home later every night. I hired a private investigator who confirmed that he was cheating."

"With Amanda Blair?"

"Yes. I wouldn't be surprised if there were others."

"I'm sorry."

"So am I." Wendy said that she filed for divorce shortly thereafter. She said it was acrimonious but didn't provide details. "I came out okay in the settlement. Among other things, I got this condo."

"It's very nice." Nady looked at the kitchen with the Sub-Zero refrigerator, restaurant-quality Viking range, and Wolf double oven. "It must have been awkward living in the same building as your ex-husband."

"I wanted stability for Jared, so I decided to stay here—at least until I could find something else. I had custody, but Tyson had visitation rights. All things considered, it worked out pretty well."

Nady kept her voice even. "Did you ever have any contact with Ms. Blair?"

"No."

"Wendy," I said, "we're trying to find out what happened to your ex-husband."

Her eyes narrowed. "The police think your client killed him."

"We believe that they're mistaken. When was the last time that you talked to him?"

"Around nine o'clock on the last night of Deal Con. We were trying to coordinate our schedules so that he could see Jared later in the week."

"How did he sound?"

"Exhausted."

I invoked a soft tone. "What was he like?"

"Complicated." Her voice turned thoughtful. "In many respects, everything you read about him was true. Brilliant mind. Visionary businessman. World-class programmer. Charismatic. Competitive. Driven. He hated to lose—at anything."

"Did he play by the rules?"

"In business, yes—at least for the most part. Tyson was more cautious than a lot of people in the crypto space. He had been through the process of building several start-ups, so he was more inclined to listen to his lawyers and follow their advice. Deal Coin filed for bankruptcy after Tyson died, but there were no criminal charges or civil cases. The company didn't implode because of fraud. Tyson and his team couldn't perfect the product fast enough. And then the crypto market cratered, and it took the company with it."

I was impressed and a bit surprised that she didn't take the opportunity to throw her ex-husband under the bus. "And his personal life?"

She responded with a derisive laugh. "Everything you've read about it was also true. It was a disaster. He had a Type A personality with no impulse control. He cheated on his first wife and then me. I would be shocked if he didn't cheat on Amanda. He was never physically abusive, but he was a manipulative control freak. And then there was the drinking and the drugs. Toward the end, he was out of control."

"Was anybody mad at him?"

"His investors lost billions and were furious, but they aren't the type of people who would have pushed Tyson over the railing at Salesforce Park. They measure success in terms of wins and losses, and they keep score with money. Venture capitalists love to recite platitudes about finding new paradigms and creating new platforms that will make the world a better place. In reality, most of them care more about the number of bedrooms in their vacation houses in Maui, the size of their yachts, and the seating capacity on their private jets."

"I understand that Tyson cut Matt Bosworth's interest in the company."

"He did. Matt lost billions, and he took it personally. He put his heart and soul into the company and ended up with nothing to show for it."

"Do you think there's any chance—,"

She stopped me. "Matt is a sweetheart. He wouldn't hurt anybody."

"We talked to Steve Warren, too. He was pretty angry, also."

"He's terrified of his father. But he isn't the kind of guy who would kill someone."

"Cynthia Mitchell lost millions, too."

"She is brilliant and insanely competitive. She also hates to lose money. She stood up to the powers that be at Andreessen. She's seen everything and knows how to deal with a loss like Deal Coin."

"Eugene McAllister lost millions, too."

"Gene's investment in Deal Coin was pocket change for him. He has a multibillion-dollar real estate portfolio. He's more interested in philanthropy and his ownership interests in the Giants and the Warriors. He wasn't happy when Deal Coin cratered, but he didn't lose any sleep over it."

"And Jack Emrich?"

Her lips turned down. "He was the only investor that I never trusted. He's an arrogant hothead who made Tyson's life a living hell. He was fired by Deutsche Bank after Deal Coin went down."

"You think he might have been angry enough to go after Tyson?"

"Doubtful. On the other hand, of the people you mentioned, he's the only one who might have been tempted to take a swing at Tyson."

We'll talk to him as soon as he returns from the U.K.

Her expression turned skeptical. "Is that your defense? You're going to accuse Tyson's billionaire investors of killing him?"

If we can't come up with something more convincing. "As far as we can tell, they were the only people in the vicinity."

Her voice filled with sarcasm. "Other than your client."

"Let me ask you about something else," I said. "We understand that Tyson was drinking heavily, taking antidepressants, and using designer drugs called 'bath salts.'"

"He was." She eyed me. "Are you asking me if I think he was suicidal?"

"Yes."

"No."

"The company was imploding. He had lost billions. He was taking Zoloft and bath salts."

Her voice became more emphatic. "No."

"You seem pretty sure."

"When I was in HR, I learned that it's impossible to get inside somebody else's head. On the other hand, I knew Tyson as well as anybody. For all of his faults—and there were many—he was the most self-confident person that I've ever known. He genuinely believed that he could solve any problem with brainpower, creativity, and perseverance. If you put me on the stand and ask me if I think he was suicidal, I will say no."

Got it. "You said that you hired a private investigator. Mind if we talk to him?"

"Fine with me. I have nothing to hide."

"What's his name?"

"*Her* name is Nicki Hanson. She's with the Hanson Agency in North Beach."

I darted a glance at Nady, who couldn't hide a smile. Nicki Hanson was the great-granddaughter of the legendary Nick "The Dick" Hanson, who founded the Hanson Investigative Agency seventy-five years ago in an office above the Condor Strip Club at the corner of Broadway and Columbus. Now in his nineties, Nick was the chairman emeritus of the biggest private eye operation on the West Coast. Nicki was every bit as tenacious as he was.

"We'll reach out to her," I said.

24

"NOBODY RECOGNIZED HIM"

Pete was sitting at my desk when I returned to the office at ten-fifteen the same night. "You're here late," he said.

"Nady and I were talking to Wendy Gore."

"Did you get anything useful?"

"Not much."

He flashed a wry grin. "You mean his ex-wife didn't confess to killing Gore?"

"Afraid not."

"I guess we'll keep going. You want your chair?"

"In a minute. Were you able to reach Nicki Hanson?"

"I left a message. She's usually very responsive."

I hung up my jacket and took a seat across from him. "What brings you here at this hour?"

"I talked to my sources in SFPD about the guy in the video. Nobody recognized him."

Crap.

He added, "I've sent it to some other people, but I'm not wildly optimistic. I talked to some of the homeless people around Salesforce Transit Center, but nobody knew who he was."

"Anything on Jack Emrich?"

"He's returning on Monday. I'll set something up." He looked at me. "You okay, Mick?"

"Just the usual pre-trial stress. Is Donna mad at you for being out so late?"

"Yes."

"You guys okay?"

"We'll be fine. We've been here many times. You going to get some more help?"

"It's on the way. Nady's trial goes to the jury tomorrow. That leaves us a full week to get ready for Reggie's trial."

"Any word from Erickson on negotiating a deal for a reduced charge?"

"No."

"Have you talked to Reggie lately?"

"I saw him this afternoon. He's holding up pretty well under the circumstances."

"Will you put him on the stand?"

"If I have to. You going home soon?"

"No." He stood up and put on his bomber jacket. "I'm going back to the bus terminal to see if I can find somebody who was there on the morning that Gore died. You?"

I glanced at my watch. "I'll probably be here for a couple more hours."

He glanced at his phone and smiled. "You got time for lunch tomorrow?"

"I'm really busy, Pete."

"It's with Nicki Hanson. She said that she'd bring her great-grandfather with her."

25

"NEVER LET THE TRUTH GET IN THE WAY OF A GOOD STORY"

The diminutive nonagenarian stood up, reset the perfect Windsor knot in his three-hundred-dollar Zegna silk necktie, tugged the sleeve of his top-of-the-line Burberry overcoat, extended a meaty hand, and spoke in a raspy, singsong voice. "Great to see you again, Mike. How the hell have you been?"

"Fine, Nick. Are you okay?"

"Indeed I am." Nick "The Dick" Hanson's rubbery face transformed into a gregarious smile as he pointed at the young woman standing next to him. "You remember my great-granddaughter, Nicki?"

"Of course." I shook her outstretched hand. "Nice to see you again."

"Same here." She smiled as she exchanged greetings with Pete.

Nicki was a foot taller than Nick. She was the head of the Hanson Investigative Agency's cybersecurity group. The thirty-year-old had a computer science degree from UC San Diego and a master's in data analytics at UCLA. Married. No kids. Her facial features bore a slight resemblance to Nick's. Her short black hair had a magenta streak.

We took our seats at one of the three mismatched tables outside of Freddie's Sandwiches in North Beach. The deli was located on the ground floor of a three-story apartment building at the corner of Stockton and Francisco. The building was painted a cheerful yellow with green and maroon trim. Freddie's was three blocks from the Wharf in a neighborhood of two- and three-story apartments, most of which dated back to the early twentieth century. Joe DiMaggio and Marilyn Monroe lived down the street and were regulars at Freddie's in the fifties.

The sun was shining at eleven-thirty on Friday morning, and I could hear the voices of the kids in the playground of Francisco Middle School across the street. I distributed four No. 1 Italian Combos made of Genoa salami, pressed ham, mortadella, and provolone on sourdough rolls. I ordered mine the same way that my dad always did: with just mustard.

I unwrapped my sandwich and spoke to Nick. "This is a little downscale for you."

The bon vivant usually enjoyed nightly three-hour dinners at Fior d'Italia, Caffe Sport, or Tommaso's.

His grin broadened. "I come here at least twice a week to support Eddy and Rosalia. They still make the best sandwiches in North Beach."

Eddy and Rosalia Sweileh have run Freddie's since 1991. In 1926, Freddie Braja opened a dry goods store selling bread, rice, and beans. In the Thirties, he added take-out sandwiches to feed the construction workers who were building the Golden Gate Bridge. The original menu included just three sandwiches: salami, salami and ham, and salami, ham, and cheese. Freddie offered only mustard because he didn't like mayo. Over the years, Eddy and Rosalia added more sandwiches, vegetables, and condiments to the menu, which now numbers more than thirty items. Nowadays, a sandwich "with everything" includes meat, mustard, tomatoes, red onions, shredded iceberg lettuce, and yes, mayonnaise.

"You warm enough?" I asked Nick.

"Fine, Mike." He playfully punched his great-granddaughter's shoulder. "Nicki and the rest of my family have conspired to make sure that I always wear my overcoat."

I winked at Nicki, then turned back to Nick. "Seems like a reasonable precaution."

"Seems like overkill."

Still energetic at ninety-five, Nick had been a PI for almost eight decades. The son of Russian immigrants whose father ran a magic shop next door to the Tosca Café and across the street from City Lights Bookstore, Nick played baseball with Joe DiMaggio on the North Beach playground. During the Great Depression, he helped his father make ends meet by sweeping up at the Valente, Marini, Perata Funeral Home on Green Street, handing out towels at the Italian Athletic Club, and bilking tourists at three-card monte.

Nick still ran the Bay to Breakers every year and worked out at the upscale Bay Club below his Earthquake-era mansion on Telegraph Hill. His agency grew into a high-tech operation employing dozens of his children, grandchildren, and great-grandchildren. A savvy businessman and astute investor, Nick accumulated a portfolio of apartment buildings rumored to be worth a cool fifty million. In his spare time, he wrote mystery novels that were embellishments of his cases. Danny DeVito played Nick in a long-running Netflix series.

I asked him about the TV show.

Nick took a big bite of his sandwich and washed it down with a San Pellegrino. "Danny just signed up for another season." He arched a bushy gray eyebrow. "My agent is pitching a series based on yours truly when I was a kid, and a full-length biopic."

"Sounds promising," I said. "Are you going to play yourself in the movie?"

"No. Confidentially, we're in talks with Robert DeNiro."

Not sure about that. "Sounds like you might be taking a few liberties, Nick."

He smiled triumphantly. "Never let the truth get in the way of a good story, Mike."

He spent twenty minutes expounding upon the growth strategy for his agency (full speed ahead), the latest on his real estate portfolio (still gaining value, albeit more slowly), and his plans for the holidays (a family reunion at his compound at Poipu Beach in Kauai). There were no indications that he was planning to slow down.

Nick took a bite of his second chocolate chip cookie. "Is Rolanda okay?"

"Fine." *Nick knows everything.* "Her doctor put her on bed rest until the baby is born."

"I heard. Boy or girl?"

"Boy."

"Excellent. Please give her my best. I heard you picked up the Reggie Jones case. Can you get an acquittal?"

"We have a decent chance of convincing the jury that it was suicide."

His expression turned skeptical. "Good luck with that."

"Did you know Tyson Gore?"

"I met him a couple of times. My former financial advisor got me into Deal Coin. Let's just say that it didn't go well."

"Did you lose a lot?"

"Not that much. Mid six-figures."

Not that much? That's real money to me.

He waved it off. "I fired my financial advisor."

I'm not surprised. "What did you think of Gore?"

"He was like everybody else in the crypto world: an arrogant dick."

Don't sugarcoat it, Nick. "What happened to Deal Coin?"

"An unfortunate combination of hubris, stupidity, sloppy business practices, and profoundly bad timing."

"Was he crooked?"

"Some of my fellow investors thought so. I had my lawyers look into it. There wasn't enough evidence to sue them for fraud. Besides, there wasn't any money left to pay damages." His voice turned philosophical. "Lesson learned, I suppose."

"Gore died after he invited a bunch of his big investors to a gathering at Kanzen."

"I heard."

"Were you invited?"

"No. I didn't put up enough money."

"Ever been to Kanzen?"

"Once or twice."

"Are you a member?"

"They approached me, but I said no. Not my style."

I wasn't surprised. Nick was a member of the Pacific Union, Olympic, and Bohemian Clubs, San Francisco's most exclusive bastions of old money.

I pulled out my phone and showed Nick and Nicki a photo of the mystery man at Salesforce Transit Center. "Any idea who this might be?"

"Afraid not," Nick said.

Nicki shook her head.

I looked at Pete, who spoke to Nick. "Wendy Gore told us that she hired your firm to find out if her husband was cheating."

"She did, and he was." He pointed at Nicki. "She handled it. It didn't take long."

"How long?" Pete asked.

Nicki grinned. "A couple of hours. I got photos of Gore walking hand-in-hand with Amanda Blair into the Four Seasons. It was the quickest tail I've ever had. Mrs. Gore was thoroughly pissed off."

"Did Gore meet Blair at the Four Seasons?"

"No, they met at the Gold Club."

"The strip club near Moscone Center?"

"That's the only Gold Club that I know."

Pete gave me a knowing look, then he turned back to Nicki. "She was a customer?"

"No, she was a dancer."

"She told us that she met Gore at a fundraiser when she was working for a caterer."

"She lied." Nicki shrugged. "Maybe she didn't want to tell you that she was working at a strip club."

"Maybe. Did you get anything else on Gore?"

"No."

"Anybody else we should talk to?"

"You might ask around at the club." She looked at me. "Do you know anybody who works there?"

A dancer named "Dazzle." "As a matter of fact, we do."

26

"YOU DIDN'T ASK"

Debra "Dazzle" Diamond's eyes sparkled like her sequined halter top and short shorts. "Did you enjoy the show?"

I returned her smile. "Yes, we did."

"Our chicken is some of the best in town. We got a nice write-up in the *Chronicle* a few months ago."

"I saw it." The Gold Club's Executive Chef, Chris Hui, was trained at the California Culinary Academy.

Her grin broadened. "Aren't you glad you aren't a priest anymore?"

"Yes, I am."

Dazzle joined us at a table in the bar at the Gold Club, the upscale strip joint down the street from Moscone Center. The lunch show was over, the midday crowd had dispersed, and the room smelled of leftover fried chicken and beer.

She gave Pete a provocative wink. "Don't see you here as much as I used to."

"Business was slow during the pandemic."

"You think people were cheating less on their spouses during Covid?"

"Probably not."

She swung her right leg onto the empty chair next to mine, exposing the ankle monitor that she had decorated in sequins. "Did you come here to tell me that the judge reconsidered and is going to let me take this stupid thing off while I'm dancing?"

"Afraid not, Dazz, but it looks nice."

"It looks ridiculous."

Yes, it does. "It's only for a couple more months."

"Right." She lowered her leg and sipped her club soda. "What can I do for you?"

"We're representing a man named Reggie Jones who is going on trial for the murder of Tyson Gore."

A look of recognition crossed her face. "The crypto guy."

"Right. Did you ever meet him?"

"Yes. He used to come in a lot."

"Good guy?"

"Just another entitled tech bro with a lot of money and a big ego. Good tipper, though. He never hit on me, but he hit on several of my co-workers. He liked them young and blonde."

I showed her a photo of Amanda Blair. "Recognize her?"

"Yes. Amanda worked here for a few months to make some extra money when she was launching her social media presence. Nice kid. Smart. Ambitious. Respectful. Good dancer."

"She met Gore here. They were in a relationship for about a year. It didn't end well."

"I'm not surprised."

I eyed her. "Why didn't you mention this to me?"

"One, I didn't know that you were representing Reggie Jones. Two, it was none of your business. And three, you didn't ask."

"Ms. Blair told us that she met Gore at a fundraiser when she was working for a caterer."

"She lied. Maybe she didn't want to tell a stranger that she met her ex-boyfriend here."

"There's nothing to be ashamed of."

"Damn right." She pointed a finger at me. "I'm proud of what I do. I'm good at what I do. And I don't apologize for what I do. Okay?"

"Okay."

"What difference does it make where she met Gore?"

"Maybe it doesn't. It makes me wonder if she lied about anything else."

"I guess you'll just have to ask her."

"We will." I pulled out my phone and showed her the photo of the man at Salesforce Transit Center. "Recognize him?"

She studied the photo. "I've seen him a few times."

"Got a name?"

"No."

"Is he in crypto?"

"No, he's in pharmaceuticals." She looked around the empty bar to make sure that nobody else was listening. "I think he might have been supplying designer drugs to the tech bros."

"Was he selling to Gore?"

"I don't know."

"Any chance you have security video of this guy?"

"Doubtful. They keep the video for just a week or two. He hasn't been around in months."

Pete leaned forward. "I showed his photo to my sources at SFPD. Nobody recognized him."

"He was discreet."

"Any idea where we can find him?"

"Afraid not."

"Have you heard from Amanda Blair since she quit?"

"No. I heard that she was making a lot of money on TikTok. Good for her."

27

"WHAT DIFFERENCE DOES IT MAKE?"

"Excuse me," I said. "Can I talk to you again for a minute, Ms. Blair?"

At nine-fifty the following morning, a Saturday, Gore's ex-girlfriend glared at me as she exited United Barbell, a CrossFit gym in a refurbished auto body shop on Fourth Street, two blocks from the ballpark.

"You're stalking me now?" she snapped.

"No, I was waiting for you."

"How did you know that I was here?"

Pete's watching you. "You mentioned to Nady that you came to Liran's class every Saturday morning."

"You could have called or texted."

"Actually, I did both."

"I just finished my workout. I need to get home."

"I'll walk with you."

"It's a public sidewalk." She pulled the hood of her Lululemon sweatshirt over her matted hair. "I told you everything I know."

"I appreciate your cooperation. It turns out that I have a few more questions."

A cool morning breeze hit my face as we walked north on Fourth through a formerly light industrial area where the warehouses have been refurbished into offices and lofts, and gleaming new apartments and condos dot every block. A new Muni line on Fourth Street connects the CalTrain Station with

Chinatown. Several old dive bars seemed out of place among the coffee bars, boba tea shops, restaurants, and boutiques.

I tried again as we walked past Marlowe, an upscale bistro in a century-old building next door to a scuba diving store called Bamboo Reef. "I wanted to ask you about something that you told us the other day."

She kept walking.

"You told us that you met Mr. Gore at a dinner where you were working for the caterer. We talked to one of your former colleagues at the Gold Club who said that you met Mr. Gore while you were working there."

She stopped. "What difference does it make?"

Probably none. "Why didn't you tell us the truth?"

She started walking again. We crossed the busy intersection of Fourth and Bryant, proceeded past the Shell Station and under the thundering noise of the I-80 Freeway, and continued north past Whole Foods on the ground floor of a new apartment building. The high-rises got taller and fancier as we got closer to downtown.

"Amanda?"

"What?"

"Why didn't you tell us that you met Mr. Gore at the club?"

"I worked there for a couple of months when I was short on cash. It isn't the sort of thing that you tell a stranger the first time that you meet them, okay?"

"Okay." I gave her a moment to catch her bearings. "Anything else we should know?"

"No."

I waited.

"I didn't go out with Tyson because he was rich. The only time I took money from him was when he paid me tips at the Gold Club. Okay?"

"Okay."

"I have no idea what this has to do with your case."

"I'm trying to learn everything that I can about Tyson Gore."

"You're trying to get your client off."

That, too.

We walked in silence to Folsom, where we turned right and headed east for two long blocks past the indoor ice rink at Yerba Buena Gardens and more apartment towers. She stopped abruptly in front of her building at 500 Folsom.

"Anything else?" she asked.

"How bad was Tyson's drug problem?"

"Pretty bad."

"Do you know where he was getting the drugs?"

"No."

Come on. "Seriously?"

"I never asked," she said. "That was Tyson's thing." ◦

I showed her the photo of the man at Salesforce Transit Center. "Ever seen him?"

"No."

"We think he might have been supplying bath salts to Tyson."

"I've never seen him."

"Who would know?"

"Matt Bosworth might."

"Thank you." I pulled up the collar of my windbreaker. "I looked at your TikTok."

Her eyes lit up. "What did you think?"

I can't believe you make six figures. "You're very talented."

"Thank you."

28

"IT DOESN'T MATTER"

Nady looked up from her laptop. "Did Blair admit that she met Gore at the Gold Club?"

"Yes."

"That's something."

I shrugged. "It doesn't matter."

"She lied."

"It doesn't provide any evidence relating to Gore's death."

"It goes to her character."

"Her character isn't on trial."

"It goes to Gore's character, too. That's relevant."

"We won't have any trouble convincing the jury that he was a jerk. It isn't evidence that somebody other than Reggie killed him."

The PD's Office was quiet at eight-forty-five on Sunday night. Nady and I were sitting in our conference room where the aroma of leftover mu shu pork and General Tso's chicken filled the room. Nady's trial went to the jury on Friday, so she was catching up on Reggie's case. Pete was leaning against the credenza. Luna was curled up in the corner. Terrence was sitting in his usual spot down the hall.

"Got a prediction on your trial?" I asked Nady.

"No."

"How's your client holding up?"

"He's expecting the worst."

Sorry I asked. I turned to Pete. "Anything on the identity of the guy in the video?"

"Not yet. I sent his picture to my best sources in SFPD and the PI community. In the meantime, I have people watching Bosworth, Warren, Mitchell, and McAllister. I'll have somebody shadow Jack Emrich when he gets back from London." He eyed me. "You really think it's worth our time to keep an eye on a bunch of rich people?"

"They were the only other people at Salesforce Park on the night that Gore died."

"Except for our client and the staff at Kanzen."

True.

"Look," he said, "I can help you convince the jury that they're a bunch of entitled billionaires who treat everybody like crap. But that isn't a crime. We still have no evidence connecting them to Gore's death."

"Then we'll just have to keep looking."

Pete put on his bomber jacket and headed toward the door.

"Where are you going?"

"To keep looking."

Nady took off her reading glasses. "Pete was in a foul mood."

"He's frustrated," I said. "He's still a cop at heart. He thinks that if he works hard enough, he'll be able to find the bad guy."

"Assuming that it isn't our client."

"True." I looked at her. "Do you think Reggie killed Gore?"

"My position hasn't changed. The truth is that I'm not sure what happened." She glanced at her laptop. "Trial starts a week from tomorrow. It's put-up time. What's the narrative?"

On my first day as a baby PD almost thirty years earlier, Rosie taught me that a successful defense requires a compelling and easy-to-understand narrative. When I hired Nady five years ago, I passed along the same advice.

"Unless we find some hard evidence that somebody else killed Gore, we start by arguing suicide," I said. "Gore's company was imploding and had lost billions. His investors had just rejected his request for more funding. He was drinking heavily and taking antidepressants and designer drugs. His ex-wives hated him. He wasn't allowed to spend much time with his kids. Amanda Blair broke up with him. His life was coming apart."

"He didn't talk about suicide with anyone. There was no suicide note."

"That isn't dispositive." I told her that I had spent the previous day with Dr. Gina Cole, the expert who performed the psychological autopsy on Gore. "I thought her analysis was compelling. She's been a strong witness in other cases."

"You think that's enough to get an acquittal?"

"It may be enough to get at least one juror to reasonable doubt."

Nady's expression turned skeptical. "I'm not so sure."

Neither am I. "Do you really think Reggie would have stayed at Salesforce Park if he had killed Gore?"

"The jury might conclude that he did it in a drunken rage."

"Maybe."

"You going to put him on the stand?"

"Only if I have to."

"And if that doesn't work?"

We're in serious trouble. "We go to Plan B. I'll try to foist the blame on somebody else who attended the gathering at Kanzen."

"Seriously?"

"There's no question that they were there. They lost a ton of money. I will put them on the stand to testify that they were angry at Gore."

She corrected me. "Each of them will testify that everybody else was angry at Gore. You really think it will work?"

I answered her honestly. "I don't know. My gut feeling is that if we can't persuade the jury that Gore was suicidal, we're going to be in serious trouble. If that's the case, we'll argue that Reggie wouldn't have stuck around all night if he had killed Gore."

"Have you heard from the DA?"

"Briefly. Erickson said that he hasn't been authorized to have any additional discussions about a plea bargain. We're meeting with Judge Tsang on Wednesday to discuss jury questionnaires and motions. I'm not going to ask for a delay or a change of venue. My guess is that the judge will agree to our motion to impose a gag order on all of the parties before and during the trial. He'll also grant our request not to have the trial televised—he's old school."

"How long do you think the trial will last?"

"No more than a couple of weeks. It'll take us at least two or three days to seat a jury. The prosecution's case will be short. The first officer at the scene, the security guard who found the body, the Chief Medical Examiner who performed the autopsy, a couple of evidence experts, and Gore's psychologist. Ken Lee will put all the pieces together and summarize their case."

"And our list?"

"Let's send subpoenas to everybody on the prosecution's list and everybody who was at Kanzen. Wendy Gore. Amanda Blair. Our evidence experts. And, of course, Gina Cole."

I walked over to the corner of the room where Luna was sleeping. I pulled out a treat and held it under her nose. Her left eye twitched. Her right eye opened. She lifted her head, shook herself awake, and yawned. Her big brown eyes opened wide, and she wagged her tail.

"Shake," I said.

She extended a paw. I handed her the treat, which she devoured with her customary enthusiasm. She looked up hopefully, but I had to disappoint her.

"I'm sorry, Luna. That's the last one."

She slunk back down to the floor.

I turned back to Nady. "I wish I had her life."

"It's good to be Luna."

"You should take her home soon."

"I will." She closed her laptop. "I think my jury is going to come in tomorrow or Tuesday, so I'll be able to devote all of my time to Reggie's case."

"Good. I could use the help."

"What are you going to do next?"

"I'm going to take another run at Matt Bosworth and Steve Warren tomorrow. Maybe they can identify the guy at Salesforce Transit Center."

29

"HE HAD A SERIOUS DRUG PROBLEM"

Matt Bosworth eyed me. "I can't talk for long."

"I just need a moment of your time."

At eight-thirty on Monday morning, we were sitting at a table in the plaza next to the central lawn area in Salesforce Park. We were the only people braving the wind.

"Have you heard anything more from the DA's Office?" I asked.

"Yes." He gulped his Philz Coffee. "Andy Erickson said that he may need me to testify that Tyson was at the gathering at Kanzen." He pulled up the collar of his Patagonia windbreaker. "And he reminded me that I'm under no obligation to talk to you."

Fair enough. "I included you on our witness list for the same reason."

"Right." He started to stand, but I stopped him. "We talked to Tyson's ex-girlfriend. Seems she has quite a following on TikTok."

"She's pretty."

"She can sing and dance a little, too. She confirmed that Tyson had substance use issues."

His tone turned blunt. "That's no secret. He had a serious drug problem. He worked his way up from coke to meth and finally to the designer stuff."

"Did you ever think about doing an intervention?"

"Yes." He shrugged. "We never did."

"Weren't you concerned that his substance use issues were having an adverse impact on the company?"

"Do you think he was the only person in the crypto space using designer drugs? He was a grown-up, Mike. He knew the consequences."

"The consequences also impacted the company."

"It didn't affect his work."

I find that hard to believe. "The side effects of bath salts include depression and even suicidal thoughts."

"I didn't see it. Tyson was always very positive."

You're trying a little too hard to convince me. "Did he ever share his stuff with you?"

His tone turned more emphatic. "I don't do that stuff."

"Do you know where he was getting it?"

"No."

"Who would know?"

He folded his arms. "I don't know."

I showed him a photo of the man on the ground level of Salesforce Transit Center on the morning that Gore died. "Ever seen him?"

He studied the photo for a long moment. "Afraid not."

"We think he may be a drug dealer."

"Sorry."

"You sure?"

A hesitation. "Yes."

Whack! The yellow golf ball soared high into the cloudless blue sky and landed in the middle of the driving range just short of the two-hundred-and-seventy-five-yard marker.

"Nice hit," I said.

Steve Warren grimaced. "I'm pulling off the ball a little."

The Stanford University driving range is in a bucolic spot in the foothills near the top of Campus Drive. The one-time home range of Tiger Woods has the usual line of Astroturf mats where golfers hit practice balls onto a manicured lawn surrounded by mature trees. At twelve-thirty on Monday afternoon the sun was out, and the warm breeze was a welcome respite from the chills of San Francisco.

"Thank you for seeing me again," I said. "You come here much?"

"A couple of times a week." He pointed at the entrance to the golf course across the street. "I have a one o'clock tee time." He quickly added, "Business."

Nice work if you can get it. "I had a few more questions for you."

"You couldn't have done this by phone or text?"

"I like to talk to people in person."

"Suit yourself." He teed up another ball and hit it straight down the range. "You play?"

"Not much anymore. I played a lot when I was a kid."

"Where?"

"Harding. Lincoln. When I was in college at Berkeley, I used to play Tilden Park every once in a while."

"They're nice for public courses." He emphasized the word "public."

I didn't grow up in Atherton, and my daddy wasn't a member at Sharon Heights. "I caddied at the Olympic Club when I was in college. If it wasn't crowded, our boss would let us play a few holes at the end of the day."

"I've been on the waiting list at Olympic for years."

Too bad. "You'll like it."

"I know. I've played there."

As someone's guest. "I wanted to let you know that I put you on our witness list."

He stopped lining up his next drive. "Why?"

"I may need to ask you some questions about what you saw at Kanzen on the night that Tyson Gore died." *And a few other things.*

"Fine. I've got nothing to hide."

"You're still on the prosecution's list. Any idea why?"

"They said that they might need me to testify about Tyson's behavior on the night that he died." He turned around, whacked another ball, and kept talking. "I'm prepared to say that he was acting normally." He smirked. "And that he wasn't suicidal."

I figured. "I heard that he had a serious drug problem."

"He had a problem. I don't know how serious it was. It didn't impact his performance."

"The company went bankrupt, and he and his investors—including you—lost billions."

"It wasn't because he was taking bath salts."

"You knew about the bath salts?"

"*Everybody* knew."

"Did he ever offer anything to you?"

"All the time. I always said no." He launched another drive. "I drink fine wine and smoke cigars and a little weed. I leave the other stuff to the kids."

"Do you know where he was getting the bath salts?"

"No."

"We think there may have been a connection to his death," I said, looking for a response.

"I don't know anything about it."

"Any chance he was in sideways with his supplier?"

"I wouldn't know." He looked at his watch. "My tee-off time is in fifteen minutes."

I showed him a photo of the guy at Salesforce Transit Center. "Have you ever seen him?"

He studied the picture. "No. Why?"

"He was at Salesforce Transit Center around the same time that Tyson left Kanzen."

He looked at the photo again. "Afraid not."

Cynthia Mitchell studied the photo of the man at Salesforce Transit Center. "I've never seen him. Have you talked to the security people at Salesforce Park?"

"Yes. They didn't have any information. Neither did the people at Kanzen."

At four-fifteen on Monday afternoon, I was admiring the view of the sparkling San Francisco Bay from Mitchell's office. I drank a bit of coffee from a mug bearing the logo of Mitchell Capital Partners. "Any suggestions about who I should ask?"

"I'm afraid that I can't help you, Mr. Daley."

"The last time we talked, you said that you did a lot of due diligence on Deal Coin and Tyson Gore. Did you do a background check?"

"That's part of our process."

"Did you hire a private investigator?"

"Yes. We have a firm on retainer to handle these issues."

"You got a report?"

"Of course. It said that Tyson was a social drinker and an occasional user of recreational drugs. We did not fully understand the magnitude of the issues at the time."

"You still invested in the company."

"I based our investment on the best information available at the time. If I ruled out investing in companies run by people who use designer drugs from time to time, my options would be severely limited."

"Knowing what you know now, would you have invested in Deal Coin?"

"No."

At least you admitted it. "Would you mind telling me the name of your PI?"

"Kaela Joy Gullion."

I recognized the name. Kaela Joy Gullion was a statuesque former model and ex-Niners cheerleader who used to be married to an offensive lineman. Pete has worked with her on several cases. Her career as a PI got off to an auspicious start when she caught her now-ex-husband in bed with another woman in the French Quarter the night before a Niners-Saints game. She flattened him with a single punch in the middle of Bourbon Street. A tourist caught it on video. "The Punch" has millions of views on YouTube.

"Any objection if we talk to her?"

"Be my guest."

30

"A COUPLE OF TIMES"

The graceful blonde tugged at the bill of her Giants baseball cap. Kaela Joy Gullion flashed a Julia Roberts smile that used to appear in fashion magazines thirty years ago. "Good to see you, Pete," she said.

Pete returned her smile. "Good to see you, too, Kaela Joy. You remember Mike?"

"Of course. Nice to see you, too." She turned back to Pete. "How old is your daughter?"

"She's a freshman in college."

"Yikes. I remember when she was born."

"And I remember when your picture was plastered on every magazine on every newsstand in San Francisco."

Her grin broadened. "Nowadays, there aren't any newsstands."

At seven-forty-five on Wednesday morning, my face was numb from a heavy mist as Pete, Kaela Joy, and I were sitting at one of the metal tables on Pier 30 behind Red's Java House, the legendary hamburger shack on the Embarcadero overlooking the Bay Bridge. Opened during the Great Depression and originally known as Franco's Lunch, the dive with five red counter stools and a half-dozen tables used to pump cheap food, coffee, and beer into the longshoremen, sailors, and laborers on San Francisco's teeming port. In 1955, two red-headed brothers named Mike and Tom McGarvey bought Franco's and renamed it Red's Java House.

Over the years, the docks closed, the ship traffic diminished, and the food shacks disappeared, but the McGarvey brothers soldiered on. They ran Red's until 1990, when they sold it to

Steve Reilly and his wife, Maria. Nowadays, Red's sits in the middle of a booming neighborhood where high-end condos line the Embarcadero from the Bay Bridge to the new UCSF Medical Center and the Warriors arena. The lunch special is still a double cheeseburger and a beer, and now you can get French fries in addition to potato chips. Ketchup still comes in squirt bottles. If you like tomatoes or lettuce, you'll have to bring your own. The *Chronicle*'s immortal Carl Nolte once called Red's the "Chartres Cathedral of cheap eats."

I nibbled at my pancake plate with eggs and bacon and drank bitter coffee from a paper cup as Pete and Kaela Joy exchanged PI gossip. Kaela Joy reported that business remained solid during Covid, which she had caught twice with mild symptoms.

The former Niners cheerleader finished her egg sandwich and finally turned my way. "You going to an acquittal for Reggie Jones?"

"We have a good shot." *We'll see.* "Cynthia Mitchell told us that you handled the due diligence on Tyson Gore."

"I did. I'm on retainer for her firm. I did a full workup and watched him for a couple of weeks. It didn't take long to figure out that he was a heavy drinker and an occasional user of designer drugs. It wasn't excessive at the time, but I understand that it got worse."

"It did. What did you think of him?"

"He was smart, self-centered, and frequently reckless. You probably know that he cheated on his ex-wives. And, of course, he lost billions when Deal Coin cratered."

"Was he dishonest?"

"To his ex-wives and girlfriends, yes. To his business partners, I don't know."

"He was taking bath salts before he died. Do you know where he got them?"

"Damian Mason. He grew up in Marin and catered to an affluent crowd. He was a go-to dealer for high-end stuff."

I showed her the photo of the man at Salesforce Transit Center. "Any chance it's this guy?"

She studied the picture. "Yes, that's Mason." She said that she saw him with Gore a couple of times.

"Any chance that Gore owed him money or pissed him off?"

"Wouldn't surprise me."

Pete finished his coffee. "Do the police know about Mason?"

"Yes. He's on their radar, but as far as I know, he's never been arrested."

"Any idea where we can find him?"

"Afraid not." She looked at the Bay Bridge and took a deep breath of the salty air. "I heard that he left town about three months ago."

Pete's mustache twitched. "Any suggestions about where we should start looking?"

She eyed him. "Talk to your sources at SFPD."

"I did."

"Talk to them again."

31

"YOU AREN'T GOING TO FIND HIM"

Joey came over to the table in the back room of Dunleavy's where Pete and I were sitting at ten-fifteen on Wednesday night. "More coffee, Mike?"

"No, thanks."

He filled Pete's cup without being asked. "Let me know if you need anything else." Sensing that Pete and I wanted to talk alone, he headed back to the bar.

Dunleavy's was quiet on a foggy night. SportsCenter was on the flat-screen, the sound off. Nobody was playing pool. The jukebox was off. A couple of regulars were sitting at the bar. Just another night in the sixty-year history of Dunleavy's.

I picked at my fish and chips. "Did you find anything on Damian Mason?"

Pete took a sip of scalding coffee and scowled. "His landlord said that he disappeared three months ago. No notice. No forwarding address."

"Did the landlord file a missing person's report?"

"No. Neither did anybody else."

"You think somebody tipped him off that the cops were looking for him?"

"Maybe. A couple of my sources at SFPD knew who he was, but they didn't have enough evidence to arrest him."

"He just disappeared?"

"At the very least, he's dropped off the grid. His cell phone went dead. His bank accounts haven't been accessed since he left. He hasn't used his credit cards."

"You can't live for long without money."

"He probably had cash squirreled away. Or maybe somebody is protecting him. I just don't know." He put down his mug. "I'll keep looking, Mick, but you need to be prepared to go to trial without him."

"I figured."

His mustache twitched as his leathery face transformed into a half-smile. "Look on the bright side. If you want to try to foist blame for Gore's death over to Mason, he won't be able to defend himself."

Swell. "We can't even place him upstairs in Salesforce Park, Pete."

"I didn't say that it was a silver bullet, Mick."

No, you didn't, and no, it isn't.

The back door opened, and the most decorated homicide inspector in SFPD history let himself inside. Roosevelt Johnson hung his overcoat on the rack and joined us. At six-four and a trim two-twenty, my father's first partner was still imposing at eighty-five.

He greeted us in the familiar baritone that I heard on Sunday nights when Roosevelt and his family used to come over for dinner. "Good to see you," he said. He arched an eyebrow above his aviator-style glasses. "Just like old times, eh? Same time. Same place. Same food. Your dad would have been pleased that we were still getting together at your uncle's saloon after all these years."

"Yes, he would."

Joey came in from the front room, poured Roosevelt a cup of coffee, and placed an order of fish and chips in front of him. "You good, Roosevelt?"

"Fine, Joe. You?"

"All good. I'll be up front if you need anything else." Joey headed to the bar.

Roosevelt reported that he was healthy, but an old knee injury was slowing him down. His wife, Janet, had passed away a couple of years earlier. His youngest granddaughter was expecting his third great-grandchild.

Finally, he turned to business. "Are you going to get Reggie Jones an acquittal?"

I never tried to BS Roosevelt. "The DA's evidence is a little thin, but I'm not wildly optimistic. Reggie was at the scene when Gore died. We have no hard evidence pointing to anybody else. Our best argument may be that Gore committed suicide."

"Was there a note?"

"No."

"Other evidence?"

"Circumstantial. Gore went through two acrimonious divorces. His business was imploding. He had lost billions. He was drinking heavily and doing designer drugs."

"Your defense seems a little thin, too."

It is. "We've commissioned a psychological autopsy from one of my best experts."

"Those things are inherently unreliable."

"The science is good, Roosevelt."

"I hope that you aren't betting your entire case on it."

"We aren't. There aren't any eyewitnesses, and the prosecution's case has holes. We might be able to get at least one juror to reasonable doubt."

His lips turned down. "Ken doesn't arrest people unless he has the goods."

Roosevelt trained Ken Lee. "It doesn't mean that he's right this time."

"We'll see. I heard that your client had Gore's wallet."

"It was on the ground next to where Reggie was sleeping. They didn't find Reggie's prints, blood, or DNA on the wallet."

"You're saying somebody else put it there?"

"Or Gore dropped it."

He responded with the familiar smile that I had seen countless times in the Homicide Detail, in court, and in my parents' dining room. "You're a good lawyer, Mike. On the other hand, it sounds like you're going to be asking the jury to connect a lot of dots."

"I am."

"Any viable alternate suspects?"

"There were several other people in the vicinity that night." He listened intently as I ran him through the list of people who had attended the gathering at Kanzen. "Everybody lost a lot of money and had big problems with Gore."

"You got any hard evidence that one of those people killed him?"

"Uh, no."

Pete pulled up his phone and showed Roosevelt Mason's photo. "This is the guy that I told you about. His name is Damian Mason. We think he was selling bath salts to Gore. We saw him in a security video taken on the street level of Salesforce Transit Center on the morning that Gore died."

"Do you have any evidence that he was upstairs in the park that morning?"

"Not yet."

"What makes you think that he had anything to do with Gore's death?"

"Maybe he and Gore had a drug deal that went south. Maybe Gore owed him money. Maybe it was something unrelated."

Roosevelt rested his chin in his palm. "Sounds like speculation to me."

It is.

Pete kept his voice even. "I've been trying to chase down Mason. I've talked to his landlord, family, friends, acquaintances, and anybody else that I could find who might have a connection. As far as I can tell, he dropped off the grid three months ago. He left his apartment in a hurry, abandoned his car and most of his belongings, and vanished into thin air. No cell phone activity, no cash withdrawals, no credit card charges, nothing."

Roosevelt nodded.

Pete looked straight at Roosevelt. "My sources told me that SFPD knew about Mason's drug dealing. They even brought him in for questioning at least once."

"They did."

"You're better connected than I am. Did your sources in SFPD provide any information that might help me find him?"

Roosevelt waited a long beat. "You aren't going to find him."

Pete took a moment to process the answer. "Is he alive?"

"As far as I know."

"Do you have any idea where he is?"

Roosevelt cleared his throat. "He was last seen heading into Mexico at a crossing in Texas. His trail went cold, and SFPD doesn't have the time or resources to keep looking for him."

I started to speak up, but Pete stopped me. He turned back to Roosevelt. "Thanks for your help. Please give my best to your granddaughter. I hope that she has a beautiful baby."

"Roosevelt looks good," Pete observed.

"Yes, he does," I said.

We were still at Dunleavy's. Roosevelt had just departed.

"What was that about?" I asked.

Pete looked up from his phone. "He was telling us that we aren't going to find Mason. You need to plan your case without him."

"You sure?"

"It's Roosevelt talking. I believe him."

I was disappointed, but I knew that he was right. I asked him if he was going home.

He put on his bomber jacket. "Your trial starts on Monday. I'm going to see if I can find you another potential suspect."

Nady walked into my office at midnight. "You're here late," she said.

"So are you. I heard you got a hung jury."

She smiled. "It's a better result than I expected."

"Congratulations. Is the DA going to refile charges?"

"Probably."

In our line of work, delaying the inevitable is sometimes the best that we can do. "Why are you here at this hour?"

"I was going to ask you the same question."

"Trial starts Monday. I've been updating our witness list and working on exhibits. We can include Mason on our list, but it's unlikely that we'll be able to locate him." I described my discussion with Roosevelt and Pete.

She took the news in stride. "We can't call a witness that we can't find. Maybe it will work to our favor. We can throw him under the bus, and he won't be able to defend himself."

"Maybe. Pete is looking for other witnesses. I'm not optimistic. In the meantime, we need to plan our case with what we already have."

"You play the cards you're dealt, Mike. You going home soon?"

"Yes. You?"

"Yes."

"Andy Erickson and I are meeting with the judge tomorrow afternoon to talk about motions and witness lists. Are you available?"

"Of course."

32

"TRY A LITTLE HARDER"

The Honorable Ignatius Tsang sat in his tall leather chair behind a government-issue desk in his meticulously arranged chambers at two-fifteen in the afternoon of Thursday, September twenty-second. His floor-to-ceiling bookcases were packed with dusty legal tomes, and a bronze rendering of the scales of justice sat on his desk. A lithograph of the U.S. Supreme Court hung next to his law school diploma from UC Berkeley. A framed photo of his wife, JoAnn, and his son, Nathan, a law professor at UCLA, sat on the credenza.

As always, he spoke to me with precision. "I understand that your colleague, Ms. Fernandez, will be home until her baby is born. Please give her my best."

"Thank you, Your Honor. I will."

Judge Tsang was a slight man in his mid-sixties with a receding hairline and a scholarly manner. The native of Taiwan had accompanied his mother and father to San Francisco when he was a baby. He grew up in Chinatown, where his parents held multiple low-paying jobs, and he focused on school. He graduated at the top of his class at Lowell High School, raced through UC Berkeley in three years, and placed first in his class at Berkeley Law. He clerked for Justice Byron White before he joined the San Francisco DA's office, where he labored for two decades while writing law review articles and teaching criminal procedure. He brought the same tenacity and intellectual rigor to the bench.

He pretended to study our pre-trial motions. Given his obsessive preparedness and photographic memory, I was confident that he could recite every word by heart.

He took off his reading glasses and spoke to me. "I have read your motions. Anything that you and Ms. Nikonova care to add?"

"No, Your Honor."

"Thank you." He looked at Andy Erickson, who was sitting in front of the dirt-encrusted window overlooking the slow lane of I-80. "You?"

"Nothing, Your Honor."

"Very good." He took a moment to gather his thoughts. "First, my gag order remains in place. I don't want you trying this case in the press."

We nodded.

"Second, I am not going to allow television cameras in my courtroom."

This came as no surprise. Judge Tsang was a traditionalist who believed—correctly, in my view—that people behave differently in court when the cameras are on.

He glanced at his computer. Then he spoke to me. "No request for a change of venue?"

"Correct."

He looked at Erickson. "You're happy to stay here in San Francisco?"

"We are, Your Honor."

"Have you and the defense exchanged witness lists?"

"We have. No last-minute additions on our side."

"Mr. Daley?"

"We have informed Mr. Erickson that we wish to include the following additional names: Ms. Amanda Blair, Ms. Elizabeth Gore, Mr. Damian Mason, Ms. Nicole Hanson, Ms. Kaela Joy Gullion, and Mr. Peter Daley. We may have some additional names, which we will provide to Mr. Erickson as soon as possible."

The judge raised an eyebrow. "Your brother is on your list?"

"He's a licensed private investigator who has joined our team."

Erickson feigned annoyance. "We fail to see how testimony from the decedent's ex-wife, ex-girlfriend, and three private investigators is relevant to this case."

I fired back. "They have information pertaining to Mr. Gore's activities and frame of mind shortly before his death."

The judge made the call. "I'm going to allow them to testify. If necessary, I will give Mr. Erickson additional leeway to question them." He turned to me. "I expect you and Mr. Erickson to exchange final lists by close of business tomorrow."

"We will."

We spent the next hour discussing jury questionnaires, evidentiary issues, chain-of-custody disputes, and draft jury instructions. Erickson said that the prosecution's case would be short—no more than two trial days after jury selection. I said that our defense would also be brief. Given the limited amount of physical evidence and the small number of witnesses, it was possible that it would take us longer to pick a jury than to present the evidence.

Judge Tsang glanced at his watch. "Anything else, Mr. Daley?"

I shot a glance at Erickson, then I addressed the judge. "Your Honor, we ask you to instruct Mr. Erickson to provide any remaining evidence as soon as possible."

Erickson feigned irritation. "We have, Your Honor."

"You provided us with more than a thousand hours of security videos, most of which were irrelevant. You were trying to take up our time."

"If we hadn't, you would be complaining that we had left something out. It's unfair to criticize us for being thorough. We fulfilled our legal obligation to provide all evidence that would tend to exonerate your client."

Judge Tsang was well aware that prosecutors frequently dump mountains of irrelevant evidence on the defense. "Mr. Erickson, if you have any additional evidence to share with the defense, I want you to do so as soon as possible and, in any event, by the close of business on Friday."

"Yes, Your Honor."

"Anything else?" the judge asked.

Erickson spoke up. "Your Honor, we renew our objection to the potential introduction of a so-called 'psychological autopsy' by the defense."

"On what grounds?"

"The science is unproven."

"That's not true," I said. "The science has been subject to rigorous academic study since the fifties. It's solid, and our expert is qualified. Your Honor has allowed the introduction of psychological autopsies in several cases in the past."

Erickson interrupted me. "The facts of this case are different."

"The facts in every case are always distinguishable." I turned back to the judge. "You have also allowed the testimony of our expert in at least one other case. We believe that the same rules should apply here."

Erickson tried again. "But, Your Honor—,"

Judge Tsang cut him off. "I am going to allow the introduction of the psychological autopsy, Mr. Erickson. And I am going to allow the testimony of Mr. Daley's expert."

Good. One for our side.

The judge looked my way. "I want to make it clear to you that I will be giving Mr. Erickson substantial latitude to question your expert witness."

"Understood."

"Anything else, Mr. Daley?"

"Are you planning to give a manslaughter instruction?"

"I haven't decided."

By law, in a first-degree murder case, Judge Tsang was obligated to instruct the jury that it might also find Reggie guilty of second-degree. He also had the discretion, but not the legal duty, to give a manslaughter instruction. The ramifications were significant. First-degree murder carries a minimum sentence of twenty-five years, second-degree, fifteen. Voluntary manslaughter has a minimum of three years, a maximum of eleven. For involuntary, the range is two to four.

A manslaughter instruction is a mixed bag. Obviously, it would lead to a shorter sentence than a murder conviction. On the other hand, it might also make it easier for the jury to reach a "compromise" guilty verdict.

He added, "I will make a final decision after the prosecution and the defense finish presenting their respective cases. Do you have a preference, Mr. Daley?"

"We're leaning in favor, Your Honor."

"Mr. Erickson?"

"It's too early for us to decide, Your Honor. We'll see how things go at trial."

"Noted."

Prosecutors are often willing to sacrifice longer sentences for surer convictions. On the other hand, Erickson was under no obligation to reveal his thinking before trial.

Judge Tsang spoke in a somber tone. "I would like you to make a final effort to work out a deal so that we don't have to empanel a jury and take up resources for a trial."

"We've tried," Erickson said.

"Try a little harder."

"This isn't a murder case," I said.

Judge Tsang's voice filled with impatience. "The charges are up to the DA, Mr. Daley. I am simply asking you to try once more to negotiate a plea bargain."

Erickson wasn't buying. "Mr. Daley refuses to be reasonable, Your Honor."

"I have known Mr. Daley for many years. In my experience, he is always reasonable."

Nice to know.

The judge's eyes twinkled. "I know how persuasive you can be, Mr. Erickson. Try to work your magic on Mr. Daley and Ms. Nikonova one more time."

"Erickson knows more than he's letting on" Nady said.

"No doubt," I replied.

I was standing next to her desk at eight-thirty the same evening. The PD's Office was quiet. Luna was sitting in the corner in anticipation of dinner. Pete was in the conference room studying video. We were less than a week from starting trial, and we were still trying to settle on a narrative and the best strategy to present our alternative suspects to the jury.

I pointed at Nady's laptop. "We have until tomorrow to add names to our witness list. I want you to load it up. All the employees at Kanzen, the entire security department at Salesforce Park, and everyone who has talked to Pete. It will make Erickson prepare for more witnesses. At the very least, maybe he'll think we know something that he doesn't."

"You're as spiteful as I am."

Perhaps. "Rosie says that I'm not as nice as I pretend to be."

"She's right. You think Erickson will offer us a new deal?"

"His boss wasn't in a dealing mood the last time I talked to her."

Pete knocked on the open door. "Got a sec?" he asked.

"It would be great if you could give me something that I can use," I said.

"Jack Emrich is back from London."

The investment banker from Deutsche Bank was at Kanzen on the night that Gore died. "Any chance that you can convince him to talk to us?"

"I already did, Mick. I promised to buy him dinner."

I was exhausted, but I had to talk to Emrich. "When?"

"Now."

33

"HE WAS WHO HE WAS"

"Good flight?" I asked.

Jack Emrich responded with a toothy smile. "Long one."

"Thank you for seeing us."

"Thanks for buying me dinner."

Pete had informed me that Emrich was thirty-eight, but his boyish features and sandy blonde hair made him look younger. He had spent the last ten hours on a flight from London, but there wasn't a hair out of place. Sporting a collarless shirt and a leather jacket, he looked like many of the young finance gurus who populate the conference rooms of investment banks and hedge funds in San Francisco and Silicon Valley. His demeanor fell somewhere between self-confident and arrogant. The native of the Chicago suburbs was a University of Michigan alum. He started his career as an analyst at Fidelity in Boston, moved to a hedge fund in New York, transitioned to a venture capital firm in Palo Alto, and finally found a home at Deutsche Bank in San Francisco, where he provided investment advice to the sovereign funds of Saudi Arabia, Kuwait, Qatar, and United Arab Emirates. Nice work if you can get it.

"Was your trip for business or pleasure?" I asked.

"Both." He said that the weather was nice in London.

"A couple of the investors in Deal Coin mentioned that you're starting a new fund."

"I am."

It didn't seem like an ideal time to ask him if he got fired by Deutsche Bank after Deal Coin crashed. "How's that going?"

"Very well."

"Good luck."

"Thanks."

The sweet aroma of barbecued ribs and steaks filled the room as we sat in an upholstered booth near the glossy bar in International Smoke. It's an upscale restaurant on the ground floor of Millennium Tower that's a collaboration between celebrity chef Michael Mina and cookbook author, television host, and entrepreneur Ayesha Curry. In a sign of the restaurant's celebrity patina, Mina and Curry opened a second location at the MGM Grand in Las Vegas.

"You live nearby?" I asked.

Emrich took a bite of his seventy-five-dollar bone-in Korean short ribs with furikake rice and cucumber kimchi and pointed up. "Upstairs."

"How are the renovations going?"

"Slowly. It's been a long and expensive process, but those of us who live here are hopeful that we're getting close to the finish line." He took a draw of his North Coast Brewing Company pilsner. "You wanted to talk about Tyson?"

"We did."

"I have nothing to hide."

Good to hear. "You're on the prosecution's witness list. Any idea why?"

"They might need me to confirm that Tyson was at Kanzen on the night that your client killed him."

I let it go. "How well did you know him?"

"Pretty well. My clients invested in several of his start-ups. We did well on the first couple of deals. Everybody lost money on Deal Coin."

"We've been told that Mr. Gore was a visionary."

"He was."

Until Deal Coin. "And that he wasn't the easiest guy to deal with."

"He was who he was."

"We understand that his behavior became erratic when Deal Coin was imploding."

"He was who he was," he repeated.

"You talked to him at Kanzen?"

"Of course."

"Did he ask you to hit up your clients for more money?"

"Yes." He shrugged. "I informed him that it wasn't going to happen."

"How did he respond?"

"He was frustrated."

"We heard that he was arguing with several of his investors."

"He was under a lot of stress."

"Did it get heated with anybody?"

He thought about it for a moment. "Matt Bosworth and Steve Warren."

"Did anybody get physical?"

"Of course not."

"Did either of them threaten Mr. Gore?"

"They're big boys, Mr. Daley. This wasn't the first time that one of their investments went south."

I turned to Pete, who took a bite of his thirty-dollar cheeseburger and spoke to Emrich in clipped cop dialect. "Did you and Tyson socialize much?"

"A little. I invited him to my firm's luxury box at the ballpark. We used to see each other at Kanzen. Our ex-wives used to get together on occasion."

"You knew that he had a drinking problem?"

"I knew that he drank socially. I saw no evidence that he did so in excess."

"Did you know that he was taking antidepressants?"

"Uh, no."

Pete ate a French fry. "Did you ever consider the possibility that he might have been suicidal?"

Emrich feigned surprise. "Are you serious?"

"His company was imploding. He and his investors had lost billions. He was drinking to excess and taking antidepressants. Did it ever occur to you that he was on the edge?"

"Not really."

"Did you know that he was doing bath salts?"

"Uh, no." He quickly added, "What Tyson did in his free time was none of my business."

"Does it bother you that a guy you entrusted with your clients' money was taking designer drugs?"

Emrich took a long draw of his pilsner. "It didn't impair his ability to perform his job."

"Deal Coin went bankrupt."

"I saw no evidence that his occasional use of recreational drugs impaired his ability to run the company."

"Not even a little?"

"A lot of corporate executives use designer drugs. Hell, a lot of lawyers do, too. It doesn't necessarily impair their performance." He looked at me. "People who do that stuff get really good at hiding it and continuing to perform their jobs. I'll bet you that there are people at the PD's Office who have alcohol and drug issues."

"Maybe." I kept my tone conversational. "How do you think your clients in the Middle East would have felt about it?"

His confident veneer showed its first crack. "They wouldn't have been happy."

"You may want to give them a heads-up that Gore's drug use might be revealed at trial." *It's definitely going to be revealed at trial.*

His expression turned serious. "I'll let them know."

If my guess is correct, you'll be on the phone with your benefactors in Riyadh to do some damage control as soon as we're finished eating.

Emrich tried to regain his swagger. "I fail to see how this is relevant to your case."

"We think there is a very good chance that Mr. Gore committed suicide."

"That's preposterous."

"We may give you an opportunity to express your views in court."

"Like I said, I have nothing to hide."

Actually, I think you do. I pulled out my phone and showed him the photo of Damian Mason. "This was taken by a security camera on the street level of Salesforce Transit Center on the morning that Mr. Gore died. Recognize him?"

A look of recognition crossed his face. "No."

You wouldn't be a good poker player. "His name is Damian Mason. Ring a bell?"

"No."

You're lying. "He's a drug dealer."

"I wouldn't know."

"The police believe that he was supplying bath salts to Mr. Gore."

"I'll take your word for it."

"You never met him?"

"Absolutely not."

A little too much bluster. I decided to bluff. "We talked to him a couple of days ago, and we've added him to our witness list."

Emrich's eyes danced from me to his plate to Pete and back to me. "I can't stop you."

"What do you think he'll say if we ask him if he knows you?"

The telltale hesitation. "He'll say that he doesn't."

"You pretty sure?"

"Yes." He finished his beer, put the glass on the table, and stood up. "Nice chatting with you guys. Thanks for dinner."

Pete was grinning as we crossed the temporary walkway through the construction zone in front of Millennium Tower. "Nice bluff, Mick. You spooked Emrich."

"Thanks."

"Unfortunately, it's going to fall apart when Emrich realizes that you aren't going to be able to produce Mason in court."

"I wanted to see how he would react when I showed him the photo."

"He recognized Mason," Pete said. "You should ask him about it in court."

"I will."

"But it isn't going to get you an acquittal."

Probably true. "Maybe he'll try to contact Mason."

"Doubtful, Mick." He pulled up the collar of his bomber jacket. "Look on the bright side. We got to have a nice dinner at a fancy restaurant. We don't get to do that very often when we're working on a case."

"True. I hope you liked it."

"I did. The food was terrific, but it's a little pricey for my taste. Maybe Ayesha's husband can get us courtside seats to a Warriors game."

"We have a better chance with Eugene McAllister. Can you keep an eye on Emrich?"

"Sure."

My phone vibrated. I had a text from Nady. It read, "Erickson wants to see us at 8:00 AM at the DA's Office."

34

"I CAN'T DO ANY BETTER"

Erickson sat behind his desk, eyes and tone somber. "Thanks for coming over on short notice."

"You're welcome," I said.

Nady and I were sitting on the opposite side of Erickson's desk at eight o'clock the following morning, a Friday. We were three days from the start of jury selection. The DA's Office was buzzing as Erickson's colleagues were preparing to head over to court.

He took off his wire-framed glasses, wiped them with a cloth, and put them back on. "You ready to go on Monday?"

"Yes." *Let him talk.*

"Judge Tsang asked us to take one more shot at a deal." He templed his fingers in front of his face. "I have a proposition for you."

I waited.

"Vanessa has authorized me to make a final offer. Your client will plead guilty to voluntary manslaughter. No enhancements. Credit for time served."

We're making progress. The maximum sentence for vol man is eleven years, but the minimum can be as low as three.

"It's a good deal, Mike," he insisted.

Yes, it is.

He added, "I can't do any better."

That's probably true. "Recommended sentence?"

"High end of the scale. We'll recommend eleven."

Not good enough. "I won't be able to sell it to my client."

"I might be able to go to the middle of the scale: six."

Let the horse trading begin. "He'll plead guilty to involuntary manslaughter. Three years."

"No." He drummed his fingers on his desk. "Your client was the only person at the scene. The decedent's wallet was on the ground next to him. He's the only legitimate suspect."

"They didn't find Reggie's prints, blood, or DNA on the wallet. Gore was drinking heavily, taking strong antidepressants, and consuming designer drugs. His company was imploding. My expert will testify that it's likely that he committed suicide."

"You can't prove it."

"I don't need to. I just have to convince one juror that there is reasonable doubt."

"Be reasonable, Mike."

"Be realistic, Andy."

"What would it take?"

"I can try to sell him on involuntary man with a minimal sentence."

"How minimal?"

"No more than three years."

"I can't do it, Mike."

"Sure you can, Andy. If Reggie killed him, why on earth did he stay in the park until the following morning?"

"He was drunk, tired, and confused."

I tried my best to sound reasonable. "We've known each other for a long time, and we've always been straight with each other." *Well, most of the time.* "You know as well as I do that you'll never make vol man, and you certainly won't make murder. Your best chance of getting a conviction is convincing the jury that Reggie got into a shoving match with Gore and accidentally pushed him over the railing at Salesforce Park. That's textbook involuntary manslaughter."

His eyes narrowed. "The offer is voluntary manslaughter with a recommended sentence of six years with credit for time served. You have a legal obligation to take it to your client. This offer will remain open until five PM on Sunday."

35

"I NEED YOU TO BE READY"

Reggie's response to Erickson's offer was a concise "No."

"We won't get a better offer," I said.

"I didn't kill Gore. I'm not going to say that I did."

He was surprisingly calm—almost serene—as we met in the drab consultation room in County Jail #3 at three-forty-five on Friday afternoon. He seemed to appreciate the reality that we were starting trial in three days. Besides discussing legal strategies, I needed to manage his expectations and emotions.

"You okay?" I asked.

"Not bad."

His orange jumpsuit was stained with perspiration. "You're sweating."

"I do that a lot."

"When was the last time you had a Covid test?"

"This morning. I'm clear."

Good. "Are you eating and sleeping?"

"Some."

"Get some rest over the weekend. The next couple of weeks are going to be stressful."

He listened attentively as I told him what to expect on Monday. He would be driven from the jail to the Hall of Justice, where I would provide a suit and tie. I asked him to be clean-shaven. I reminded him that appearances are critical. "Everybody will be watching you. I want you to be respectful and engaged. People will pay close attention to your facial expressions. I need you to look the judge, the jurors, and the witnesses in the eye. Judge Tsang is a stickler for decorum, so it is absolutely critical that you avoid any disruptions or make any remarks."

He nodded.

I explained that the trial would start with jury selection, a tedious but critical process which would last at least a few days. "We'll do opening statements after we pick the jury. The prosecution goes first. Then it will be our turn." I told him that the trial would probably be finished in less than two weeks.

"Did you find the guy in the security video?"

"No. Our sources at SFPD informed us that he's probably left the country."

"You can still blame him for killing Gore, right?"

"Yes, but we have no evidence putting him upstairs in Salesforce Park that morning."

He exhaled heavily. "What's the plan?"

"We'll start by trying to persuade the jury that the prosecution doesn't have enough evidence to prove its case beyond a reasonable doubt. If I can punch enough holes in the prosecution's case and everything goes exceptionally well, we won't put on a defense."

His eyes lit up. "What's the likelihood?"

"No better than twenty percent." I explained that we would start by calling forensics experts to confirm that the police found no blood, fingerprints, or DNA connecting him to Gore. We would follow up by having our expert present her psychological autopsy and opine that Gore committed suicide.

"You think the jury will buy it?"

"Hard to say. Our expert is very good, but psychological autopsies are a tough sell. If it looks like the jury is buying it, we'll stop there. If not, I'll put up some of the people who were at Salesforce Park that morning to see if I can foist the potential blame to one of them."

"You got any real evidence?"

Uh, no. "Everybody there had lost a lot of money and was pissed off at Gore."

"And if that isn't enough?"

I lowered my voice. "I need you to be ready to testify. I want you to deny that you killed Gore."

He froze. "I thought it was a bad idea for a client to testify in his own defense."

In most cases, it is. The conventional wisdom says that it's too risky to put a client on the stand because the prosecution will have the opportunity to go after him.

"Depends on the circumstances," I said. "I will ask you just a couple of questions. I think it would be helpful for the jury to hear you say that you didn't kill Gore."

He scowled. "I'm not sure if I can do it."

"Yes, you can, Reggie."

"What about Erickson?"

"You have nothing to worry about as long as you tell the truth."

He didn't respond.

I eyed him. "You *have* been telling me the truth, haven't you?"

"Yes." He took a couple of deep breaths. "You think this is going to work?"

"I think we have a good shot to get the jury to reasonable doubt."

36

"DID YOU HEAR THE NEWS?"

"The Terminator" knocked on the open door to the conference room in the PD's Office at eight-fifteen on Sunday night. Nady was sitting next to me. Rolanda had joined us on Zoom.

"You need anything?" he asked.

I looked up from my laptop. "We're good, T."

"Okay if I head home?"

"Sure."

"I'll be here early tomorrow if anything comes up." The hulking former boxer returned to his desk, put on his oversized parka, and headed out the door.

I looked at Rolanda in the box on my screen. "You feeling okay?"

"Fine, Mike. I'm getting tired of watching Netflix, and I'm not getting much sleep."

"You're in the homestretch."

"Tell that to the baby. You ready for trial tomorrow?"

"Absolutely." I explained that Nady and I had spent the day finalizing juror questionnaires, witness lists, exhibits, and trial strategy.

"Are you working with a jury consultant?"

"No time or budget." I smiled. "We're going to rely on Nady's instincts."

"They're very good. Have you finished your closing argument?"

"Working on it now."

You might think that on the night before trial, I would be focused on my opening. In reality, I completed it yesterday.

When I was a rookie PD, Rosie taught me that you should also write your closing before the trial starts. It helps you focus on the story that you want to tell the jurors.

"What's the narrative?" Rolanda asked.

"We'll start with the argument that the DA doesn't have enough evidence to prove beyond a reasonable doubt that Reggie killed Gore." I told her that we would focus on the fact that the police found no fingerprints, blood, or DNA evidence connecting Reggie to Gore or the wallet.

"And the dried blood on Reggie's hands and face?"

"He fell down the day before Gore died."

"Says Reggie. Then what?"

"Suicide." I said that our expert would present her psychological autopsy and opine that Gore had taken his own life.

Rolanda's voice was skeptical. "That's going to be an uphill climb. Psychological autopsies are inherently suspect and a tough sell to a jury."

The unyielding voice of reality. "If it isn't enough, I'll call everybody who was at Kanzen and try to get the jury to consider blaming one of them."

"You'll sound desperate."

Yes, I will. "I don't have to prove that somebody else killed Gore. I just need to make a case to one juror that it's plausible." I looked over at Nady. "You included all the names on our witness list, right?"

"Right." She looked up from her computer. "McAllister won't be able to testify."

"Why not? We sent him a summons."

"Did you hear the news?"

"What news?"

"McAllister had a stroke at the Giants game last night. He's going to be in the hospital for a couple of weeks."

My head throbbed. "That doesn't help."

Rolanda eyed me from her box on Zoom. "You aren't going to try to blame Gore's death on a guy who just had a stroke, are you?"

"No." *And now I won't have the chance.* "We have other options."

"Proof?"

"Innuendo."

"Wonderful."

Pete walked into the conference room, took off his bomber jacket, put his laptop on the table, and poured himself a cup of lukewarm coffee.

"Any update on Mason?" I asked.

"I'm not going to be able to find him, Mick. My sources in Narcotics confirmed what Roosevelt told us. Somebody must have tipped Mason that SFPD was looking for him. He made a quick exit to Mexico. He was spotted crossing the border."

I just lost my second witness in the last two minutes. "We can only call the witnesses who are available."

Pete smirked. "But you can still blame the ones who aren't."

True.

Nady spoke up again. "You going to put Reggie on the stand?"

"Only if we're desperate."

"Where are you?" Rosie asked.

"The Golden Gate Bridge," I said, using the hands-free. "I'll be home in twenty minutes."

Traffic was light as I drove northbound at eleven-fifteen on Sunday night. The fog covered the towers, and I could barely make out the Alcatraz beacon. The Berkeley Hills had disappeared.

"You ready to roll?" Rosie asked.

"As ready as I'm going to be. I'll tell you about it when I get home."

She waited a beat. "You need to stay at the apartment tonight."

Uh-oh. "You mad at me?"

"No." She cleared her throat. "I was at a meeting at the Mayor's Office on Friday evening. I found out earlier tonight that two people who were there tested positive for Covid. I just tested positive, too."

Crap. "I'll call you when I get to the apartment."

37

"THIS COULD GET UGLY"

"How are you feeling?" I asked.

Rosie looked at me from the box on Zoom. "My throat is sore, but otherwise fine. You?"

"Fine."

I was sitting at the table in the one-bedroom apartment behind the Larkspur Fire Station that I had rented when Rosie and I got divorced. It was four blocks from Rosie's house. I hadn't bothered to upgrade my furniture since I had moved in twenty-five years earlier: a butcher-block table, two spindle chairs, a gray sofa, a secondhand end table, and a bedroom set from Scandinavian Design. It wasn't much to look at, but it was nicer than the thrift-store furniture in my room in the back of a century-old house in Berkeley when I was in law school.

"What do you need?" I asked.

"Nothing at the moment. I signed up for a PCR test at Marin General in the morning. Dr. Yee said that she would get me a prescription for Paxlovid. I have plenty of food. I'll be fine."

"I was hoping that we were finished with Covid."

"We'll be finished with Covid when Covid decides that it's finished with us. I just got word that the Mayor tested positive, too. It looks like City government will be working from home for a few days."

I looked over at the sofa, where my snow-white cat, Wilma, was sleeping. Wilma used to live in the apartment next door. When my neighbors had twin boys, she started coming over to my place for peace and quiet. It turned out that the twins were allergic to cats, so my neighbors asked me to adopt Wilma since she was spending most of her time over here anyway. I was happy to do so, and Wilma was delighted to have a quiet place to herself and a human to make sure that her water bowl and kibble dish were full.

"Who have you seen since the meeting?" I asked.

"You, my mother, my brother, Grace, Rolanda, and Rolanda's baby. Everybody has tested negative other than you."

So far, so good. I looked at the at-home test sitting next to my computer. "I'm negative."

"Good." Her voice filled with resignation. "I'm going to feel like crap if I gave it to somebody."

"Everybody's vaccinated and boosted, Rosie."

"I just sent an email to everybody at the office. I asked everybody to get tested. You'll let Pete know?"

"Already did. He's clean, too. So is Donna."

"That's a relief."

"We'll deal with it, Rosie. At least you weren't exposed right before Grace's wedding."

"We aren't going to postpone again, Mike—even if I have to watch it on Zoom."

"We'll worry about it in December. For now, you need to stay home for a few days. I'll take care of the office until you return."

"You have a trial starting in the morning."

"I've gotten pretty adept at multitasking. Terrence will take care of anything that I don't have time to handle. He runs the office anyway."

"Yes, he does. Are you and Nady ready to go in the morning?"

"Of course."

"How does it look?"

"Not great. In fact, this could get ugly. Pete got word that Damian Mason was last seen entering Mexico, and it's unlikely that we'll be able to find him. He was probably our best alternative suspect."

"And now he won't be able to defend himself."

"I don't have any hard evidence that he had anything to do with Gore's death. I can't place him upstairs in Salesforce Park."

"You don't need to prove it. You just need to suggest it. What's the narrative?"

Rosie listened attentively as I walked her through our defense strategy. She asked a few pointed questions and offered a couple of suggestions.

"Will you put Reggie on the stand?" she asked.

"If we're desperate. If that doesn't work, I'll go to smoke and mirrors."

"Thought so." Her voice softened. "Do you think you can pull a rabbit out of your hat?"

"There's always a chance."

She eyed me. "Do you think Reggie killed Gore?"

"I don't know for sure, but it seems pretty unlikely to me that he would have stuck around all night if he had."

"Fair enough. You should go out and get some air in the morning."

"I was planning to go for a walk to clear my head."

"Give my best to Zvi."

Our friend, neighbor, and hero, Zvi Danenberg, was a relentlessly upbeat ninety-seven-year-old retired science teacher who exercised by climbing the one hundred and thirty-nine steps connecting Magnolia Avenue in downtown Larkspur with the houses on the adjacent hill. He used to do it every day, but he slowed down to twice a week after he celebrated his ninety-fifth birthday, and his doctors advised him to preserve what was left of his overworked knees. I joined him from time to time in my never-ending quest to improve my conditioning. In his spare time, Zvi maintained a magnificent collection of classical records that he had accumulated over eight decades. I was honored when he invited me to view the room in his house that he devoted to his albums.

"I'll pass along your regards," I said. "Unfortunately, your positive Covid test means that we won't be able to engage in our customary pre-trial ritual. For the record, I am profoundly disappointed."

"So am I."

Since Rosie and I rarely slept on the night before trial, we usually tried to relieve the stress by engaging in pre-trial bedroom activities.

"I'm sorry, Mike," she said. "That wouldn't be prudent in the circumstances."

"Agreed. Is there such a thing as 'Zoom sex'?"

She chuckled. "I don't think so."

"You'll make it up to me if I get an acquittal?"

Her eyes gleamed. "I'll make it up to you no matter what."

38

"LET'S GET STARTED"

At nine-ten on a windy Monday morning, Nady and I kept our heads down as we lugged our laptops, trial bags, and exhibits past a handful of reporters who were waiting for us on the front steps of the Hall of Justice.

"Mr. Daley? Is your client going to cut a deal?"

"Mr. Daley? Is there anything that you would like to say to Tyson Gore's children?"

"Mr. Daley? Is it true that the Public Defender has tested positive for Covid?"

I stopped, turned around, and recited the platitude that every defense attorney says before the start of every trial. "I am pleased to have the opportunity to defend my client in court. I am confident that he will be exonerated."

The reporters quickly shifted to Vanessa Turner, who was heading up the steps next to the area where the smokers congregated. Our media-savvy DA looked into the cameras and spoke in an appropriately somber tone. "The evidence against Reginald Jones is overwhelming and will result in a first-degree murder conviction. My administration has made it a priority to prosecute criminals to the fullest extent of the law. We are sending a message that there will be meaningful consequences for criminal behavior."

She touted her alleged success at ridding our streets of crime. In reality, she had been in office for only a few months, and things hadn't changed. In San Francisco politics, perception and spin are often more important than reality.

As Turner played to the cameras, Nady and I slipped inside the Hall.

Judge Tsang's courtroom smelled of mildew as two deputies escorted Reggie to the defense table, where he sat down between Nady and me. Freshly shaved and wearing the charcoal suit and striped tie that I had picked out for him from the donated clothes closet at the PD's Office, he appeared more resigned than nervous.

I whispered, "Stay calm and look the judge and the jurors in the eye."

"When do you need me to testify?"

"Not until we present our defense. The earliest would be at the end of this week."

I looked around the airless room. Reggie had no rooting section. There were no members of Gore's family in the gallery, either. His parents were deceased, his ex-wives had no desire to appear, and his children were too young. Erickson sat at the prosecution table with a junior prosecutor and Inspector Lee. As the lead homicide inspector, Lee was the only witness allowed in court before his testimony.

The gallery was half-full. In a display of institutional support, Turner sat behind Erickson in the front row. I figured that she would stay through the start of jury selection. Rosie usually showed up at the start of major trials, but she was, of course, unavailable. I liked having Pete sit in the gallery because he had good instincts for jury selection, but he was on our witness list, so he could not. A reporter from the *Chronicle* sat by himself in the third row, along with two reporters from the local TV stations. I recognized one crypto blogger in the back row. Evidently, the cable news networks didn't deem our case juicy enough to cover. As always, the ragtag assortment of courtroom junkies, retirees, law students, and homeless people took seats in the gallery. Only two people wore masks—a sign that we were perhaps finally inching out of the Covid era.

I felt an adrenaline rush as Judge Tsang's longtime bailiff called us to order. "All rise."

Here we go.

A standing fan pushed around the heavy air as Judge Tsang emerged from his chambers, surveyed his domain, and walked to his leather chair. He turned on his computer, glanced at his docket, and lifted a hand. "Please be seated."

Nowadays, most judges never touch their gavels.

He addressed the bailiff. "We are in session and on the record. Please call our case."

"The People versus Reginald Jones. The charge is first-degree murder."

"Counsel will state their names for the record."

"Andrew Erickson and Edward George for the People."

"Michael Daley and Nadezhda Nikonova for the defense."

"Thank you." The judge cleared his throat. "Pursuant to updated City Covid policy, I must still ask everyone in court to wear a face covering. Please remove your mask when you address the court. In an abundance of caution, I would also request that you maintain distance when possible. I will allow potential and seated jurors to wear masks if they desire, and I will make accommodations for additional spacing if requested. Any questions?"

Silence.

"Let's get started and pick a jury."

Trials are won and lost at jury selection. It's the most important and least scientific part of the process. It's also the most frustrating for prosecutors and defense attorneys alike because we have little control over it. Successful jury consultants charge well-heeled clients hundreds of thousands of dollars to analyze questionnaires, prepare demographic studies, dissect body language, and, supposedly, pick the perfect panel. In Reggie's case, it was an unaffordable luxury, so Nady and I would have to rely on intuition.

Conventional wisdom says that defense lawyers should choose jurors who are attentive, thoughtful, and, most important, susceptible to persuasion. The oversimplified version of this trope suggests that we should try to pick idiots. I'm as cynical as the next guy, but I've never fully bought into it. I prioritize people who appear likely to listen carefully, keep an open mind, and follow the jury instructions. Reggie's case would likely turn on a thoughtful analysis of the concept of reasonable doubt. I was also going to argue that Gore committed suicide based on a psychological autopsy. This would require some sophisticated thinking and receptiveness to scientific concepts the validity of which are subject to debate. As a result, I was inclined to seat a few jurors with college degrees. As always, I wouldn't know if I chose wisely until the trial was over.

Under Judge Tsang's skillful supervision, we selected twelve jurors and four alternates by the close of business on Wednesday. At ten-fifteen on Thursday morning, those who hadn't come up with a convincing sob story were seated in the box, feigning nonchalance, their eyes revealing nervousness. All were attentive—for now.

Our lineup included nine women, seven with college degrees. We had two African-Americans, two Latinas, and one Filipino. Three worked for tech firms, two worked for the City, one was a postal clerk, one was a supervisor at PG&E, one was a lawyer with a big firm downtown, and three were retirees. I was hoping that the lawyer would take a leadership role.

Judge Tsang thanked the jurors for their service. Then he read the standard instructions which he could have recited by heart. "Do not talk about this case to anyone or among yourselves until deliberations begin. Do not do any research on your own or as a group. You may take notes, but do not use a dictionary or other reference materials, investigate the facts or law, conduct any experiments, or visit the scene of the events to be described at this trial. Do not look at anything involving this case in the press, on TV, or online."

He added the now-standard admonition that was unnecessary when I started as a Deputy Public Defender almost three decades ago. "Do not post anything on Facebook, Twitter, Instagram, Snapchat, WhatsApp, or other social media. If you tweet or text about this case, it will cost you."

A couple of jurors nodded.

The judge looked at Erickson. "Do you wish to make an opening statement?"

He wasn't required to do so, but I have never seen a prosecutor decline the invitation.

"Yes, Your Honor." He stood, buttoned his charcoal suit jacket, strode to the lectern, opened his laptop, and addressed the jury. "My name is Andrew Erickson. I am an Assistant District Attorney. I am grateful for your service, and I appreciate your time and attention."

Reggie tensed.

Erickson activated the flat-screen TV and showed a glossy photo of a smiling Tyson Gore from the now-deleted Deal Coin website. "Tyson Gore was a successful entrepreneur, Silicon Valley visionary, respected CEO, valued mentor, generous philanthropist, and loyal friend. He was a loving father of four young children who will never see him again. He was only thirty-eight years old when the defendant murdered him in Salesforce Park on a cold morning in March."

I could have objected on the grounds that Erickson hadn't proved that Gore was murdered, but it's bad form to interrupt early in an opening.

Erickson pushed out a melodramatic sigh. "Tyson's death is an unspeakable tragedy."

I leaned over and whispered to Reggie, "He's about to point at you. When he does, I want you to look him right in the eye."

On cue, Erickson pointed at Reggie—just the way every prosecutor is taught. "The defendant, Reginald Jones, is sitting at the defense table."

To his credit, Reggie stared right back at him.

Erickson lowered his arm. "We will demonstrate beyond a reasonable doubt that the defendant struck Tyson during a botched robbery in Salesforce Park. We will prove that the defendant pushed Tyson over a railing, and Tyson fell seventy feet into a construction zone. He died upon impact."

He was following the conventional playbook. He would refer to Gore by name to humanize him. The jurors didn't know that Gore had cheated on his wives, ignored his kids, picked up women at the Gold Club, and lost billions of his investors' money. Likewise, Erickson would never mention Reggie's name in an effort to dehumanize him. To the jurors, he would always be "the defendant." It may seem trivial, but trial work is theater, and every detail counts.

Erickson continued. "Tyson's children, friends, and colleagues are devastated. We cannot bring him back, but we can bring his murderer to justice."

I was still reluctant to interrupt, but I wanted the jurors to know that I was paying attention. "Objection to the term 'murderer.' My client is innocent until proven otherwise."

"Sustained. The jury will disregard the use of the term 'murderer.'"

Sure, they will—especially since you just repeated it.

Erickson plowed ahead. "Tyson was the visionary CEO of a company called Deal Coin. Experts in the financial world believed that it would have been the first company to find mainstream uses for crypto currencies. At its peak, it was worth billions."

At the end, it was worthless.

"Tyson spent the last weekend of his life speaking at Deal Con, a convention at Moscone Center. It was a three-day celebration of a wildly successful company."

And a last-ditch effort to raise funds to keep it from filing for bankruptcy.

"After Deal Con ended, Tyson invited his most important investors to a small celebration at a private club called Kanzen in Salesforce Park. The defendant was hiding in the bushes nearby when Tyson and his investors entered the club. The defendant must have seen them. It was obvious that they were affluent. He saw an opportunity to rob them when they departed. And that's exactly what happened. The defendant accosted Tyson after he left Kanzen. He took Tyson's wallet, which the police found on the ground next to the defendant. We know that he attacked Tyson because we found dried blood on his face and hands. He pushed Tyson over the railing. Tyson fell four stories. The Medical Examiner determined that Tyson died upon impact."

Erickson spent ten minutes walking the jurors through the crime scene, the discovery of the wallet, and the Medical Examiner's analysis of cause of death. The jurors were locked in.

Reggie leaned over and whispered, "Can you stop this?"

No. "It'll be our turn shortly."

Erickson shot a disdainful glance my way, then he faced the jury. "Mr. Daley is going to try to convince you that the defendant didn't attack Tyson. Or he'll claim that the defendant's bruises were the result of a fall unrelated to his attack on Tyson. Or perhaps he'll try to persuade you that it was just happenstance that Tyson's wallet was found a few feet from the defendant. Or maybe he'll suggest that Tyson's death was an accident or even a suicide. Mr. Daley is simply doing his job—to distract you. That's why I ask you to evaluate the evidence carefully."

Erickson returned to the lectern. "You are going to hear a lot about 'reasonable doubt.' It's a key legal concept. But common sense is just as critical. It's your job to evaluate the evidence, deliberate carefully, and, most important, use your common sense. I am confident that you will do so. I promise to provide more than enough evidence for you to find beyond a reasonable doubt that the defendant is guilty of murdering Tyson Gore."

He returned to the prosecution table and sat down.

Judge Tsang looked my way. "Opening statement, Mr. Daley?"

"Yes, Your Honor." I could have deferred until after Erickson had completed his case, but I wanted to connect with the jurors right away.

I walked to the lectern and placed a single piece of paper in front of me. "My name is Michael Daley. I am the co-head of the Felony Division of the Public Defender's Office. Reggie Jones has been wrongly accused of a crime that he did not commit. It's your job to correct this error and see that justice is served."

I moved closer to the jurors. "Reggie is a San Francisco native and a former employee of UPS. He isn't perfect, but he's a good man who caught some bad breaks. When he was healthy, he was a productive member of society who worked hard at a physically demanding job, paid his taxes, and played by the rules. He is honest. He is kind. And he is resilient.

"Reggie doesn't want me to make excuses for him, but I want you to understand why he was sleeping in Salesforce Park on the morning that Tyson Gore died. Reggie suffered a debilitating injury at work and developed alcohol and drug issues. Unable to keep his job, he ended up living in several homeless encampments not far from here. He entered treatment programs several times to fight his addictions, but he always relapsed. He ran out of money and spiraled into homelessness.

"Reggie was in Salesforce Park on the morning that Tyson Gore died because he had nowhere else to go. He just wanted a quiet place to sleep. He had fallen down the previous day and injured himself. That's why he had dried blood on his face and hands. He brought a bottle of tequila to the park and found a spot in the bushes to spend the night. Reggie drank the tequila and passed out. He didn't wake up until a security guard found him the following morning. Reggie didn't see or hear anything during the night. It is true that the guard found Tyson Gore's wallet next to the spot where Reggie was sleeping, but there is no evidence that Reggie tried to steal it. Why would Reggie have attacked Mr. Gore? How did a frail fifty-five-year-old homeless man who had consumed a bottle of tequila possibly have the strength to attack Mr. Gore, let alone push him over the railing? Most important, there is no evidence that he did so."

The jurors were listening, but I couldn't tell if they were buying what I was selling.

"The Medical Examiner concluded that Mr. Gore died of a crushed skull after he fell over a railing and landed in a construction zone. I have no reason to doubt her conclusion as to the cause of death. However, there is no evidence that Reggie pushed Mr. Gore."

I took a deep breath. "Mr. Erickson correctly noted that Tyson Gore was the billionaire founder of a cryptocurrency company. However, he left out the fact that Mr. Gore's company had lost billions of his investors' money and was on the verge of bankruptcy. Mr. Gore was desperately trying to raise additional capital before he died. He was unsuccessful, and his investors were irate. Mr. Gore was under an extraordinary amount of stress because of the impending failure of Deal Coin. The media had started calling it 'Dead Coin.' He had gone through two acrimonious divorces. He was also drinking heavily, taking antidepressants, and using illegal designer drugs known as 'bath salts.' You will hear from a respected expert who conducted a detailed psychological analysis of Mr. Gore. She will explain to you why she believes that Mr. Gore committed suicide."

Erickson spoke in a respectful tone. "I must object, Your Honor. This is beyond the scope of what is appropriate for an opening."

Yes, it is.

The judge addressed the jury. "I am going to sustain Mr. Erickson's objection. An opening statement should not be treated as fact. It merely constitutes a road map of what the anticipated evidence will show."

As if they're going to forget what they just heard.

I lowered my voice. "Mr. Erickson and I agree on one thing: Tyson Gore's death is a great tragedy. On the other hand, it would compound the tragedy to convict an innocent man of a crime that he did not commit."

"Objection," Erickson said. "Argumentative."

"Overruled."

"The law requires Mr. Erickson to prove his case beyond a reasonable doubt. That's a critical legal concept. It's also a high standard. Reggie is under no legal obligation to prove his innocence. Nor is he required to put on a defense. Mr. Erickson asked you to use common sense. So will I. Bottom line: Mr. Erickson will not be able to prove his case beyond a reasonable doubt. As a result, you cannot convict Reggie of murder."

There was no reaction from the jurors as I walked back to the defense table.

The judge spoke to Erickson. "It's almost noon, so I am going to recess for lunch. Please be ready to call your first witness when we return."

39

LAYING THE FOUNDATION

Erickson stood at the lectern after the lunch break. "Could you please state your name and occupation for the record?"

"Gilberto Torres. I am a foreman with Bayshore Concrete. I have worked for the company for thirty-four years."

Torres was a stocky silver-haired man with a pockmarked face and a dignified manner. The native of the Mission wore a gray suit appropriate for weddings, funerals, church, and court. He evoked an understated confidence reflecting decades of experience at Bayshore.

"What type of work does your company do?" Erickson asked.

"We provide concrete, rebar, and heavy materials for infrastructure and construction projects." He said that the company had worked on Salesforce Transit Center, Chase Center, the new Central Subway, and several buildings in the UCSF Medical Campus south of the ballpark.

Erickson activated the flat-screen and asked for permission to approach Torres, which Judge Tsang granted. Erickson stopped a few feet from the front of the box—you never crowd a friendly witness. "Your company is working on the retrofit of Millennium Tower?"

"Correct."

"Was Bayshore involved in the original construction?"

"No." A half grin. "If we had been, a retrofit wouldn't have been necessary."

Muffled chuckles in the gallery.

"You were supervising the Millennium Tower site on March seventh of this year, weren't you?"

I spoke up in a respectful tone. "Your Honor, I would be grateful if you would remind Mr. Erickson not to lead the witness."

Erickson nodded. "I will rephrase the question, Mr. Daley."

"Thank you." It was a minor point, but I wanted to signal to the jury that I expected Erickson to stick to the rules.

Erickson turned back to Torres. "Were you working at the Millennium Tower site on the morning of Monday, March seventh, of this year?"

"Yes." He said that he arrived at five-forty-five AM to supervise a crew of a dozen people. "They were scheduled to arrive at six-thirty AM."

"What did you do when you arrived?"

"I checked in with security at Millennium Tower, unlocked the gates so that our trucks could unload, and surveyed the site to make sure that it would be ready when our crew arrived."

"Did you find anything out of the ordinary?"

"Yes." He waited a beat—just the way he and Erickson had rehearsed it. "A body."

"A dead body?"

"Objection," I said. "Mr. Torres is not qualified to render a medical conclusion."

"I'll rephrase," Erickson said. "Was the person moving?"

"No."

"Did you check for a pulse?"

"Yes. As far as I could tell, there was none."

"Did it appear to you that the person was dead?"

"Yes."

Erickson had put the first points on the board. In a murder case, you need a decedent. He displayed a photo of the crime scene taken from above. A red X was superimposed on a pile of gravel in the construction zone between Millennium Tower and Salesforce Transit Center. "Could you please show us where you found the body?"

"At the red X."

Erickson was conducting a by-the-book direct exam. He was asking Torres precise questions. Torres was giving him short answers.

"What did you do next?" Erickson asked.

"I called 9-1-1, Millennium Tower Security, Salesforce Security, and my boss." He said that the police and EMTs arrived within five minutes. "I found out later that the man was pronounced dead by the EMTs. He was identified as Tyson Gore. I gave my statement to the police."

"Do you have any idea how the victim ended up in a pile of gravel?"

"No."

"No further questions."

The judge looked my way. "Cross-exam, Mr. Daley?"

"Just a few questions, Your Honor. May we approach the witness?"

"You may."

I stood, buttoned my jacket, and headed to the front of the box. "Mr. Torres, you didn't know the decedent, did you?"

Erickson stood up as if he was thinking about objecting but reconsidered. It was a legitimate question, and on cross, you're allowed to lead the witness.

"No," Torres said.

"He was already on the pile of gravel when you arrived?"

"Yes."

"You don't know how he got there, do you?"

"No."

"And you don't know when he got there, either, do you?"

"No."

"Was anybody else around?"

"No."

"You don't know how he died, do you?"

"It looked like he had fallen onto the pile of gravel and hit his head."

"But you have no personal knowledge of how or when that might have happened, do you?"

"No."

"In fact, he could have been walking on the gravel and fallen, right?"

"I guess it's possible."

"Or he could have jumped from Salesforce Park? It could have been suicide, right?"

"Objection," Erickson said. "Calls for speculation."

Yes, it does.

The judge eyed me. "The objection is sustained."

"No further questions."

Erickson spent the next hour meticulously laying the foundation for his case. The first officer at the scene testified that he arrived within five minutes after the 9-1-1 call, a moment ahead of the EMTs. He called for backup, began administering first aid, and started to secure the area. The lead EMT reported that Gore had no pulse when he arrived. Efforts to resuscitate him were unsuccessful. He was pronounced dead at the scene at six-forty-five AM, almost an hour after Torres discovered the body. The head of security at Millennium Tower testified that there was no surveillance video of the area where Gore died because the cameras had been removed during construction.

I objected to Erickson's questions from time to time, but there were few items that I could legitimately dispute. On cross, I got each witness to confirm that they had no personal knowledge as to how Gore's body ended up on a pile of gravel. They acknowledged that they had no way of knowing whether Gore had jumped voluntarily or been pushed. Most important, they admitted that they had no knowledge of any involvement on Reggie's part. It wasn't going to get us an acquittal, but it might have inched us a little closer to reasonable doubt.

Having finished with the preliminaries, Erickson finally took his first step to tie Reggie to Gore's death by calling the security guard who found Reggie in the bushes. "The People call Kevin Sanders."

40

"I WAS MAKING MY REGULAR ROUNDS"

Kevin Sanders sat in the box and gulped his second cup of water, eyes squinting, a glint of perspiration on his forehead. "I was making my regular rounds in Salesforce Park at six AM on Monday, March seventh."

Erickson was standing a few feet in front of him, hands in his pockets. "How often did you walk around the park during your shift?"

"Approximately every hour."

"Did you see anything out of the ordinary?"

"Yes."

Erickson had instructed Sanders to answer only the specific questions that he asked, which is an effective way to calm an inexperienced witness. While this often results in rather stilted testimony, the young security guard was doing a nice job of following directions.

"What did you see?" Erickson asked.

"A man sleeping in the bushes."

"Is that man here in this courtroom?"

"Yes."

"Could you point him out?"

Sanders pointed at Reggie. "The defendant."

Erickson had tallied another point: Sanders had connected Reggie to the crime scene.

Erickson displayed an overhead photo of Salesforce Park on the TV and got Sanders to point out the exact spot where he found Reggie. Sanders noted that it was about a hundred feet from Kanzen and directly above the construction site where Gore's body was found.

Erickson moved closer to the box. "What did you do after you found the defendant in the bushes?"

"I reported the incident to my supervisor, Mr. Dave Evans. He said that he would send up another security ambassador to provide assistance. Per our policy, he instructed me to approach the man, politely request his identification, and remain in place until backup arrived."

"How did the man react when you woke him up?"

"He was startled and disoriented. Then he got angry."

"Did he attempt to run?"

"No. He had trouble standing up. His legs were shaky."

"Did you think he was sick?"

"Objection," I said. "Mr. Sanders is not qualified as a medical expert."

Erickson feigned irritation. "I'm not asking Mr. Sanders for a medical diagnosis. I'm just asking about the defendant's appearance."

"Overruled."

It was the correct call. I had objected to break up Erickson's rhythm.

Sanders took another sip of water. "I thought that he was under the influence or hungover."

"Was he cooperative?"

"Not really. He didn't want to talk. I told him that I needed to take his name and contact information. He refused to give it to me. Then I got another message from my boss. He said that there had been some trouble in the construction zone at Millennium Tower. The police wanted to talk to everybody in the area, so he told me to wait for them." He said that Sergeant David Dito arrived five minutes later. "He took my statement. Then he talked to the defendant alone."

"Then what?"

"He waited for additional officers to arrive. They started searching the area. Sergeant Dito escorted the defendant downstairs. He was going to take him in for questioning."

"Did you have any idea what was going on?"

"By then, my boss had informed me that a body was found in the construction zone. The police were trying to figure out if the defendant had anything to do with it."

"No further questions."

"Cross-exam, Mr. Daley?"

"Yes, Your Honor." I moved to the front of the box and kept my tone conversational. "You saw Reggie at approximately six-twenty AM?"

"Yes."

"He was asleep?"

"Correct."

"You had walked by the same area late the previous night and earlier that morning?"

"Yes."

"How many times?"

"Every hour, so probably about eight times."

"But you didn't see him during your earlier rounds?"

"No." He added, "It was dark, and he was hiding in the bushes."

"So you have no firsthand knowledge of when he got there?"

"No."

"When you woke him up, did he try to run?"

"No."

"He made no attempt to run away after you told him that he had to wait until the police arrived?"

"Correct."

"Did that strike you as odd?"

"I don't understand."

"You understand that Reggie has been charged with the murder of Tyson Gore, right?"

"Right."

"If he was guilty, don't you think he would have tried to run away when you told him that the cops were coming?"

"Objection," Erickson said. "Calls for speculation."

Yes, it does. And we're going to be calling for a lot of speculation before this trial is over.

"Sustained."

I inched a little closer. "Did you see Tyson Gore that morning?"

"No."

"Which means that you didn't see Reggie attack him, right?"

"Right."

"Did you talk to anybody who saw Reggie attack him?"

"No."

"So you have no personal knowledge of whether my client attacked Tyson Gore, right?"

"Right."

"And you have no personal knowledge as to whether Mr. Gore was pushed over the railing or jumped on his own, right? Or it could have been an accident, right?"

"Right."

"And it's even possible that he committed suicide, isn't it?"

"Objection. Calls for speculation."

"Sustained."

I had made my point. "You knew that there were others at the gathering at Kanzen late on Sunday night and early Monday morning, didn't you?"

"Yes."

"Did you see any of them?"

"No."

"Did you hear any of them?"

"No."

"Did you consider the possibility that one of them might have attacked Mr. Gore?"

He looked perplexed. "It never occurred to me."

"No further questions."

Susan Gallardo sat in the box, poised, professional. "I am the general manager of Kanzen, a private club located in Salesforce Park."

Erickson stood in front of the box. "Were you working on the night of March sixth and the early morning of March seventh of this year?"

"Yes. I was supervising a private event for Mr. Tyson Gore."

"Mr. Gore was present the entire time?"

"Yes."

Another point for Erickson: he had placed Gore within a hundred feet of Reggie.

"What time did the event start?" Erickson asked.

"A few minutes after eleven PM." She said that it ended shortly after two AM.

"Could you please identify who else was there at the end?"

"Of course." Gallardo listed Matt Bosworth, Steve Warren, Eugene McAllister, Jack Emrich, and Cynthia Mitchell. She also noted that a bartender and two servers were present in addition to herself. "I let my staff go home early. I was the last one to leave."

"What time did everybody depart?"

"Between one-thirty and two-ten."

"Do you recall when Mr. Gore left?"

"Yes. Two-ten AM. He was the last person to leave other than myself." She said that she left about five minutes later.

"Did you see Mr. Gore after you departed?"

"No."

"Did he mention where he was going?"

"Home."

"To his condo across the street at Millennium Tower?"

"Yes."

"Did you happen to notice which direction he went after he left Kanzen?"

"Yes." Gallardo said that she let Gore out before she locked the door. "He turned to his left and started walking."

Erickson pointed at the overhead photo of Salesforce Park that was on display on the flat-screen. "So he left Kanzen and headed toward the Millennium Tower side of the park?"

"Correct."

Erickson pointed at the red X identifying the spot where Sanders had found Reggie. "He must have walked by this spot in the Redwood Forest, right?"

"Correct."

"Did you leave through the same door?"

"Yes. I walked to a stairway and headed home to my condo a few blocks away."

"No further questions."

The judge nodded. "Your witness, Mr. Daley."

"Thank you." I walked to the front of the box. "Have you ever met my client?"

"No."

"You didn't see him that morning?"

"No."

"So you didn't see him interact with Mr. Gore?"

"I did not."

"And you therefore didn't see him attack Mr. Gore, did you?"

"No."

"So you have no personal knowledge of what happened to Mr. Gore that night, do you?"

"No."

"And it's possible that he might have committed suicide, isn't it?"

"Objection. Speculation."

"Sustained."

"And it's also possible that one of the other individuals that you identified in your earlier testimony might have killed Mr. Gore, isn't it?"

"Objection. Speculation."

"Sustained."

"You would agree that all of the individuals that you named had just left Kanzen and were still in the immediate area, right?"

"Right."

"No further questions, Your Honor." I returned to my seat.

Reggie leaned over and whispered, "Can't you do more?"

"On cross, I can only ask questions about matters raised during direct. I'll get more during our defense. Be patient. We're scoring points."

"We need to win."

The judge looked at Erickson. "Please call your next witness."

"The People call Sergeant David Dito."

41

"THIS WALLET?"

Sergeant David Dito's uniform was pressed, his star polished as he sat in the box, bearing erect, demeanor professional. I remembered when he was a happy-go-lucky kid running around in his parents' backyard a few blocks from the house where I grew up. He was now a veteran cop on track to another promotion. The self-assured sergeant wouldn't touch the cup of water that he had poured for himself. Nervous witnesses gulp water. Experienced cops do not.

Erickson was at the lectern. "How long have you been a sworn officer?"

"Twelve years and four months. I have held the rank of sergeant for three years."

Erickson led Dito through his CV: graduated from St. Ignatius and UC Davis; top of his class at the Academy; postings at Northern, Taraval, and Southern Stations; multiple commendations.

Erickson moved forward and stopped a respectful distance from the box. "You were on duty at Southern Station on Monday, March seventh?"

"Yes." Dito said that he began his shift at five-thirty AM. "I was being debriefed by the overnight sergeant when dispatch received an emergency call. A body had been found in the construction area at Millennium Tower. I answered the call at five-fifty-one AM. I checked out a unit and drove to the scene. I was among the first officers there when I arrived at six-oh-two AM. I assisted the officers who were already administering first aid until the EMTs arrived. I called for additional backup."

"Was the decedent pronounced dead at the scene?"

"Yes, he was. At six-forty-five AM."

Erickson led Dito through a crisp description of how he and his subordinates secured the scene (in accordance with SFPD procedure), organized a search for witnesses (none found), and briefed Inspector Lee when he arrived (uneventful).

Erickson kept his voice even. "At approximately six-twenty AM, did you receive a call from Salesforce Park Security?"

"Yes. Mr. Dave Evans informed me that a security guard named Kevin Sanders had found a man named Reggie Jones in Salesforce Park. I told Mr. Evans to instruct his subordinate to stay with Mr. Jones until I arrived. I proceeded upstairs to interview Mr. Sanders, who informed me that he had found the defendant sleeping in the bushes in Salesforce Park above the location where Mr. Gore's body was found."

"Could you describe Mr. Sanders' demeanor?"

"He was pretty shaken up."

"Did you also interview the defendant?"

"Yes, although it was difficult to do so at first. He was angry and disoriented. He was also upset that Mr. Sanders had asked him to remain at the scene until I arrived."

"Did the defendant explain why he was there even though the park was closed?"

"He said that he was sleeping."

"Did you notice any blood on his person?"

"Yes. There was dried blood on his hands and face. He claimed that he had been injured when he fell down the day before."

"Did you believe him?"

Dito's expression turned skeptical. "I didn't find him credible."

"Did you find anything on the ground where the defendant was sleeping?"

"An empty tequila bottle, a sleeping bag, and a backpack containing the defendant's clothing, toiletries, and other personal effects. The defendant brought them to Southern Station, where they were inventoried."

"Anything else?"

"A wallet."

Erickson walked over to the evidence cart and picked up a plastic evidence bag, which encased Gore's wallet. He introduced it into evidence and handed it to Dito. "This wallet?"

"Yes."

"Was there any money inside?"

"No."

"Identification?"

"Yes." Dito turned to face the jury. "We found Tyson Gore's driver's license and several credit cards."

"No further questions, Your Honor."

"Cross-exam, Mr. Daley?"

"Yes, Your Honor." I strode past Erickson as he was returning to his seat. "Sergeant Dito, you didn't see my client interact with Mr. Gore, did you?"

"No."

"You didn't see him try to rob Mr. Gore or push him?"

"No."

"You didn't interview anybody who saw my client interact with Mr. Gore?"

"No."

"So you have no personal knowledge of what, if anything, happened at Salesforce Park on the morning of March seventh, do you?"

"No."

"It's possible that somebody other than my client tried to rob Mr. Gore, isn't it?"

"Objection. Speculation."

"Sustained."

Fine. "It's also possible that somebody other than my client pushed Mr. Gore over the railing, isn't it?"

"Objection. Speculation."

"Sustained."

One more time. "And it's also possible that Mr. Gore committed suicide by jumping from Salesforce Park into the construction zone below, isn't it?"

"Objection. Speculation."

"Sustained. Please move on, Mr. Daley."

"Yes, Your Honor." I moved in a little closer. "The fact of the matter is that you don't know what happened to Mr. Gore that morning, right?"

Dito measured his words. "I have no personal knowledge of what happened to Mr. Gore. Likewise, I did not interview anybody who admitted to killing Mr. Gore that morning."

"Including my client, right?"

"Right."

"Did you or any of your colleagues find my client's fingerprints, blood, sweat, or DNA on Mr. Gore's body?"

"No, but the body was covered in dust, so it would have been very difficult to obtain usable samples."

"Did you or any of your colleagues find my client's fingerprints, blood, sweat, or DNA on Mr. Gore's wallet?"

"No."

"Seems to me that it was a substantial leap to accuse my client of murder based on some very tenuous connections."

"Objection," Erickson said. "There wasn't a question there."

"Withdrawn," I said. "Did my client have any money on him when you found him?"

"Twelve dollars and change."

"You really think he killed Tyson Gore over twelve bucks?"

"Objection. Calls for more speculation."

"Sustained."

I asked Dito if he arrested Reggie.

"No. I escorted him to Southern Station for questioning. Inspector Kenneth Lee placed him under arrest two days later."

"You didn't think that Inspector Lee was rushing to judgment?"

"I have great respect for Inspector Lee."

"So do I, but it doesn't mean that he's always right."

"Move to strike."

"Withdrawn," I said. "Did my client attempt to flee?"

"No."

"Did he ask to see a lawyer?"

"No."

"You're saying that you think he killed Mr. Gore a few hours earlier, yet he made no attempt to flee and didn't even ask for a lawyer?"

"Yes."

I gave the jury a skeptical look. "Other than the traces of dried blood on my client's hands and face, did you find any other blood in the area?"

"No."

"You looked, right?"

He tensed. "Right."

"Right," I repeated, sarcastically. "No further questions, Your Honor."

Erickson passed on redirect.

Judge Tsang looked at his watch. "It's after four o'clock, so I am going to adjourn for the day. We will resume at ten o'clock in the morning."

42

"I FOUND NO EVIDENCE"

At ten-forty-five the following morning, a Friday, Dr. Joy Siu was wearing her white lab coat as she sat in the box, makeup perfect, manner professorial. "I have been the Chief Medical Examiner of the City and County of San Francisco for ten years. Before that, I was a tenured professor and Chair of the PhD program in anatomic pathology at UCSF."

There was nothing to be gained by letting her recite her resume into the record. "Your Honor, we will stipulate that Dr. Siu is a recognized authority in her field."

"Thank you, Mr. Daley."

Erickson introduced the autopsy report into evidence and presented it to Siu. "You performed the autopsy of Mr. Tyson Gore on Tuesday, March eighth, of this year?"

"I did." She confirmed that she had prepared the report.

"Were you able to determine the cause of death?"

"I was." Siu pretended to glance at her report. "Massive brain trauma. The decedent was pushed over the railing of Salesforce Park and landed in the construction zone in front of Millennium Tower. He died upon impact."

"Any chance of survival?"

"Unlikely. In addition to a fractured skull, the victim broke more than two dozen bones, including all of his ribs and several vertebrae."

"Defensive wounds?"

"Not that I could identify." She confirmed that Gore's body was found in a pile of gravel and was covered in dust. "It was a very grim crime scene."

Erickson had what he needed. "No further questions."

"Cross-exam, Mr. Daley?"

"Yes, Your Honor." I shot a glance at Nady, who touched her nose—a reminder to keep Siu's testimony short. Then I approached the box. "Good morning, Dr. Siu."

"Good morning, Mr. Daley."

"You testified that you believe that Mr. Gore was pushed over the railing at Salesforce Park and landed in the construction zone below?"

"Yes."

"Did you find my client's blood on Mr. Gore's body?"

"That would have been impossible. The body was caked in dust."

"So you didn't find my client's blood on the body, right?"

"That would have been impossible," she repeated.

"Your Honor," I said, "would you please instruct Dr. Siu to answer?"

"Please, Dr. Siu?"

"The answer is no."

Good. "Did you find my client's blood on Mr. Gore's clothes?"

"No."

"Did you find my client's DNA anywhere on Mr. Gore's body or clothes?"

"No."

"You found no evidence that my client touched Mr. Gore, did you?"

"No, Mr. Daley."

I looked over at the jury for an instant, then I turned back to Siu. "So you found no evidence that my client pushed Mr. Gore, do you?"

"I was unable to identify your client's fingerprints, blood, or DNA on Mr. Gore's body."

Good. "Did you consider the possibility that somebody other than my client pushed Mr. Gore?"

"Yes, Mr. Daley. I found no evidence."

"Did you consider the possibility that it might have been an accident?"

"Yes, Mr. Daley. I found no evidence."

"Did you consider the possibility that Mr. Gore might have committed suicide?"

"Yes, Mr. Daley. I found no evidence."

"You knew that his company was imploding, and he was facing bankruptcy, right?"

"Objection," Erickson said. "This question is beyond the scope of Dr. Siu's knowledge."

"Your Honor," I said, "it is within the scope of the knowledge of anybody who has read a newspaper in the past year."

"Overruled."

I wasn't sure that Judge Tsang would give me that one.

Dr. Siu nodded. "I read that Mr. Gore's company was experiencing financial difficulties."

"And he was under a lot of stress as a result?"

Erickson stood up as if to object, but he reconsidered.

"I would suspect that was the case," Siu said, "but I have no personal knowledge."

I pointed at her autopsy report. "Your report included a toxicology report?"

"Yes."

"Among other things, it showed that Mr. Gore had been drinking heavily immediately before his death, didn't it?"

"He was below the legal limit."

Fine. "He was also taking a commonly prescribed antidepressant called Zoloft, wasn't he?"

"Yes."

"He was also taking illegal designer drugs known as bath salts, wasn't he?"

"Yes."

"You are aware that the side effects of bath salts can include hallucinations, agitation, violent behavior, paranoia, and even suicidal thoughts, right?"

"Yes."

"Did you consider the possibility that the combination of stress, alcohol, antidepressants, and designer drugs might have caused Mr. Gore to contemplate suicide?"

"I considered the possibility, but I found no evidence that he did."

"You didn't have a chance to question him about it, did you?"

"Of course not, Mr. Daley. However, I did question the therapist who recommended Zoloft. She saw no signs that Mr. Gore was suicidal."

"Except for the fact that his company had lost billions, he was drinking heavily, and he was taking strong antidepressants and designer drugs, right?"

Erickson objected. "Asked and answered."

"Sustained."

"Dr. Siu, you can't say with any certainty that Mr. Gore did not commit suicide, can you?"

"Objection. Dr. Siu can't be expected to prove a negative."

"Sustained." Judge Tsang kept his tone modulated. "Anything further for this witness, Mr. Daley?"

"No, Your Honor."

"Please call your next witness, Mr. Erickson."

"The People call Dr. Madeline Swartz."

43

"HE SHOWED NO SIGNS"

Erickson stood at the lectern. "You're a medical doctor?"

"PhD." Dr. Madeline Swartz sat in the box, demeanor professional, voice soothing. "I earned my undergraduate degree from Stanford and my doctorate from Duke. I have been a practicing psychologist and life coach for twenty-five years." Erickson led her through a concise recitation of her CV. "Many of my patients are executives in the tech industry in San Francisco and Silicon Valley."

"Your services must be in high demand."

She feigned modesty. "They are."

The gallery was almost empty at eleven-fifteen on Friday morning. The regulars had left to get a jump on the lunch lines across Bryant Street.

Erickson moved to the front of the box. "You knew the victim, Tyson Gore?"

I noted the subtle shift in Erickson's language. He was trying to evoke sympathy for Gore by referring to him as "the victim" instead of "the decedent."

"I was his therapist and life coach," Swartz said.

"You must have known him very well."

"I saw him almost every week for seven years. I probably knew him better than anybody except his immediate family and closest business associates."

And his ex-wives, ex-girlfriends, and mistresses.

Reggie leaned over and whispered, "Why is she here?"

"Erickson is making a pre-emptive attempt to discredit our expert, who will say that Gore committed suicide."

"Why did Mr. Gore first come to see you?" Erickson asked.

"He was having relationship issues with his first ex-wife and stress at work. I'm afraid that I cannot be more specific without violating confidentiality."

"Of course." Erickson furrowed his brow. "Could you please describe in general terms the types of issues that you discussed?"

"His relationships with his ex-spouses and children. Stress management. Optimizing performance. Balancing his career and his family obligations."

"You also addressed substance use issues?"

"From time to time." She cleared her throat. "It's a matter of record that Mr. Gore used alcohol regularly and recreational drugs occasionally. I worked with him to manage those issues."

"Were you successful?"

"Off and on."

"Mr. Gore was under a lot of stress, wasn't he?"

"Yes—especially near the end of his life when the crypto market got shaky, and his company started to lose valuation. I helped him deal with it."

"Was he clinically depressed?"

"In my judgment, no."

"Yet you recommended that he take a strong antidepressant called Zoloft?"

"I suggested that he might give it a try." She said that Gore asked his physician to prescribe the medication. "It seemed to help."

"Did you ever consider the possibility that he might have been suicidal?"

"I considered the possibility, but he showed no signs. Based upon my experience and training and my long-term relationship with Mr. Gore, I concluded that he was not."

"No further questions."

I moved to the front of the box and invoked a non-confrontational tone. "You saw Tyson Gore almost every week for seven years?"

"Yes."

"So you saw him more than three hundred times?"

Swartz did a quick computation in her head. "Approximately."

"You counseled him through two contentious divorces?"

"Yes."

"And several start-ups?"

"Yes."

"You knew that he had been unfaithful to his wives?"

"Objection," Erickson said. "Relevance. Mr. Gore is not on trial."

Yes, he is. "Mr. Erickson questioned Dr. Swartz about her significant and long-term relationship with the decedent. He opened the door. I should be able to follow up."

"Overruled. Please answer the question, Dr. Swartz."

She didn't fluster. "I was aware of Mr. Gore's issues involving infidelity."

"And the fact that he was a regular at a strip club called the Gold Club?"

"On occasion."

"And he had met his most recent companion, Ms. Amanda Blair, at the Gold Club?"

"Objection. Relevance."

Come on. "I promise to show relevance in a moment, Your Honor."

"I'll give you a little leeway, Mr. Daley. The objection is overruled."

Swartz folded her arms. "Mr. Gore met Ms. Blair at the Gold Club."

"She was a dancer?"

"Yes."

"He was still married at the time?"

"He was."

"He cheated on Ms. Blair, too, didn't he?"

"Yes."

I glanced at Nady, who tugged her ear—the signal to move on. Jurors don't like it when you put the decedent on trial—even if he was a serial philanderer.

I kept my voice even. "You are aware that immediately before his death, Mr. Gore's business was imploding?"

"He told me that there were serious issues."

"The company had lost about forty billion dollars in valuation, hadn't it?"

"That's what I read in the papers."

"Mr. Gore must have been very upset about it, wasn't he?"

"He was concerned."

I'll say. "You are aware that shortly before he died, Mr. Gore held a gathering at a private club called Kanzen at which he asked his biggest investors for emergency funding? And that his solicitations were unsuccessful?"

"I read about it in the paper."

"Which means that his business was going under."

"Objection," Erickson said. "Mr. Daley is testifying. Moreover, this is an area that's outside Dr. Swartz's expertise."

I fired back. "Dr. Swartz was very familiar with Mr. Gore's business."

"Overruled."

"Yes," Swartz said. "Deal Coin was in serious trouble."

"So much trouble that the press had dubbed it 'Dead Coin,' hadn't it?"

"I heard that term."

I inched closer to the box. "Mr. Gore's business was blowing up. He and his investors had lost billions. His personal relationships had imploded. He had alcohol and drug problems. He was taking antidepressants—at your suggestion. And he had just failed in a last-ditch effort to raise the money to keep his company afloat."

Erickson was on his feet. "Objection. Mr. Daley is testifying again."

Yes, I am.

The judge eyed me. "Did you wish to ask a question, Mr. Daley?"

"Yes." I turned back to Swartz. "Given the circumstances that I just described, isn't it likely that Mr. Gore was suicidal that night?"

She spoke with authority. "Tyson Gore was a supremely self-confident and successful businessman who had dealt with several failed business ventures over his career. He always bounced back. He was not, in my judgment, suicidal."

"You didn't even consider the possibility?"

"I considered it, Mr. Daley. I ruled it out."

"Come on, Dr. Swartz."

"Objection. There wasn't a question there."

No, there wasn't.

"Sustained."

"No further questions, Your Honor."

"Cross-exam, Mr. Erickson?"

"No, Your Honor."

The judge looked at the clock. "It's almost noon. This is probably a good time to break for lunch. How many more witnesses do you plan to call, Mr. Erickson?"

"Just one, Your Honor."

It would undoubtedly be Inspector Lee. And the timing wasn't an accident. Erickson would keep Lee on the stand and wrap up just before Judge Tsang adjourned for the weekend. Then the jury would have two full days to think about everything they'd heard.

44

"BE BETTER"

Reggie was agitated when we regrouped in the consultation room during the lunch break. "What the hell were you doing in there?" he snapped.

"Trying to get at least one of the jurors to seriously consider the possibility that Gore committed suicide."

"By pissing on him?"

"By pointing out that he was drinking heavily, taking antidepressants, using designer drugs, and was under an ungodly amount of stress after his business lost billions."

The air was stale in the windowless room down the hall from Judge Tsang's court. A burly sheriff's deputy was posted outside the door. Nady stared at her laptop and picked at a kale salad. I had forced myself to eat half of my tuna sandwich even though I wasn't hungry. Reggie hadn't touched his turkey sandwich.

Reggie's voice filled with frustration. "Erickson is pounding us."

"The prosecution always has the upper hand at the beginning. It'll be our turn soon."

He wasn't convinced. "Be better."

"I'm doing everything that I can, Reggie. The jurors are paying attention." I pointed at his sandwich. "Eat something."

"I'm not hungry."

"I need you to be strong and alert during the afternoon session."

"I'm not hungry," he repeated.

I couldn't force him to eat. I turned to Nady. "Any word from Pete?"

"Not since this morning. He's still looking."

On we go.

The deputy tapped on the door. "Ten minutes, Mr. Daley."

"Thank you."

Reggie pushed his sandwich aside. "What's going to happen this afternoon?"

"Erickson is going to put Inspector Lee on the stand to summarize his case."

"You'll go after him?"

"Absolutely."

45

"YOU JUST ASSUMED?"

Erickson stood at the lectern at three-fifteen on Friday afternoon. "Inspector," he said, "could you please show us exactly where Sergeant Dito found Mr. Gore's wallet?"

"Of course." A confident Inspector Lee stood next to the flat-screen and used a Cross pen to point at an enlarged overhead photo of the Redwood Forest in Salesforce Park. "Here."

"And the spot where the security guard, Kevin Sanders, found the defendant that morning?"

"Here."

"How far was the wallet from the defendant?"

"Less than three feet."

"Less than three feet," Erickson repeated. "Was anybody else in the vicinity at the time?"

"Other than the security guard, no."

Judge Tsang's courtroom was filled with an intense silence. The twelve jurors and four alternates were focused on Lee, who had been on the stand for two hours. He and Erickson were executing a textbook direct exam. Their rehearsed presentation resulted in a meticulous presentation of the evidence. I objected frequently, emphatically, and, for the most part, unsuccessfully.

Lee returned to the box and described his first conversation with Reggie at Salesforce Park, and his later conversations with him at Southern Station. He assured us that he had secured the scene and supervised the collection of evidence in accordance with SFPD's best practices. He confirmed that there had been no lapses in chain of custody. He stated that he had taken statements from everybody in the immediate vicinity.

Erickson stood at the lectern. "How was the defendant's demeanor?"

"At first, he refused to cooperate. He later reconsidered and admitted that he had been at Salesforce Park on the morning that he killed Tyson Gore."

Nice try. "Objection. Inspector Lee is offering a conclusion that is not supported by the evidence. It's up to the jury to decide what happened that morning."

"Sustained."

Erickson had made his point. "Did the defendant offer any explanation as to what happened to Mr. Gore?"

"No."

"Did he offer an explanation as to how Mr. Gore's empty wallet happened to be sitting on the ground within arm's length?"

"No."

"Inspector, could you please summarize your conclusion as to what happened in Salesforce Park on the morning of March seventh of this year?"

"Yes, Mr. Erickson." Lee turned and spoke directly to the jury. "Tyson Gore invited some of his investors to a small gathering at Kanzen on the night of Sunday, March sixth. The defendant was illegally trespassing less than one hundred feet away in the Redwood Forest at Salesforce Park, which was closed. The defendant saw Mr. Gore and his investors pass by and enter Kanzen. It was apparent that they were affluent. The gathering ended around two AM. Mr. Gore was the last person to leave other than the general manager of Kanzen. On his way home, he walked by Redwood Forest, where the defendant was waiting for him. The defendant accosted Mr. Gore and took his wallet. They fought, which resulted in the defendant suffering bloody bruises on his face and hands. The defendant then pushed Mr. Gore over the railing. Mr. Gore fell seventy-five feet to his death on a pile of gravel in the construction zone between Salesforce Park and Millennium Tower. Mr. Gore died instantly."

"You believe that the defendant caused Mr. Gore's death?"

"Yes. But for the fact that the defendant robbed him and pushed him over the railing, Tyson Gore would be alive today."

"No further questions." Erickson nodded at the jury, closed his laptop, and walked to the prosecution table.

"Cross-exam, Mr. Daley?"

"Yes, Your Honor." I walked over to the evidence cart, picked up Gore's wallet, and handed it to Lee. "You didn't find my client's fingerprints on this wallet, did you?"

"No."

"His blood?"

"No."

"His DNA?"

"No."

"So you have no evidence connecting him to this wallet, do you?"

"It was within reach of the defendant."

"It doesn't mean that Reggie took it."

"It seems obvious to me."

"Not to me."

"Objection."

"Withdrawn. The Medical Examiner didn't find my client's fingerprints, blood, or DNA on Mr. Gore's body or clothing, did she?"

"Mr. Gore landed on a pile of gravel and dust. It would have been impossible to find a usable sample."

"My client is fifty-five years old, in bad physical condition, and had consumed a fifth of tequila that night. Do you really think he could have pushed Mr. Gore over the railing?"

"Yes."

"You just assumed that my client attacked Mr. Gore and stole his wallet, didn't you?"

"His face and hands were bloody. The wallet was next to him."

"If his hands were bloody, why didn't you find my client's blood on the wallet?"

Lee hesitated for an instant. "The blood on his hands was dry. No traces transferred to the wallet."

"Come on, Inspector."

"Objection."

"Withdrawn. The wallet could have fallen out of Mr. Gore's pocket as he was walking by. Or maybe somebody else took it from him from him and tossed it next to Reggie."

"I don't think so, Mr. Daley."

"The fact remains that you just don't know, right?"

"It seems obvious to me."

"Not to me."

"Objection."

"Sustained."

"Did you consider the possibility that Mr. Gore had committed suicide?"

"I found no evidence, and Mr. Gore's therapist thought it was unlikely."

"And you had already decided that Reggie was guilty, right?"

"Objection."

"Withdrawn." I hammered Lee on the collection of the evidence and the lack of a direct physical connection between Reggie and Gore, but he remained resolute. The jury was paying attention, but I saw no signs that I was convincing them. I was also limited in my questioning to subjects raised by Erickson on direct exam. I would have to wait until I presented our defense before I could talk about other potential suspects. After twenty minutes, I turned to the judge. "No further questions, Your Honor." I made my way back to the defense table.

"Redirect, Mr. Erickson?"

"No, Your Honor. The prosecution rests."

The judge looked my way. "I am going to adjourn for the weekend."

No surprise.

He added, "Mr. Daley, do you wish to make a motion before we recess?"

"Yes, Your Honor. The defense moves for a directed acquittal under Penal Code Section 1181.1 and requests that the charges against Mr. Jones be dropped as a matter of law because there is insufficient evidence to find the defendant guilty beyond a reasonable doubt."

"Denied."

No surprise there, either.

He added, "We'll resume at ten o'clock on Monday morning when you should be prepared to start the defense case."

46

"WE NEED TO GIVE THEM MORE"

Reggie was frustrated. "What the hell were you doing yesterday? Why didn't you talk more about suicide? And what about the other people who were at Kanzen that night?"

I kept my voice even. "We've talked about this, Reggie. On cross-exam, I can only ask about issues that Erickson raised on direct. We'll address everything else when we start our defense on Monday."

"You said that we wouldn't need to put on a defense."

"I said that we might not if we could poke enough holes in Erickson's case to convince the jury that he hadn't proved his case beyond a reasonable doubt. We need to give them more." *Or at least muddy the waters.*

His eyes darted to Nady. "You agree?"

"Yes."

Reggie slumped back in his chair.

At ten-forty-five the following morning, a Saturday, Reggie, Nady, and I were meeting in the attorney-client consultation room in the bowels of San Bruno Jail. The air smelled of Lysol. I had tested negative for Covid before I drove across the bridge, but I was coming down with a cold. My throat was scratchy. My stomach churned.

Reggie scowled. "How long will our defense take?"

"A couple of days," I said. "We'll start by putting on a couple of experts who will confirm that they didn't find your prints or DNA on Gore's wallet. We may put the manager of Kanzen on the stand to testify that Gore was under a lot of stress at the gathering there. Then our psychological expert will testify that she believes that Gore committed suicide. Then I'll put

Lee back on the stand and try to convince the jury that he shouldn't have ruled out suicide and the possibility that the other people at Kanzen were involved."

"Are you planning to call any of those people to testify?"

"I haven't decided."

Nady and I disagreed on this point. I was inclined to throw some dirt on Matt Bosworth and Steve Warren, and maybe even Cynthia Mitchell. Nady believed that it would be better to allude to their possible guilt when I questioned Lee. If we put them on the stand, they'll deny that they killed Gore, which could undercut us. As a practical matter, other than the fact that they were at Kanzen and lost a lot of money, we had no evidence connecting them to Gore's death.

"Do you still want me to testify?" Reggie asked.

Probably. "I haven't decided."

His expression turned resolute. "I'll be ready if you need me, Mike."

"Good."

"Mike?"

"Yes?"

"How do you really think it's going?"

Hard to say. "There's a good chance that we'll convince at least one juror to acquit, and the jury will hang. If everything goes really well, we'll get the jury to reasonable doubt, and you can get out of here."

Terrence "The Terminator" knocked on the open door of my office at eight-fifteen the same night. "You need anything else?"

"No, thanks, T. You should go home."

"I'll meet you here in the morning."

"Tomorrow is Sunday."

"Your trial resumes on Monday morning."

"We'll manage. Take the day off."

"I'll have plenty of days off after I retire."

"You can't retire, T."

"Yes, I can." He gave me a sly smile. "You should retire, too."

"Not yet. Rosie and I have to pay for Grace's wedding in December, and Tommy is still in college. Besides, a wise lawyer once told me that it's a bad idea to make any major life decisions while you're in trial."

"Rosie?"

"Correct."

His smile broadened. "I'm not in trial."

"You aren't in court, but when I'm in trial, so are you. We'll talk about it again after Reggie's trial is over."

"Sounds like a good plan, Mike." He headed out the door.

Nady looked up from her laptop. "You going to be able to persuade him to stay?"

"Not sure."

"Are *you* going to stay?"

"If Rosie runs for another term." I eyed her. "You aren't thinking of leaving, are you?"

"Not as long as you and Rosie and Rolanda are here." She grinned. "Just so you know, I'm not planning to be working when I'm your age."

Ouch. "I'm not that old."

"Old enough to know better. I think I can make it to fifty. After that, Max and I plan to be living someplace warm with a pool and drinks with umbrellas." She pointed at Luna, who was sleeping in the corner of my office. "We've already talked it over with the boss. She thinks it's a fine plan." _

"Sounds good to me."

Her tone turned thoughtful. "I do this because I like helping people, it's an interesting and challenging job, and it's what I'm trained to do. You and Rosie do it because you love it."

True. "It's who we are."

"I didn't say that it was a bad thing. We need people like you to make the system work."

"And you."

"Thank you." She turned back to business. "We should keep Reggie's defense short."

"Agreed."

"Are you going to put him on the stand?"

"I'm leaning in favor. I'll have him give a quick and forceful denial."

"Erickson will keep him up there for an hour and take him apart."

"The jury will be impressed if he defends himself."

"We'll see. You heading home?"

"I'm going to talk to Pete first."

Joey picked up my empty mug. "You need anything else, Mike?"

"I'm good."

He refilled Pete's coffee cup without being asked.

Pete and I were sitting at our father's table in the back room of Dunleavy's at ten-fifteen on Saturday night. The weekend crowd was modest. The TV was tuned to ESPN. The jukebox was quiet.

"You look tired," Joey said to me.

"Comes with the territory when you're in trial."

"You're getting too old for trial work, Mike."

I grinned. "Shut up, Joey."

"My offer still stands if you want to tend bar for me."

"Maybe I'm too old to tend bar."

"Big John was still tending bar at eighty-seven. You going to get an acquittal?"

"I'm not sure." I pointed at Pete. "Depends on whether he can find any helpful evidence."

Joey smiled at Pete, who was checking messages. "You want to come work for me, too?"

He looked up. "Sounds pretty good to me. Let me think about it."

Joey headed back to the bar.

"You got anything I can use?" I asked Pete.

"Working on it, Mick."

"We start our defense on Monday."

"I'm aware of the timing. I'll check in with my sources at SFPD. I'll talk to Kaela Joy again. And I'll call Nicki Hanson. Maybe one of them knows somebody who knows something that might help." He took a sip of coffee. "I'm just a PI, Mick. I can't do miracles."

"Unfortunately, neither can I."

"You're the ex-priest. You should ask your former colleagues to conjure up something for you."

"It can't hurt." I crumpled my napkin. "Did you find anything else on Damian Mason?"

"A second source confirmed that he went to Mexico and vanished. It's a big country. I probably won't be able to find him."

Roosevelt was right. "Anything more on the people at Kanzen?"

"Eugene McAllister is doing better, but he won't be able to testify."

"Is he going to be okay?"

"I don't know. He's at UCSF. It would be a bad look to try to blame Gore's death on a guy who just had a stroke."

True. "I won't."

"Good. Do you need me to testify?"

"Doubtful." Pete was on our witness list in case I needed him to corroborate my discussions with Kevin Sanders, David Dito, Matt Bosworth, and Steve Warren. He was excellent in court, but it isn't ideal to call your brother as a key witness.

He finished his coffee. "Try to slow-walk things for a few days. I'll see if I can come up with something."

Rosie's mother smiled at me from her box on Zoom. "Are you going to get a not guilty verdict for Reggie Jones?"

"Not sure, Sylvia. It's going to be close, but I think I can get the jury to reasonable doubt."

"You'll come up with something. You always do."

At eleven-forty-five on Sunday night, I was sitting in my kitchen and staring at my laptop, where I had joined Sylvia and Rosie on Zoom. Grace had signed off after we completed our weekly update on wedding plans. Grace wanted to add more people to the guest list, which had ballooned from a hundred and twenty to a hundred and seventy-five. After two years and two Covid-related postponements, Rosie and I capitulated. The great thing about planning a wedding is that you can solve almost any problem by writing bigger checks.

I looked at Rosie, who was wearing a Cal hoodie. "How are you feeling?"

"Better than yesterday. I tested positive again this morning." She had started Paxlovid treatments. "They seem to be helping."

"Good. We need you to be one hundred percent for the wedding."

"I'll be fine, Mike. Did you test yourself again?"

"Yes. Negative."

"Good." She spoke to her mother. "You?"

"Negative, Rosita."

"Good. Did you go to church this morning?"

"Yes."

"Mama!"

"I tested negative before I went to church. I wore a mask. I tested again when I got home. I'm fine."

"Do you need more tests?"

"I still have a dozen from the last batch that you sent me." Sylvia reported that she won at mah-jongg earlier Sunday night, but the game was less satisfying than usual because the young woman who supplied her cannabis couldn't make her regular delivery. "It's been a while since I played without a buzz. I have to sign off, dears. I'll talk to you tomorrow." Her box disappeared.

Rosie's voice was tired. "You okay?" she asked me.

"I'm getting a cold, but I'll be fine. You?"

"Sore throat. Otherwise, I'm good."

"We need you back at the office."

"Soon, Mike. You got any news on Reggie's case?"

"Not much." I filled her in on the plans for our defense. "Hopefully, it will be just enough to get the jury to reasonable doubt."

"You don't sound wildly confident."

"The jury has been attentive, but impossible to read. It could go either way."

"Are you going to put Reggie on the stand?"

"Probably. I want to have him issue a short and forceful denial."

"Probably the right call." She grinned and repeated her mother's words. "You'll come up with something. You always do."

47

"NONE"

The slender man with the jet-black hair, trim gray mustache, and severe crow's feet spoke deliberately. "My name is Sridar Iyengar. I recently retired after thirty years at the San Mateo County Crime Lab."

Nady stood at the lectern. "What is your area of expertise?"

"Fingerprints."

Judge Tsang's courtroom was tense at ten-forty-five on Monday morning as we began our defense. Nady and I decided that she would question the first witnesses to give the jury a chance to listen to a fresh voice. She would play the good cop to my bad cop. More important, she had an excellent touch.

She lobbed another softball. "Could you please tell us about your background?"

"Certainly." Sridar's mustache twitched as he explained that he was a first-generation native of San Francisco whose parents were born in India and moved to the Bay Area to be closer to his grandfather, a researcher at UCSF. "I earned my Bachelor's in criminology from San Francisco State University and spent my entire career at the San Mateo County Crime Lab."

Erickson spoke from his seat. "The People stipulate as to Mr. Iyengar's expertise in fingerprint analysis."

The judge was pleased. "Thank you, Mr. Erickson."

It was a good move. Sridar was, in fact, one of California's foremost authorities on fingerprints. He was also my former neighbor, long-time friend, and one of the most meticulous guys I've ever known. His mom and dad operated an Indian restaurant a few doors from Dunleavy's, which became an unlikely hit among the predominantly Irish, Italian, and later Chinese families. His scholarly demeanor and engaging manner made him an ideal expert witness, and he became my go-to guy after he retired. I recommended him to other defense attorneys, and his post-retirement side hustle turned into a lucrative second career.

Nady pointed at the TV. "Are you familiar with these fingerprints?"

"Yes. The first is a left thumbprint of the defendant, Reggie Jones, taken by the police at his booking. The second is a left thumbprint included in the police report prepared by Inspector Kenneth Lee in connection with the death of Tyson Gore. It was lifted from Mr. Gore's wallet."

"Do the two prints match?"

"No."

"Did you find any prints on the wallet that matched Mr. Jones's?"

"None."

So far, so good.

Nady displayed another print on the TV. "Was this also in the police report?"

"Yes. It was lifted from the collar of Mr. Gore's leather jacket."

"Does the print match Reggie's?"

"No."

The jury paid close attention as Nady led Sridar through a description of a series of prints lifted from Gore's belt buckle, watch, and shoes. Sridar confirmed three prints as belonging to Gore. The fourth was too smudged to identify.

"Mr. Iyengar," Nady said, "did you review all of the fingerprints included in the police reports?"

"Yes."

"Did you find any fingerprints on Mr. Gore's person or belongings that matched my client, Reggie Jones?"

"None."

"No further questions."

"Cross-exam, Mr. Erickson?"

Nady had astutely framed Sridar's testimony to demonstrate that there was no evidence that Reggie had touched Gore's person or belongings. Erickson couldn't disprove a negative, and he had already stipulated to Sridar's expertise, so he had little room to maneuver.

"We have no questions for this witness, Your Honor," he said.

Nady was back at the lectern five minutes later. "What is your occupation?"

Dr. Carla Jimenez removed her mask and spoke with authority. "I am a senior forensic DNA Analyst at the Serological Research Institute in Richmond, California. I have worked at SERI for twenty-four years."

"You're a medical doctor?"

"PhD. I earned my bachelor's degree in chemistry and biological science from San Francisco State, and a master's and then a PhD in forensic science from UC Davis. My area of expertise is forensic serology and forensic DNA."

"You've been called as an expert witness before?"

"Many times. I have testified in hundreds of cases in state and federal courts nationwide as well as in federal and military courts."

And she's very good at her job.

We had asked Rosie's high school classmate to add a few more morsels of doubt to Erickson's claim that Reggie had pushed Gore over the railing at Salesforce Park. Carla Jimenez graduated second in her class at Mercy High, worked her way through State, and was accepted into UCLA Medical School. She deferred her admission to work in a research lab in the Department of Forensic Science at UC Davis, where her professor offered her a scholarship to earn a master's and then a PhD. She went to work at SERI, the preeminent lab for DNA analysis in Northern California. She was testifying *pro bono* as a favor to Rosie and a promise that we would take her out for dinner at Chez Panisse in Berkeley when Rosie was feeling better.

Nady moved closer to the box. "You've received a great deal of recognition over the years, haven't you?"

"I am a Fellow of the American Board of Criminalistics in Forensic Biology with subspecialties in Forensic Biochemistry and Forensic Molecular Biology. I am also a member of the California Association of Criminalists, the Northwest Association of Forensic Scientists, the California Association of Crime Laboratory Directors, and the Association of Forensic Quality Assurance Managers."

Erickson finally spoke up. "We will stipulate that Dr. Jimenez is a highly qualified expert in the fields of forensic serology and forensic DNA."

What took you so long?

Nady walked to the evidence cart, picked up an official-looking document, introduced it into evidence, and handed it to Carla. "You're familiar with this report?"

"Yes. It is a DNA analysis of samples obtained from the person, clothing, and wallet of the decedent, Tyson Gore. It was prepared by Mr. George Romero of the Forensic Services Division of the San Francisco Police Department's Criminalistics Laboratory."

"You believe that it was prepared in accordance with highest industry standards?"

"I do. Mr. Romero has an excellent reputation."

Nady introduced a DNA analysis based on a sample from Reggie that we had provided to Inspector Lee, who, in turn, forwarded it to Romero for analysis. Then she continued with Carla. "We asked you to compare the DNA sample from our client, Reggie Jones, with DNA found on the decedent's person, clothing, and wallet, didn't we?"

"Yes. I found no matches to Mr. Jones's DNA."

"Did you find any DNA evidence connecting Reggie Jones to the decedent?"

"None."

That's all that we need.

Nady nodded triumphantly. "No further questions."

"Cross-exam, Mr. Erickson?"

"No, Your Honor."

"Do you wish to call another witness, Ms. Nikonova?"

"One moment, Your Honor." Nady came over to the defense table and spoke in a whisper. "You want to stop now?"

"Not yet. We need to stick to the plan and give the jury a path to suicide."

"Fine." Nady turned and spoke to the judge. "The defense calls Ms. Susan Gallardo."

48

"INTENSE"

Nady stood in front of the box. "You organized the gathering at Kanzen on the night of March sixth and the early morning of March seventh at the request of Tyson Gore?"

Susan Gallardo sat in the box, her arms folded. "Yes."

"Did Mr. Gore tell you the reason for the meeting?"

"He said that it involved sensitive matters relating to his company."

"You were there the entire time?"

"Yes." Gallardo reconfirmed the names of the bartender and servers who worked at the gathering. "People were more interested in talking than eating and drinking, so I let my staff go home before the gathering ended."

Nady punched a button on her laptop and displayed a printout of the guest list. "Mr. Gore provided this list to you?"

"Yes." At Nady's prompt, Gallardo read off the names: Matt Bosworth, Steve Warren, Eugene McAllister, Jack Emrich, and Cynthia Mitchell.

Nady arched an eyebrow. "All of those people lost millions or even billions of dollars on Deal Coin, didn't they?"

"Objection," Erickson said. "That's outside the scope of the witness' knowledge."

Yes, it is.

"Sustained."

Nady kept her eyes on Gallardo. "How would you describe Mr. Gore's demeanor that evening?"

"Objection. Calls for speculation."

"No, it doesn't," Nady snapped. "I'm not asking Ms. Gallardo to read Mr. Gore's mind. I'm simply asking her for her observations about his outward appearance."

"Overruled."

"He was exhausted," Gallardo said. "He also appeared frustrated."

"Did he say why?"

"He was under a lot of pressure. It probably had something to do with the fact that he was having trouble raising money for his company, but I don't know for sure."

Good enough.

"How was the mood?" Nady asked.

"Intense."

"How so?"

Nady was taking a calculated risk. You're supposed to ask specific questions for which you already know the answer. In this case, she was trying to draw Gallardo out.

Gallardo considered her response. "I was not privy to individual conversations because we respect our members' confidences. On the other hand, it appeared that Mr. Gore was trying to convince his investors to put more money into his company. It looked like it wasn't going well."

"Did anybody get angry?"

"I would describe several conversations as passionate."

"Did anyone raise their voice?"

"Mr. Bosworth and Mr. Warren were pretty animated. Mr. Emrich seemed more frustrated than angry. Mr. McAllister and Ms. Mitchell seemed direct, but they remained calm." Nady tried to get her to elaborate, but Gallardo said that she couldn't recall any details.

"How was Mr. Gore's demeanor when he left the gathering?" Nady asked.

"He looked pretty upset to me."

"No further questions, Your Honor."

"Cross-exam, Mr. Erickson?"

"Just a couple of questions, Your Honor." Erickson made his way to the lectern. "Ms. Gallardo, did anybody yell at Mr. Gore?"

"No."

"Did anybody threaten him?"

"No."

"Did anybody call him names or storm out?"

"No, Mr. Erickson."

"No further questions."

"Please call your next witness, Ms. Nikonova."

"One moment, Your Honor." Nady came back to the defense table and spoke in a whisper. "It might be enough, Mike. Do you still want to call the people who were at the gathering at Kanzen?"

I ran a quick mental calculus. "Yes, but let's not overplay our hand. See if you can get them to confirm that they lost a ton of money and were pissed off about it. Then try to get them to say that Gore was upset that night. It will enhance our suicide argument."

"Do you want me to accuse them of murder?"

"No. They'll just deny it, which will hurt our credibility."

Nady turned back to the judge. "The defense calls Matthew Bosworth."

49

"HOW MUCH DID YOU LOSE?"

"How long did you know Tyson Gore?" Nady asked.

A supremely confident Matt Bosworth sat in the box. "More than twenty years. We met in college and were the best men at each other's weddings. We co-founded several start-ups and were business partners for many years."

In his double-breasted suit, Egyptian cotton white shirt, and polka dot tie, "Boz" looked like a partner at a downtown law firm. The jurors were dialed in.

"You and Mr. Gore co-founded Deal Coin?" Nady asked.

"We did."

"It didn't end well."

"That's often the nature of a start-up."

"How much did you lose?"

"A lot."

"How much is a lot?"

"I'd rather not say."

"Millions?"

"It's confidential, Ms. Nikonova."

"Tens of millions? Hundreds of millions? Billions?"

"Objection," Erickson said. "Relevance."

"Overruled."

Seems Judge Tsang is just as curious as I am.

"Eight figures," Bosworth said.

"How much did Mr. Gore lose?"

"More than I did."

Nady kept her voice businesslike. "Mr. Gore reduced your percentage interest in Deal Coin shortly before he died, didn't he?"

"We needed to free up some room for new investors."

"You must have been unhappy about it."

"Nobody is ever happy about taking a haircut, Ms. Nikonova."

"You were at the gathering at Kanzen in the early morning of March seventh?"

"Yes."

"What was the purpose of that meeting?"

"Deal Coin was experiencing some minor liquidity issues. Tyson and I met with some of our investors to request additional short-term funding to mitigate the impact."

"Were you able to raise the funds that morning?"

A hesitation. "No."

"Your investors had already started withdrawing funds, hadn't they?"

"Yes."

"And the company filed for bankruptcy shortly thereafter, didn't it?"

"We had no choice."

"Would it therefore be fair to say that the company was experiencing more than a 'minor' liquidity issue?"

"We didn't view it that way."

"Seems your investors did."

"Objection. Argumentative."

"Sustained."

Nady inched closer to Bosworth. "Mr. Gore must have been extremely worried about getting the new funding."

"He was concerned."

"I would have been panic-stricken."

"Objection. There wasn't a question there."

"Withdrawn." The corner of Nady's mouth turned up. "Earlier today, the general manager of Kanzen testified that the gathering was intense."

"That's fair."

"Mr. Gore was under a lot of pressure to obtain the new funding, wasn't he?"

"Yes."

"Because he knew that if he didn't, he would lose billions and the company was likely to go under, right?"

"It was a possibility."

"It was more than a possibility, Mr. Bosworth. That's exactly what happened, isn't it?"

"Yes."

Stay the course, Nady. Don't overplay your hand.

Nady's tone turned sharper. "You knew that Mr. Gore had a drinking problem, didn't you?"

"Yes."

"And he was taking antidepressants? And designer drugs known as 'bath salts'?"

"Yes."

"You must have been concerned about your friend's physical and mental health."

"I was, but Tyson was very strong."

"You knew that he was drinking heavily, taking antidepressants, and consuming illegal drugs. You knew that he had gone through two acrimonious divorces. You knew that his business was failing and he and his investors—including you—were on the verge of losing billions."

"Objection. There wasn't a question there."

"Sustained." The judge looked at Nady. "Please, Ms. Nikonova."

Nady hadn't taken her eyes off Bosworth. "Did you consider the possibility that your longtime friend and business partner was suicidal?"

"Absolutely not." Bosworth's voice filled with a full measure of Silicon Valley bravado. "Tyson was a brilliant businessman who was eternally optimistic—even when our companies had difficulties. He was the most confident person that I've ever known. He believed that Deal Coin would succeed. So did I. On that basis, I can assure you that he wasn't suicidal."

"No further questions."

Nady was back at the lectern a few minutes later. "How much money did your firm lose on Deal Coin, Mr. Warren?"

"A lot"

Even in a ten-thousand-dollar Italian suit and a Hermès tie, Steve Warren still looked like a kid who had been sent to the principal's office instead of a hotshot Silicon Valley venture capitalist. Then again, he wasn't really a hotshot VC; his father was.

"How much is a lot?" Nady asked.

"I'd rather not say."

"Your Honor?"

"Please answer the question, Mr. Warren."

"Low ten figures."

"That would be over a billion dollars?"

"Correct."

Nady peppered Warren with questions about Gore's drinking, drug use, and consumption of antidepressants. He was more nervous than Bosworth, his answers more tentative. Warren reconfirmed that Gore stood to lose billions if Deal Coin went under.

Finally, Nady got into his face. "You must have been concerned about Mr. Gore's physical and mental health, right?"

Warren sighed. "Yes."

"And your investment?"

"Of course."

"Did you consider the possibility that Mr. Gore was suicidal that morning?"

Warren tried to project authority by speaking louder, which made him less convincing. "I saw no evidence that he was."

Nady feigned disbelief. "No further questions."

Emrich was next up. In a custom-tailored Armani suit and a designer tie, he looked the part of a successful hedge fund promoter. True to form, he spoke with relentless self-confidence. "I was aware that Tyson had some issues with alcohol and drugs. However, I never saw it impact his job performance. He was a visionary entrepreneur and a charismatic leader."

Please.

Nady somehow managed to avoid rolling her eyes. "Mr. Gore was going to lose billions if he didn't raise additional capital for Deal Coin, wasn't he?"

"It was a possibility."

"You and your co-investors were also about to lose billions, weren't you?"

"Also a possibility."

"That's exactly what happened, isn't it?"

Erickson started to stand but reconsidered.

"Yes," Emrich said.

"You would therefore agree that Mr. Gore was under a lot of stress?"

"Of course."

"He was also dealing with the fallout from two acrimonious divorces and child custody issues?"

"Yes."

"And he was drinking heavily, and taking antidepressants and designer drugs, wasn't he?"

"Yes."

"Did you consider the possibility that he might have been suicidal?"

Emrich's tone shifted from confident to dismissive. "No, Ms. Nikonova. Tyson was one of the most self-confident people I've ever known. I saw no signs that he was suicidal."

Cynthia Mitchell was poised, professional, and direct when she took the stand a few minutes later. "If I had the chance to do it again, I wouldn't have invested in Deal Coin."

Nady spoke to her from the lectern. "You would acknowledge that Tyson Gore was under a lot of stress when you saw him at Kanzen on March seventh of this year?"

"Of course."

"And you were aware of his drinking issues, drug use, and personal problems?"

"They've been documented, Ms. Nikonova."

"He must have been desperate to raise additional funding."

"That's fair."

"Did you sense that he was on the edge?"

"A little."

"Did he demonstrate any signs that he was suicidal?"

"Objection," Erickson said. "Calls for an expert opinion that it is outside of Ms. Mitchell's expertise."

"Your Honor," Nady said, "I'm not asking Ms. Mitchell to express a medical conclusion. I am simply asking for her observations of Mr. Gore's behavior that night."

"Overruled."

Mitchell measured her words. "Mr. Gore's behavior was erratic. While I am not a trained psychologist, I think it's fair to say that the stresses were a lot to handle."

"No further questions, Your Honor."

Erickson declined cross-exam. Judge Tsang asked Nady to call her next witness.

"The defense calls Dr. Gina Cole."

50

"MULTIPLE SIGNS OF PSYCHOLOGICAL TRAUMA"

Nady stood at the lectern after the lunch break. "Please state your name for the record."

The African-American woman with the short hair, subdued gray suit, and hoop-style earrings sat in the box, arms folded, manner authoritative. "Dr. Gina Cole."

"Are you a medical doctor?"

"PhD in psychology. Undergrad from USC, master's and doctorate from UCLA. I have been a practicing psychologist for twenty-seven years."

"Are you in private practice?"

"I founded a nonprofit called the Psychological Trauma Center in Berkeley." She cleared her throat. "My area of expertise is suicide prevention."

Rosie and I had met Gina during our first tour at the PD's Office. She had grown up in the Fillmore and developed an interest in suicide prevention after her younger brother took his own life in jail while awaiting trial for shoplifting. During college, she volunteered at the Los Angeles Suicide Prevention Hotline. After she finished grad school, she moved back to the Bay Area and formed the Psychological Trauma Center to provide counseling in underserved areas and conduct academic research on the causes of suicide.

Nady led Gina through her stellar credentials. Then she provided copies of a lengthy document to Erickson, Gina, and the judge. "Your Honor, we would like to introduce into evidence this psychological autopsy report prepared by Dr.

Cole relating to the death of Tyson Gore. We previously provided a copy to Mr. Erickson."

"Objection," Erickson said. "With all due respect to Dr. Cole, this report and her testimony relating thereto is inadmissible as expert testimony under the *Daubert* standard."

Erickson was referring to a U.S. Supreme Court case called *Daubert v. Merrell Dow Pharmaceuticals*, which sets forth the federal standard for challenging the admissibility of an opposing party's expert. California has adopted a similar requirement. It says that expert witnesses can give opinions as long as they are qualified by "knowledge, skill, experience, training, or education." The judge must decide whether the expert's opinion will make the evidence more understandable, is based on sufficient facts or data, and reflects reliable principles and methods.

Judge Tsang raised his hands and formed the letter "T" the same way that a football coach would signal a time-out. "Counsel will approach."

Erickson, Nady, and I dutifully walked up to the bench. Judge Tsang covered his microphone and spoke to Erickson in a stern whisper. "I resolved this issue during pre-trial motions. We aren't going to relitigate it here."

"Respectfully, Your Honor, the science of psychological autopsies is unproven."

"Your Honor," Nady said, "we briefed this issue weeks ago. You ruled that Dr. Cole is qualified to opine as to whether Mr. Gore committed suicide. If Mr. Erickson wishes to challenge your ruling, he may do so on appeal."

Erickson tried again. "But, Your Honor—,"

The judge stopped him with an upraised hand. "I've ruled. Please step back."

As Andy headed back to the prosecution table, he gave me a sheepish half-smile, and I responded with a subtle nod. It was yet another reminder that trial work is theater, and the jurors are the audience. He knew that Judge Tsang wouldn't reconsider his earlier ruling. He was trying to plant a morsel of doubt about the psychological autopsy in the jurors' minds.

Nady approached the box. "Are you familiar with this document?"

"Yes, Ms. Nikonova. It's a psychological autopsy report that I prepared for Tyson Gore."

"How many such reports have you prepared?"

"Over a hundred. I have appeared as an expert witness with respect to such reports dozens of times."

"Could you please confirm that the Public Defender's Office hired you?"

"Yes."

"How many hours did you spend on this project?"

"Approximately two hundred."

"How much did you charge us for your services?"

"Nothing. We are a nonprofit that receives funding from charitable organizations and private foundations. As a result, we are able to provide our services on a *pro bono* basis."

Nady nodded at the jurors. She wanted them to understand that we hadn't simply bought Gina's opinion. Then again, she wouldn't be on the stand if we thought she was going to say anything other than that Gore committed suicide.

Nady asked Gina if she was ever called upon to perform psychological autopsies in circumstances not involving criminal cases.

"Yes, Ms. Nikonova. Many of my cases involve disputes over estates where the litigants disagree as to whether the decedent was of sound mind when he or she executed a will. I am also called upon to help resolve issues over life insurance policies, which contain a 'suicide clause' prohibiting payment of death benefits if the decedent took his or her own life within a certain period after the policy was issued."

"The science for psychological autopsies has been around for a long time, hasn't it?"

"Since the fifties." Gina explained that the concepts were developed by a clinical psychologist named Edwin Schneidman, the founder of the Los Angeles Suicide Prevention Center. Schneidman became interested in the causes of suicide while working at a Southern California V.A.

Hospital. He wrote several books on the subject, founded the American Association of Suicidology, and was among the first "suicidologists." "He coined the term 'psychological autopsy,' and he developed rigorous standards for conducting a retrospective investigation to determine whether a decedent committed suicide."

"You performed a psychological autopsy for Tyson Gore using such standards?"

"I did."

"What does such an investigation entail?"

Gina turned and faced the jury—just as we had rehearsed. "Broadly speaking, the evaluation requires careful consideration of six concepts: cause, mode, motive, intent, lethality, and sane versus insane suicide. 'Cause' explains how a person actually died. In Mr. Gore's case, this was not in dispute: he died of massive head injuries when he jumped from Salesforce Park and landed on a pile of gravel approximately seventy feet below."

She explained that "mode" referred to the circumstances that led to the cause of death. "We use the acronym 'NASH,' which stands for 'natural, accidental, suicide, or homicide.' 'Motive' addresses why the decedent committed suicide. 'Intent' represents the resolve of the individual in carrying out his death—whether consciously or unconsciously." She said that "lethality" represents the probability that an individual will successfully kill themselves in the near future. "Dr. Schneidman believed that high lethality represented an unequivocal decision by an individual to kill himself, such as a self-inflicted shotgun wound."

"Or jumping off the top level of a four-story bus terminal?" Nady said.

"Correct."

I glanced at the jurors, whose eyes were locked onto Gina's. They were listening.

Nady asked Gina to describe how she conducted the psychological autopsy.

"I gathered as much information as I could about the decedent. I reviewed his medical history, although not everything was available because of doctor-patient confidentiality. I talked to people who knew him the best. Ordinarily, that would include family members, but Mr. Gore's parents are deceased, and he had no siblings. As a result, I focused upon his friends, business associates, and acquaintances."

"Were you able to speak to either of his ex-wives?"

"I spoke briefly with his first ex-wife, but she was reluctant to provide details." Gina described conversations with Bosworth, Warren, Emrich, and Mitchell. She painted a picture of a man who was driven in business and unable to maintain long-term connections. "He had almost no relationship with his ex-wives or children. His most recent romantic relationship, with a woman named Amanda Blair, had dissolved. There were anger management and impulse control issues. I didn't find evidence of physical abuse, but there were suggestions of emotional cruelty. Mr. Gore was a control freak and a manipulator. It must have been very difficult for his former spouses and his children."

"How many people did you talk to?"

She glanced at her report. "Twenty-two."

"You are aware that Mr. Gore was drinking heavily and taking antidepressants and illegal designer drugs?"

"Yes. Obviously, those were relevant facts in my analysis. While those issues are not necessarily dispositive markers of a suicidal mind, they are important considerations. In addition, Mr. Gore's business associates said that he was consumed by the possibility that Deal Coin would go bankrupt, and he would lose his fortune. In my view, the combination of factors created a potentially lethal environment."

"What did you conclude?"

Gina took a deep breath. "Tyson Gore was a brilliant but angry and troubled man who demonstrated multiple signs of psychological trauma. His personal life was a disaster, and his company was on the verge of bankruptcy. On the night that he died, he had been unsuccessful in trying to raise additional money to keep his business afloat. He was drinking heavily and consuming antidepressants and illegal drugs. When you factor in all of the foregoing, it is my opinion that it is likely that Mr. Gore committed suicide."

"No further questions."

"Cross-exam?"

"Yes, Your Honor." Erickson moved to the front of the courtroom and positioned himself directly in front of Gina. "You never met Mr. Gore, did you?"

"No."

"Or his parents?"

"They're deceased."

"The only family member that you spoke to was his first ex-wife for a few minutes?"

"Correct."

"His most recent girlfriend wouldn't talk to you?"

"That's right."

"Neither his doctor nor his therapist would talk to you, either?"

"They cited patient confidentiality."

Erickson spent the next twenty minutes attacking her analysis and suggesting that she lacked the information to make any meaningful judgments about Gore's state of mind. In fairness, it was a legitimate line of questioning, and I would have done exactly the same thing. Thankfully, Gina was an experienced witness who remained calm and responded in a respectful, but authoritative voice.

Erickson walked back to the lectern, summoned a skeptical expression, and spoke in a pointed tone. "Dr. Cole, I have great respect for you and the good work that you do, but I have serious trouble believing that you were able to find sufficient information to make any meaningful determinations about Tyson Gore's state of mind immediately before he died."

"Objection," Nady said. "There wasn't a question."

"Sustained."

Erickson was still looking at Gina. "You are aware that Mr. Gore's longtime therapist, Dr. Madeline Swartz, concluded that he did not commit suicide?"

"I have great respect for Dr. Swartz, but I disagree with her analysis."

"You would acknowledge that Dr. Swartz knew Mr. Gore personally for many years."

"I do."

"Yet you believe that you are more qualified than she is to make a determination as to whether Mr. Gore was suicidal?"

"I don't know if I'm more qualified, Mr. Erickson. I looked at the facts available to me, and I concluded that it is likely that Mr. Gore committed suicide."

"No further questions."

"Re-direct, Ms. Nikonova?"

"No, Your Honor."

"Please call your next witness."

She looked at the prosecution table. "The defense recalls Inspector Kenneth Lee."

51

"YOU DIDN'T CONSIDER ANYBODY ELSE"

At two-forty on Monday afternoon, the battle was fully engaged. I stood in front of the box, my eyes locked onto Ken Lee's. "You interviewed Mr. Gore's family, friends, and business associates?"

"Yes."

"You knew that his business was imploding, and that he had lost billions of his own money and that of his investors?"

"I did."

Nady had played her role as "good cop" to perfection. Things were likely to become contentious with Lee, so we decided that I should bring the heat.

I inched closer. "He organized the gathering at Kanzen to hit up his biggest investors for additional funding to keep Deal Coin afloat, didn't he?"

"So I understand."

"Nobody came through with additional money?"

"Correct."

"Which means that his business was on the verge of failure, and he was likely to file for bankruptcy, right?"

"Right."

"You were also aware that Mr. Gore had been through two acrimonious divorces, was having difficulties with his children, and had recently broken up with his girlfriend?"

"I was."

"He was drinking heavily, taking antidepressants, and consuming designer drugs?"

"Yes."

"You would therefore acknowledge that Mr. Gore was under an ungodly amount of stress, wouldn't you?"

"I would think so."

I took a deep breath. "Yet you didn't consider the possibility that he committed suicide?"

Lee didn't fluster. "I considered the possibility, Mr. Daley. Based on lengthy discussions with his friends, family, business associates, and therapist, I believe that he did not do so."

"You were here during Dr. Cole's testimony?"

"I was."

"You heard her expert opinion that Mr. Gore had committed suicide?"

"I did."

"Yet you ruled out the possibility that he committed suicide?"

"After full consideration of the evidence, I concluded that he did not."

"But you don't know for sure, do you?"

"I found no compelling evidence that he did."

"That conclusion fits squarely within the narrative of this case that you and Mr. Erickson are trying to prove, doesn't it?"

"Objection. Argumentative."

"Sustained."

I glanced at Nady, who gave me a subtle nod. Time to muddy the waters a little more.

"Inspector," I said, "there were other people at the gathering at Kanzen that night, weren't there?"

"Yes."

"All of whom walked right by the Redwood Forest after the party?"

"Yes."

"Yet you didn't consider anybody else as a potential suspect, did you?"

"I found no evidence."

"And it wouldn't have been consistent with your pre-established conclusion that Reggie was guilty, right?"

"Objection. Argumentative."

"Sustained."

I headed back to the lectern, activated my laptop, and put a slide reading "Other people at Kanzen." It displayed photos of Bosworth, Warren, Emrich, and Mitchell. We didn't include Eugene McAllister on the belief that it wouldn't play well to suggest that a man who had suffered a stroke might have been a murderer.

I turned back to Lee. "You interviewed all of these people?"

"Yes."

"They were all investors in Deal Coin who attended the gathering at Kanzen?"

"Right."

"And they all lost millions or even billions?"

"Yes."

"Matt Bosworth was the co-founder of Deal Coin whose investment was reduced by Mr. Gore. He lost almost a billion dollars when the company tanked, right?"

"Yes."

"So he was undoubtedly angry at Mr. Gore, wasn't he?"

"Objection. Speculation."

"Sustained."

"Yet you didn't consider him a possible suspect in Mr. Gore's death?"

"I found no evidence."

I pointed at the photo of Warren. "His venture capital firm and its investors lost over a billion dollars on Deal Coin, didn't they?"

"So I was told."

"Mr. Warren had to inform his investors, many of whom were his father's friends and associates, that he had lost billions of their money. I'll bet that he was pretty angry, too."

"Objection. Speculation."

"Sustained."

I invoked a sarcastic tone. "If you had lost more than a billion dollars, you would have been angry, wouldn't you?"

"Objection. Speculation."

"Sustained."

"Yet you didn't consider the possibility that Mr. Warren might have been involved in Mr. Gore's death, did you?"

"I found no evidence, Mr. Daley."

"Seems to me that you didn't look very hard."

"Objection."

"Withdrawn." I went through a similar exercise with respect to Jack Emrich and Cynthia Mitchell. Lee kept his tone even and stuck to his talking point that he had found no evidence implicating any of them. In fairness, there wasn't any.

Erickson finally rose to his feet and feigned exasperation. "Your Honor, I must object to this line of questioning. Mr. Daley is trying to create confusion by suggesting that people in the vicinity were involved in Mr. Gore's death."

That's true.

"The problem," Erickson continued, "is that he has no evidence."

That's also true. I addressed Judge Tsang, but I was really talking to the jury. "Your Honor, I am simply pointing out that several other people walked by the Redwood Forest early that morning. Every one of them had lost a lot of money and was angry at Mr. Gore. Several had harsh words with Mr. Gore at Kanzen. It is therefore relevant to point this out to the jury and to note that Inspector Lee jumped to conclusions when he ruled them out as suspects."

"You're going to have to come up with some real evidence, Mr. Daley. Mr. Erickson's objection is sustained. Do you have anything else for this witness?"

"Just a couple more questions, Your Honor." I glanced at Nady, who nodded. I punched a button on my laptop, and the video of Damian Mason appeared on the flat-screen, the date and time stamped in the corner. "Did you review this security video?"

"Yes. It was taken on the ground level of Salesforce Transit Center at two-twenty AM on Monday, March seventh." He confirmed that it was the morning that Gore died.

"Were you able to identify the person in this photo?"

"His name is Damian Mason."

"He is a known drug dealer, isn't he?"

"Objection," Erickson said. "Relevance."

"I'll show relevance in a moment."

"Overruled."

Lee nodded. "We believe that Mr. Mason may have been involved in the sale of drugs. I would note, however, that he has never been arrested."

"Did you interview him?"

"We could not locate him. We believe that he has left the country."

"And you have no idea where he is?"

"I'm afraid not."

I pretended to study Mason's photo. "Among other things, Mr. Mason sold designer drugs known as 'bath salts' to Tyson Gore, didn't he?"

"I don't know."

"You think it's just coincidence that he was at Salesforce Park on the morning that Mr. Gore died?"

"Objection. Speculation."

"Sustained."

"Why else would he have been there?"

"Objection. Speculation."

"Sustained."

I eyed the jury, then I turned back to Lee. "Did you consider the possibility that he might have had an issue with Mr. Gore? Maybe a dispute about money?"

Erickson stood to object to my blatantly speculative question, but Lee stopped him with an upraised hand. "I don't know why he was there, Mr. Daley."

"Did you consider the possibility that he killed Mr. Gore?"

"As a matter of fact, I did. I found no evidence that Mr. Mason went upstairs to Salesforce Park. And I found no evidence that he had any contact with Mr. Gore that morning."

"But you couldn't rule out the possibility, right?"

Lee's tone became more emphatic. "There was no evidence, Mr. Daley."

"Let's be honest, Inspector. You didn't consider anybody else, did you?"

"Objection," Erickson said. "Foundation. This line of questioning is unsubstantiated and evidence-free."

"Sustained." The judge looked my way. "Anything else, Mr. Daley?"

"Just one more thing, Your Honor." I turned back to Lee. "How long have you been a homicide inspector?"

"Fourteen years."

"How many homicides have you investigated over that time?"

"I don't recall."

"Ballpark estimate. A dozen? Two dozen? Fifty?"

"More than fifty. Fewer than a hundred."

"You've interviewed hundreds of suspects, right?"

"Right."

"Did any of them try to run when you caught them?"

"Some."

"You would probably take that as a sign of their guilt, right?"

"Probably."

"When you interviewed my client, did he make any attempt to run?"

"No."

"Did he ask to talk to a lawyer?"

"Not until we placed him under arrest."

"Didn't that strike you as odd?"

"Not really."

"If you had killed Tyson Gore, would you have stayed all night until a security guard found you?"

"Objection. Speculation."

"Sustained."

Once more. "If the cops came up to talk to you, you would have tried to run, wouldn't you?"

"Objection. More speculation."

"Sustained."

"Come on, Inspector," I said. "Do you really think Reggie would have stuck around if he had killed Tyson Gore?"

"Objection. Even more speculation, Your Honor."

"Sustained. That's enough, Mr. Daley."

"No further questions, Your Honor."

"Cross-exam, Mr. Erickson?"

"No, Your Honor."

"Do you wish to call any more witnesses, Mr. Daley?"

"One moment, Your Honor." I walked over to the defense table and huddled with Nady. "Is it enough?" I whispered to her.

She glanced at Reggie, whose eyes were filled with panic. "Yes," she said.

My heart was pounding. "I'll put Reggie up for a minute and get a forceful denial."

"It's not worth it, Mike." Nady's eyes narrowed. "Erickson will go after him. In this instance, less is more. It's time to stop."

My eyes shifted from Nady to Reggie and back to Nady. My instincts told me to put Reggie on the stand, but my rational side said that Nady was right, and it was time to sit down.

I turned around and addressed the judge. "We have no further witnesses, Your Honor. The defense rests."

"Thank you, Mr. Daley." Judge Tsang looked at the clock. "It's past four PM, so I am going to adjourn for the day. We will proceed with closing arguments first thing tomorrow morning. I need you and Mr. Erickson to provide any final comments on our jury instructions by six PM."

52

"HARD TO SAY"

"Any word?" I asked.

"Not yet." Nady looked up from her computer. "Calm down, Mike. You've always said that juries take their own sweet time. At least they're still thinking about it."

"Maybe we should have put Reggie on the stand."

"You've also taught me that you shouldn't second-guess yourself while the jury is out. We made the right call on Reggie. The risks outweighed the potential benefits. Let it go."

I knew that she was right.

Three days later, at five-fifteen on Thursday evening, Nady, Pete, and I were in the conference room at the PD's Office. Rosie had joined us on Zoom. Luna was sleeping in the corner. We had finished closing arguments on Tuesday morning. Erickson went through a meticulous summary of the evidence and gave an emotional plea for justice. I argued that he hadn't proved his case beyond a reasonable doubt, and I tried once again to convince the jury that Gore had committed suicide. The jurors were listening, but I couldn't tell whether they found either of us terribly convincing. In the movies and on TV, an impassioned closing can sway a jury. In real life, not so much.

Judge Tsang gave the jury our carefully negotiated instructions and sent them off to deliberate. In addition to first- and second-degree murder charges, he gave them the option to convict on voluntary or involuntary manslaughter. Despite my long-standing advice to the contrary, Nady and I had spent the last two days second-guessing ourselves—a profoundly unproductive exercise. In reality, we simply had to wait.

I looked at Pete. "Anything on Damian Mason?"

"It doesn't matter anymore, Mick."

"Just curious."

"I got a text from Kaela Joy. She said that one of her sources told her that he may have been spotted at the border coming back into the U.S."

"You really think it was Mason?"

"I don't know. What if it was?"

"We might be able to do something on appeal or ask for a new trial."

"You won't need to do anything if you get an acquittal."

"True."

Rosie spoke to us from her box on my screen. "How is Reggie holding up?"

"Not great," I said. "I'm going to see him in the morning. How are you feeling?"

"Better, but still testing positive. How do you think this is going to go, Mike?"

"Hard to say. My boss once told me that it's a fool's errand to try to predict what a jury is going to do."

"You must have a gut feeling."

"I do, but I don't want to jinx it."

"Were you this superstitious when you were a priest?"

"Yes."

"The jury has been out for almost three days."

"Doesn't mean a thing."

Experts on juries have conflicting views about whether a lengthy deliberation is a good sign. Some gurus insist that convictions come quickly, while acquittals and hung juries take longer. Others say just the opposite. I don't know who is right. As I've gotten older and more cynical, I've started to believe that they tell the lawyers what they want to hear.

"I think we made a compelling case for reasonable doubt," I said.

Rosie was getting impatient. "Conviction, acquittal, or hung jury?"

Hung jury. "I'm not saying."

"Come on, Mike."

"I'm not saying," I repeated.

Rosie asked Nady. "What do you think?"

"I'm more superstitious than Mike. I'm not saying, either."

Rosie tried Pete. "What about you?"

He looked up from his phone. "I wasn't even in court."

"Doesn't matter. You're the jury whisperer. You always get it right."

Pete rolled his eyes. "Acquittal."

"Any particular reason?"

"Never question the jury whisperer."

Terrence knocked on the open door. "I got a text from Judge Tsang's clerk. The jury reached a verdict. They want everybody back in court at ten o'clock tomorrow morning."

53

"HAVE YOU REACHED A VERDICT?"

Judge Tsang's courtroom was silent except for the buzz of the fluorescent lights, the hum of the standing fan, and the sound of Andy Erickson tapping his pencil on the prosecution table. Vanessa Turner sat behind him in the front row of the full gallery. People always show up for the fourth quarter.

Reggie was sitting between Nady and me. I tried to reassure him, but he appeared resigned to his fate—whichever way the jury went.

I glanced at Pete, who was sitting in the back row. He nodded subtly, but he never showed emotion in court.

Judge Tsang touched his microphone. "The defendant will please rise."

Reggie lifted himself to his feet. Nady and I stood up with him. Attorneys are not required to stand during the reading of the verdict, but I've always done so in a show of solidarity.

The judge spoke to the foreperson. "Have you reached a verdict?"

The attorney from the big law firm answered him. "We have, Your Honor."

My stomach churned. Time moved slowly as she handed the slip of paper to the bailiff, who delivered it to the judge. He studied the verdict for a moment, nodded, and handed it to the clerk.

"Please read the verdict."

"On the charge of murder in the first degree, the jury finds the defendant not guilty. On the charge of murder in the second degree, the jury also finds the defendant not guilty."

So far, so good.

"On the charge of voluntary manslaughter, the jury finds the defendant not guilty. On the charge of involuntary manslaughter, the jury finds the defendant not guilty."

Yes! The jury whisperer was right again!

Reggie clenched his fists and threw his arms into the air. He thanked Nady and me, then he fell back into his seat.

The judge asked the foreperson the obligatory question of whether the verdict was unanimous.

"Yes, Your Honor."

In response to Erickson's request, Judge Tsang agreed to poll the individual jurors. He asked each of the jurors if they agreed with the verdict read. All of them responded in the affirmative.

"Thank you for your service," the judge said. After he excused the jurors, he spoke to Reggie. "You are free to go, Mr. Jones. We wish you well."

"Thank you, Your Honor."

Everybody stood as Judge Tsang left the courtroom.

Reggie hugged Nady and me. "I don't know what I would have done without you," he whispered. "Thank you."

"You're welcome," I said.

He sat down and tried to get his bearings. Then his eyes filled with panic. "Now what? I don't have a place to stay. I don't have any money. I don't want to go back onto the street."

I invoked my priest-voice. "First, we're going downstairs to get you discharged. Second, we'll take you to San Bruno to collect your belongings. Third, we'll sit down with one of our transition specialists and get you set up with a temporary place to live and a little money."

"Thanks." He swallowed. "Then what?"

I could only offer a cliché. "One step at a time, Reggie."

I looked over at the prosecution table, where a dejected Andy Erickson closed his laptop, his eyes down. Ken Lee had already departed. So had Vanessa Turner. I nodded respectfully in Andy's direction. He nodded back.

I texted Rosie and Terrence with the good news. Then I turned around and looked at Pete, whose stoic expression hadn't changed.

He mouthed the words, "Nice work. I'll call you." Then he left the courtroom.

54

"YOU GOT A GOOD RESULT"

"You got a good result," Rosie said.

"Thank you," I replied.

"You don't seem excited. Public Defenders don't get a lot of victories. Enjoy it while you can."

I sipped my Diet Dr Pepper. "Just tired."

Nady and I were sitting in my office at six-thirty on Friday night. Terrence had gone home. Rosie and Rolanda had joined us on Zoom. A victory celebration was in order, but I was too exhausted.

"Did you get Reggie a place to stay?" Rosie asked.

"Yes. We set him up at a motel for a couple of days. He's working with one of our transition facilitators who provided some clothes and a little cash. She's going to start setting him up with access to other services on Monday."

"You think he'll be back on the street soon?"

I answered her honestly. "I wouldn't be surprised. I hope he can stay off booze."

"It is what it is. Did you have a chance to talk to the jurors?"

"Briefly."

Jurors are frequently willing to talk to the attorneys after trial. I've always found it helpful to get their feedback if they're willing.

"Bottom line," I said, "they didn't think that Erickson proved his case beyond a reasonable doubt."

"Good enough," Rosie said. "Did they think that Reggie did it?"

"There wasn't any consensus. Most thought it was unlikely that he would have stuck around if he had really pushed Gore over the railing. About half believed that Gore committed suicide. It sounds like they took their deliberations seriously and followed the judge's instructions. That's all that we can ask."

Contrary to what you often see on TV, I have found that most jurors take their responsibilities seriously and try to do the right thing.

"You got a good result," she repeated. "At the end of the day, their reasoning doesn't matter."

It matters to me.

She read my expression through the little Zoom box. "Do you think Reggie killed Gore?"

"No. My best guess is that Gore committed suicide." I looked at Nady. "What do you think?"

"I think somebody pushed him over the railing. Gore had a massive ego. He wouldn't have done it to himself."

"You think Reggie did it?"

"Doubtful. He wouldn't have stayed if he did. He's never hurt anybody. I think he was telling the truth when he said that he was passed out."

"Then who?" I asked.

She shrugged. "I don't know."

"Neither do I." *If you're right, a killer is still out there.*

"Did you talk to Erickson?" Rosie asked.

"Briefly. To his credit, he was gracious."

"Does he still have a job?"

"For now. He thinks our new DA will blame him for Reggie's acquittal."

"That's not fair."

"Nothing is fair in politics."

"He didn't have great cards to play."

"Neither did we. This trial could have gone either way."

Her expression turned thoughtful. "You okay?"

"I'll be fine. I just have a feeling that we missed something."

"Go home soon and take the weekend off."

I glanced at Luna, who was sleeping in the corner. "I will."

Pete's voice was raspy as I held my cell to my ear. "You up, Mick?"

"Yes."

I glanced at my watch as I sat at the table in the kitchen of my apartment at ten-forty-five on Friday night. Wilma glared at me from her spot on the sofa, annoyed that Pete's call had interrupted a nap that had started four hours earlier.

"You doing anything?" Pete asked.

"I was thinking seriously about going to bed."

"I'm heading into the City. I'll pick you up on my way."

"What's going on?"

"I got a text from Kaela Joy. Her source at the border confirmed that Mason returned to the U.S. She said that she might have something for us."

55

"KEEP YOUR VOICE DOWN"

Kaela Joy sat behind the wheel of an old Jeep Cherokee that she drove instead of her top-of-the-line BMW when she wanted to avoid drawing attention to herself. She tugged at her black Giants cap, glanced at her Apple Watch, and hunkered down. "Any minute now," she said.

Pete was sitting in the passenger seat. "Good."

I was in the back seat at eleven-forty-five on a foggy Friday night. Kaela Joy was parked in an alley off Beale Street, between Mission and Howard, across the street from the east entrance of Salesforce Transit Center. The street was empty.

"Are you going to tell me what's going on?" I asked.

"Keep your voice down," she whispered.

"Our windows are rolled up, and nobody is around."

She turned around and glared at me. "We think that's about to change."

I sat in silence for five minutes before I spoke up again. "Come on, guys. Please?"

Kaela Joy exchanged an irritated glance with Pete, then she spoke to me in a tense whisper. "We think that we're about to witness a crime."

"Are we safe?"

"Hopefully."

"Do you think it might be a good idea to call the cops?"

"We already have."

"What does this have to do with me?"

"Nothing. It may have something to do with Reggie Jones."

I looked at the back of Pete's head, but he didn't say anything.

Kaela Joy put her hands on the wheel and stared across the street in silence.

A man dressed in black emerged on foot from behind a truck parked across the street. He walked to the entrance to Salesforce Transit Center. He paused, pulled out his vape pen, took a hit, and waited.

Kaela Joy tapped Pete's shoulder and whispered, "Right on time."

He nodded.

"Who?" I asked.

"Damian Mason."

"What's going on?"

"Keep your voice down," Pete hissed.

"What now?" I asked.

"We wait."

A moment later, Susan Gallardo exited the terminal and walked over to Mason. They spoke for a moment. He gave her a package the size of a softball. She handed him an envelope.

"Are we going to do something?" I asked.

"Absolutely," Pete said. He turned to Kaela Joy. "Would you like to do the honors?"

She smiled. "You go ahead."

He pulled out a burner phone, hit the speed dial, and waited.

The recipient answered on the first ring. "Sergeant David Dito speaking."

"I would like to make an anonymous report of criminal activity taking place right now on Beale between Mission and Howard, at the eastern entrance of Salesforce Transit Center."

"Thank you."

Pete ended the call.

A moment later, four police cars emerged from around the corner and parked haphazardly on Beale. Eight officers emerged, weapons drawn. They quickly surrounded Gallardo and Mason, who put their hands up and were handcuffed and arrested without incident. The operation ended five minutes after it started.

"What just happened?" I asked.

Kaela Joy took off her baseball cap, turned around, and smiled. "Mason was just arrested for selling bath salts to Gallardo. Gallardo was just arrested for buying bath salts from Mason and selling them to the members and guests of Kanzen."

"How did you know?"

"Cynthia Mitchell is considering an investment in Matt Bosworth's new venture, so she asked me to keep an eye on him. I watched him for a few days and talked to a few people. It didn't take long to figure out that Mason was supplying bath salts and other designer drugs to Gallardo, who was, in turn, selling them to the members at Kanzen at a rather substantial markup."

"Including Bosworth?"

"Yes." She smirked. "Cynthia has decided not to invest in his new company."

"Good call. What does this have to do with Reggie?"

"According to my sources, Gore was also purchasing bath salts from Gallardo, who was supplied by Mason. When Deal Coin cratered, Gore became delinquent in his payments to Gallardo who was, in turn, delinquent in her payments to Mason."

Pete interjected. "Gore was paying Gallardo in Deal Coin, and she was paying Mason in Deal Coin. When Deal Coin became worthless, the financial arrangements became unworkable."

Kaela Joy spoke up again. "Not surprisingly, Mason's suppliers wanted real money. My sources at the border believe that Mason went down to Mexico with a suitcase full of cash to keep his cartel bosses happy."

"Mason came back to collect cash from Gallardo?"

"So it seems."

Pete chuckled. "It seems that even drug dealers are figuring out that crypto isn't an ideal currency for doing business, and they're insisting on being paid in real money, too."

"How does this relate to Gore's death?"

Kaela Joy answered. "Cynthia told me that Gore and Gallardo got into a brief argument at Kanzen. She couldn't hear the details, but she thought it was about money. At the time, she assumed that Gore was late on paying his dues or some dinner bills to Kanzen. After I told her about Gallardo's business relationship with Gore, she thought that they might have been arguing about drug money that Gore owed Gallardo. You saw Mason in the security video on the morning that Gore died. It's possible that he was waiting for Gore, but I think there's a better chance that he was waiting to collect money from Gallardo, who never showed up."

My heart was pounding. "Do you have any evidence that Gallardo or Mason had something to do with Gore's death?"

"I don't, but I provided this new information to Sergeant Dito, Inspector Lee, and Andy Erickson. I'm sure that they will ask Gallardo and Mason about it tonight."

56

"YOU KNOW HOW IT GOES"

Andy Erickson took a long draw of his Anchor Steam. "Is Rosie out of quarantine?"

"Yes," I said. "Thanks for asking. She tested negative a couple of days ago, and she's feeling fine."

"Good to hear."

Mars Bar was quiet a week later on Friday, October fourteenth. At eight-fifteen PM, the Happy Hour crowd had dispersed, and the DJ was preparing for the evening rush. The TV was tuned to ESPN. A couple of people were shooting pool.

I took a bite of my cheeseburger. "I haven't heard anything more about Susan Gallardo and Damian Mason."

Andy nibbled on a pork slider. "There will be an announcement at the appropriate time."

"Your office *is* going to file charges against one or both of them, right?"

"Yes." He looked around to make sure that nobody was within earshot. "Attorney-client?"

"Of course."

"Vanessa has a team that's getting ready to present evidence to the grand jury."

"Are you on the team?"

"No."

Too bad. "Charges?"

"Multiple felony counts of drug dealing. Maybe more."

"Did Gallardo or Mason have anything to do with Tyson Gore's death?"

"That's the working theory, but they're still gathering evidence. Mason was definitely selling designer drugs to Gallardo, who was, in turn, reselling them at a substantial markup to people at Kanzen. Gore was one of her regular customers. When Deal Coin started going sideways, Gallardo started asking for cash instead of Deal Coin. Gore had cash flow issues and owed Gallardo almost a hundred grand. She owed fifty grand to Mason, who was getting pressure from his suppliers. We believe that Mason was waiting for Gallardo downstairs on the morning that Gore died, hoping to get paid, but Gallardo never showed up. Our people think Gallardo confronted Gore at Kanzen and demanded money. He didn't pay, and she followed him outside. They got into it in the Redwood Forest, and she pushed him over the railing."

"Is there surveillance video showing any of this?"

"Unfortunately, no. We have her on video leaving Salesforce Park via the stairway near the Redwood Forest. As far as we can tell, she never met up with Mason."

I asked about Gore's wallet.

"Not sure. Maybe Gallardo grabbed it during a struggle. Maybe it fell out of Gore's pocket. Or maybe he pulled it out to show her that he didn't have any cash. Either way, it ended up on the ground next to your client."

"Other corroboration?"

"Mason claims that he heard Gore and Gallardo yelling at each other."

"He was four stories below the park."

"There was nobody else around except Reggie, who was passed out. Salesforce Park is quiet at night."

"Is Mason prepared to testify against her?"

"We think so. He knows that he's going to be convicted of multiple felony drug charges that will put him in prison for at least twenty years, and we think he's prepared to cut a deal. The feds are talking about filing charges, too. Mason's lawyer said that his client may be willing to testify against Gallardo in exchange for a reduced sentence."

"Do you think there's enough to make a murder charge stick?"

"Vanessa thinks so, but I'm not so sure."

"It sounds like it may be tough to prove murder beyond a reasonable doubt." *Just like Reggie's case.*

He nodded. "I pointed that out to Vanessa, but she wasn't interested in my opinion." He shrugged. "You know as well as I do that anything can happen at trial. Either way, it's likely that Mason and Gallardo won't be hanging out at Kanzen for a long time."

"Sounds like we may get to the right result after all."

"Hopefully."

I had a long draw of my Guinness. "Will you get any credit for helping to find the truth?"

"Not a chance. If Gallardo and Mason are convicted, Vanessa will take the credit. If not, she'll figure out a way to deflect the blame—again."

"That's not fair."

"You know how it goes."

I took a moment to digest Andy's information. "An employee of the DA's Office probably shouldn't be sharing what is undoubtedly confidential information about an ongoing investigation."

"Given your representation of Reggie Jones and your knowledge of the circumstances, I thought you deserved to know. I trust that you will be discreet."

"I will."

He finished his beer. "And I wanted to let you know that I am no longer an employee of the DA's Office."

I'm not surprised. "I'm sorry. You resigned?"

"Vanessa fired me. She wasn't comfortable working with somebody who had run against her."

"That's BS. You're one of the best prosecutors in the office, Andy."

"You know how it goes," he repeated. "This didn't exactly come as a huge surprise—especially after your client was acquitted."

"You okay?"

"I'll be fine. I've already talked to some of my friends at the DA's Offices in Alameda, San Mateo, and Contra Costa. They're interested."

"Good."

"I'm also thinking of running for DA again." He grinned. "Now that I'm no longer employed by the DA's Office, I'm free to take potshots at Vanessa."

"I think you would make a fine DA."

"Thank you."

"Let me know if there's anything I can do to help. I would be happy to be a reference and write you a recommendation."

"I'm not sure that a letter from a PD will help, but I'll take you up on it."

"I'll put something together over the weekend." I looked my longtime adversary in the eye. "You should come to work for us."

"Are you serious?"

"Yes. You're an excellent lawyer, you know the system, and you know everybody at the DA's Office. You would be a great addition."

"I don't know, Mike. I've spent my whole career putting bad guys away. I'm not sure that I would be comfortable working the other side of the street."

"As an added bonus, you'll have plenty of opportunities to stick it to Vanessa."

His eyes lit up.

I grinned. "The way I see it, the only potential downside is that you'll have to get used to losing more cases than you win. It comes with the territory when you're a PD."

His expression indicated that he might be interested.

"Rolanda is going to be on bed rest for three months," I said, "and then she's going to be on maternity leave. Rosie has a full plate running the office, and Nady and I have more than we can handle. We could use another experienced hand."

"Have you cleared this with Rosie?"

"Yes. In fact, it was her idea."

"Can I think about it?"

"Of course. Can I buy you another beer?"

"No, thanks, Mike. I need to get home to the kids."

"You'll let me know soon?"

"I will." He stood up, put his jacket on, and extended a hand. "Mike?"

"Yes?"

"Thanks."

57

"BE HEALTHY. BE HAPPY. BE SAFE."

Grace kicked off her three-inch heels and sat down between Rosie and me at the otherwise empty head table in the social hall at St. Peter's. "It was a beautiful wedding, Daddy."

"Thanks, honey." It had been years since our daughter had called me "Daddy." "I'm glad you had a nice time."

Her dark brown eyes gleamed. "It was perfect."

At eleven-forty PM on Saturday, December thirty-first, most of the guests had departed, the band was packing up, and the caterer's people were collecting dirty dishes, empty wine goblets, and soiled tablecloths. Grace's husband, Chuck, was helping his parents carry their belongings to the car. The tireless Sylvia was holding forth at the dessert table and regaling the Fernandez side of the family with stories. Joey, Pete, and my baby sister, Mary, were leading the Daley contingent in a final round at the bar. The bartender had closed up shop, but Joey had smuggled in a bottle of Glendalough Irish whiskey. I smiled when I saw him pour a shot for Tommy, notwithstanding the fact that he hadn't yet turned twenty-one. Nobody was going to report us to the cops. We had provided Uber gift certificates to anybody who wanted them, and we had encouraged people to avoid driving.

Grace flashed a radiant smile that was identical to Rosie's. It was striking how much she looked like her mother when Rosie and I got married at St. Peter's almost thirty years earlier. "You should go home," she said to Rosie. "It's been a long day."

Rosie smiled. "I want to take it in for a few more minutes, honey."

"So do I."

I looked around at the workmanlike social hall in the weathered old church where my mom and dad had been baptized and married, Rosie and I had been baptized and married, and now Grace had been baptized and married. The memories came flooding back.

"It took us almost two years to get here," I said to Grace. "I'm not in any hurry to leave."

Rosie reached over and squeezed Grace's hand. "I'm sorry that you didn't get your big wedding party at the Fairmont."

"No need to apologize, Mama. I wouldn't have changed a thing."

When we started planning Grace's wedding, we put down a deposit for a black-tie event at the Fairmont. It was the wedding that Rosie had always dreamed of. Rosie and I got married in a humble gathering here at St. Peter's, featuring a band headlined by Rosie's cousin and food catered by the Roosevelt Tamale Parlor around the corner. Covid put the kibosh on our original plans for Grace, and we weren't able to rebook the Fairmont. She was disappointed at first, but she decided that a smaller event at St. Peter's was more our style.

Rosie looked at our beautiful daughter. "When your kids get married, you and Chuck can throw a big wedding at the Fairmont."

"Maybe we will." Grace's expression turned serious. "You're awfully quiet, Dad."

"Just tired."

"What is it?"

"I know that it's your wedding night, but I was hoping that the father of the bride could ask you for one small favor."

Her eyes brightened. "Of course."

"Three generations of our families have been baptized in this church. When you and Chuck have children, it would make me very happy if you would make it four."

"We wouldn't think of doing it anywhere else." She got a faraway look in her eyes. "Do you and Mom ever talk about getting married again?"

Uh-oh. I quickly deferred to Rosie.

She thought about it for a moment. "On occasion."

"What's stopping you?" Grace asked.

"Superstition."

"Seriously?"

Rosie reached over and touched my arm. "We've gotten along a lot better since we stopped being married. We're reluctant to mess with something that's working."

"You work together. You live together most of the time. You never stopped sleeping together. Why don't you make it official?"

Rosie looked my way and smiled, then she turned back to Grace. "Your father and I don't handle change very well. Maybe that's why you and Chuck got married in the same church that your parents and grandparents did."

Grace was bemused. "You know that doesn't make one iota of sense."

No, it doesn't.

Rosie's eyes filled with maternal love. "Some things don't make sense, Grace. As you get older, you'll start to realize that your parents have their, uh, idiosyncrasies just like everybody else. I hope you'll forgive us for ours and learn to live with them."

"Of course."

I looked across the room and saw Father Guillermo Lopez having a shot with Joey, Pete, and Tommy. At forty, Gil was one of the younger priests at the historic church. He had grown up around the corner and attended Saint Ignatius and USF before heading to the seminary. Smart, savvy, charismatic, and intensely political, he was primed to lead the community deep into the twenty-first century.

"Father Lopez spoke very nicely," I said.

"Yes, he did," Grace said. "So did you."

"Thank you."

"I'll bet you were a good priest."

"Not bad."

"Why did you decide to become a lawyer?"

It was the first time that she had asked me. "The priesthood wasn't a good fit for me. I didn't think I was qualified to save people's souls."

"You're too modest."

"You're too kind."

She smiled. "I'm glad that you decided to leave the priesthood. If you hadn't, you never would have met Mom, I wouldn't have been born, and we wouldn't be here tonight."

True. "I would say that it all worked out very well."

"So would I." Her voice turned thoughtful. "I liked the last couple of lines in your speech. How did it go?"

"You want three things for your children. Be healthy. Be happy. Be safe."

"Did you make it up?"

Rosie answered her. "He stole it from Big John. At every family event—including our wedding—Big John was always asked to make a toast. And that's what he always said."

I added, "He claimed that he heard it from his grandfather, your Great-Great-Grandpa Johnny, who came over from Ireland, but I think he came up with it himself. He had a gift for saying the right thing."

"You miss him, don't you?"

"I sure do. This is our first family wedding in almost ninety years that Big John didn't attend."

"He's with us in spirit."

"Yes, he is." I pointed at Joey, who was refilling Father Gil's glass. "The family tradition lives on and is in good hands."

I thought of my mom and dad; my older brother, Tommy; Big John and Aunt Kate; Sylvia and her late husband, Eduardo; and all of our family members who had celebrated almost a century of major life events in this building. I was looking at Joey and Tommy when I realized that Sylvia had joined us.

"You ready to go home, Mama?" Rosie asked.

"Actually, I need a ride to Marin."

Rosie stood up. "Is everything okay?"

"Fine, Rosita. Did you get Tony's text?"

"No." Rosie glanced at her phone. "I ran out of battery."

Sylvia flashed the Fernandez family smile. "Rolanda went into labor. Zach is taking her to Marin General. Tony said that he will meet us there. If we leave now, we can be there when the baby is born."

58

"ONE MORE ROUND"

Joey walked up to our table in the back room of Dunleavy's, tossed his dishtowel over his shoulder just the way Big John had taught him, and flashed a wistful smile. "One more round?"

I shook my head. "Thanks, Joey. I think we're good for now."

"Let me know if you change your mind." He headed back to the bar.

Dunleavy's was quiet at nine o'clock the following night, a Sunday, which happened to be New Year's Day. The football games were finished, and the holiday crowd had dissipated. Rosie, Sylvia, Pete, and I were splitting two orders of fish and chips. I was nursing a Guinness. Rosie and Pete drank coffee. Sylvia was sipping sherry. Tommy was playing pool with Donna and Margaret. Nady and Max were throwing darts with Terrence "The Terminator." Luna was sleeping in the corner in Lucky's old spot. Grace and Chuck were on their way to New Zealand for their honeymoon.

Just another Sunday night at Dunleavy's.

Pete looked up from his phone. "Anything more on Damian Mason or Susan Gallardo?"

Rosie answered him. "Mason cut a deal to plead guilty to a single count of felony drug trafficking in exchange for a reduced sentence of seven years. He's also going to testify against Gallardo, who is going to be indicted on drug dealing and a second-degree murder charge."

Pete grinned. "Happy New Year."

"Looks like we're going to get another good result."

Pete looked my way. "Nice work, Mick."

"Thanks, Pete. You, too."

"Any word on Reggie?"

"We got him into transitional housing with on-site alcohol and drug counseling. He's stayed clean since the trial ended. There are no guarantees, but so far, so good."

"I hope he makes it."

"Me, too."

I watched as my brother-the-ex-cop-turned-private-eye headed over to the pool table to get schooled by his daughter-the-budding-pool-shark.

Sylvia turned my way. "Another crypto company went under on Friday."

"I heard. It's been a rough couple of months." In November, a high-flying firm called FTX had lost almost forty billion dollars and gone bankrupt. Its thirty-year-old wunderkind founder, the son of two Stanford law professors, was arrested for fraud. Several other crypto firms had filed for bankruptcy. "There will be more, Sylvia. They're calling it the 'crypto winter.'"

"Sounds like Tyson Gore's company wasn't the only one built on a shaky foundation."

"So it seems."

She smiled triumphantly. "I told you that crypto was a hustle."

Joey walked in and pointed at the empty chair next to mine. "May I join you?"

"Of course."

He took his seat. "I can't believe you people are still awake. You were up all night."

Rosie chuckled. "We always end up here, Joey. And yes, it's been an eventful weekend."

I did my best impression of Nick "The Dick." "Indeed it has."

Joey smiled. "Are Rolanda and the baby okay?"

Sylvia answered him. "Everybody's fine. They're going home tomorrow."

"Excellent. The new year is off to a fine start."

Sylvia pulled out her iPhone and beamed with great-grandmotherly pride as she showed Joey a dozen photos of her new great-grandson, Antonio Eduardo Fernandez

Epstein, who arrived after putting his mother through twelve hours of labor. He was named after his grandfather, Tony, and his great-grandfather, Eduardo, Sylvia's late husband.

"A handsome lad," Joey said.

"A big lad," Sylvia replied. "Nine pounds two ounces. Twenty-one inches long."

"Another football player."

Sylvia smiled. "I'm hoping for a doctor."

Joey pointed at Rosie and me. "Or a lawyer."

"We'll see."

Joey turned to Rosie. "Grace's wedding was beautiful. It reminded me of yours. I was just a kid, but I had a great time."

Rosie winked. "Did your grandfather give you a shot of whiskey at our wedding the way you gave one to Tommy last night?"

Joey didn't fluster. "Family tradition."

Sylvia's eyes twinkled. "Joseph, would you mind if I ask you something?"

"Of course, Sylvia."

"Are you seeing anybody?"

"You mean a woman?"

"Yes, dear. I was wondering if you have a girlfriend."

"Not at the moment."

And not for the last ten years.

"Would you be interested in meeting somebody?" Sylvia asked.

Joey hesitated. "Uh, sure. I guess."

"Good. You met my friend, Margarita, at the wedding. Her granddaughter lives in the Mission and works for a start-up. She's smart, ambitious, and single." Sylvia held up her phone and showed Joey a photo. "She's also very pretty."

"Yes, she is."

"Margarita and I think you would enjoy each other's company."

"You're trying to fix me up?"

"Yes, dear. She doesn't have any children, but she's divorced." Sylvia eyed him. "Is that a problem?"

"That's fine." He grinned. "You may recall that Rosie was divorced when she met Mike. Do you think we'll like each other?"

"Yes, dear. I have very good instincts." She winked at Rosie. "I convinced Rosita to go out with Michael. She was reluctant at first because she was his supervisor, and the PD's Office had a policy against dating a subordinate."

Rosie interjected. "It didn't take much convincing."

Joey smiled at Sylvia. "You may recall that Rosie and Mike are also divorced."

She waved him off. "I didn't say that my instincts were perfect. Besides, that's just a legal technicality under California law. Rosita and Michael never got an annulment from the Church, so in the eyes of God—and me—they're still married."

"I'm not sure that I'm built for marriage."

"I'm not asking you to get married. I'm simply asking you to give her a call. I have been assured that if you ask her out for dinner, she will say yes. After that, it's up to you. And no burgers or pizza, either. I expect you to take her someplace nice."

"I'd love to meet her," Joey said.

"Excellent. I'll text you her information." Sylvia stood up. "You'll excuse me while I watch my grandchildren play pool." She headed toward the pool table.

Joey leaned back in his chair and spoke to Rosie. "Your mom is still a pistol."

"I haven't won an argument with her in fifty-six years." She arched an eyebrow. "I think you'll like Margarita's granddaughter."

"I hope so." He got up and grabbed his dishtowel. "I have some extra fish and chips in the kitchen. I'll put together a care package for you."

"We can't possibly eat anything more this weekend."

"Save it for tomorrow. You'll thank me."

We will.

As Joey headed to the kitchen, Rosie turned to me. "If Joey and Margarita's granddaughter hit it off, we'll throw them an engagement party here at Dunleavy's and do the wedding at St. Peter's."

"Let's not get ahead of ourselves."

"Never underestimate Mama's instincts."

"I hope it works out." I looked at the photo of Big John above the bar. "So would he." I reached over and squeezed her hand. "It's been a good weekend, Rosie." I pointed at Big John's picture. "He always said that he was born lucky. So are we. He said that we should be thankful for all of the nice people who pass through our lives."

"He was very wise." Her eyes gleamed. "What do you think of our new great-nephew?"

"He was born lucky, too. And he's a keeper."

"Yes, he is." Rosie took a sip of water and her expression turned serious. "Now that the wedding is over, I need to talk to you about something." She glanced at the TV, then she turned back to me. "Rolanda and I had a little conversation about work this afternoon."

"She had a baby less than twelve hours ago. Couldn't it wait?"

"She's very good at multitasking. Besides, she wanted to talk."

Uh-oh. "She isn't going to quit, is she?"

"No, but she wants to extend her maternity leave. And she wants to work a reduced schedule for at least a year after she comes back."

"Fine with me."

"Me, too, but it means that I may need you to work a little harder." She pointed at my heart. "Can your ticker handle an increased workload?"

"You bet. It's as good as new."

"Good to hear. You know how we've talked about Rolanda running for PD when my term is up?"

"Yes."

"She thinks that running for PD with a two-year-old and a newborn is a little more than she can handle. I'm inclined to agree with her."

"So am I."

"She asked me if I would be willing to run for one more term. She promised that she would run for PD at the end of my next term."

"The timing would be better," I said.

"Agreed. That will be my third and final term, Mike. Believe it or not, I'd like to do some travelling while I'm still reasonably young and healthy. I'd like to do it with you."

"Sounds like an excellent plan."

She eyed me. "I do have some conditions if I run."

You always do.

"First, I won't do it unless you agree to stay on for one more term."

"Agreed."

"Second, I need you to make sure that Rolanda and Nady don't leave. It may mean that I'll need to appoint Nady as co-head of the Felony Division in your place at some point."

"Works for me. Anything else?"

She pointed at Terrence. "I need you to convince him to stay, too."

"I'll talk to him again." I winked. "I can be very persuasive."

"I know." She flashed the perfect smile that hadn't changed in all of the years that I had known her. "So we're good to move forward?"

"Yes, we are." I glanced at Sylvia, who was standing next to the pool table. "Have you told your mother?"

"Yes. She isn't crazy about it, but she'll come around—eventually."

I looked into her eyes. "Let me guess. You were waiting until after the baby was born to talk to her about it because you knew that she would be in a good mood, right?"

"Maybe."

"You made up your mind to run again months ago, didn't you?"

"Possibly." Her eyes twinkled. "You know that I like to plan ahead."

I'm not surprised.

She reached across the table and squeezed my hand. "I love you, Mike."

"I love you, too, Rosie. I think this calls for a toast."

"It does."

I turned around and called out to Joey, who was standing under Big John's photo. "One more round, Joey."

He responded with a wide smile. "Coming right up, Mike."

Acknowledgments

As I have noted in the past, I am extraordinarily fortunate to have a very supportive and generous "board of advisors" who graciously provide their time and expertise to help me write these stories. As always, I have a lot of thank yous!

Thanks to my beautiful wife, Linda, who reads my manuscripts, designs the covers, is my online marketing guru, and takes care of all things technological. I couldn't imagine navigating the chaos of the publishing world without you.

Thanks to our son, Alan, for your endless support, editorial suggestions, thoughtful observations, and excellent cover art and formatting work. I will look forward to seeing your first novel on the shelves in bookstores in the near future.

Thanks to our son, Stephen, and our daughter-in-law, Lauren, for being kind, generous, and talented people.

Thanks to my teachers, Katherine Forrest and Michael Nava, who encouraged me to finish my first book. Thanks to the Every Other Thursday Night Writers Group: Bonnie DeClark, Meg Stiefvater, Anne Maczulak, Liz Hartka, Janet Wallace, and Priscilla Royal. Thanks to Bill and Elaine Petrocelli, Kathryn Petrocelli, Karen West, and Luisa Smith at Book Passage.

A huge thanks to Jane Gorsi and Linda Hall for your excellent editing skills.

A huge thanks to even more people for your excellent editing skills: Rich and Leslie Kramer, Lloyd and Joni Russell, Kay Hagan-Haller, Ann Grubbs, and Michael Moody.

Another huge thanks to Vilaska Nguyen of the San Francisco Public Defender's Office for your thoughtful comments and support. If you ever get into serious trouble, he's your guy.

Thanks to Joan Lubamersky for providing the invaluable "Lubamersky Comments" for the fifteenth time.

Thanks to Tim Campbell for your stellar narration of the audio version of this book (and many others in the series). You are the voice of Mike Daley, and you bring these stories to life!

Thanks to my friends and former colleagues at Sheppard, Mullin, Richter & Hampton. I can't mention everybody, but I'd like to note those of you with whom I worked the longest: Randy and Mary Short, Chris and Debbie Neils, Joan Story and Robert Kidd, Donna Andrews, Phil and Wendy Atkins-Patterson, Geri Freeman and David Nickerson, Bill and Barbara Manierre, Betsy McDaniel, Ron and Rita Ryland, Bob Stumpf, Mathilde Kapuano, Susan Sabath, Guy Halgren, Ed Graziani, Julie Penney, Christa Carter, Doug Bacon, Lorna Tanner, Larry Braun, Nady Nikonova, and Joy Siu.

Thanks to Jerry and Dena Wald, Rabbi Neil Brief, Gary and Marla Goldstein, Ron and Betsy Rooth, Jay Flaherty, Debbie and Seth Tanenbaum, Jill Hutchinson and Chuck Odenthal, Tom Bearrows and Holly Hirst, Julie Hart, Burt Rosenberg, Ted George, Phil Dito, Sister Karen Marie Franks, Chuck and Nora Koslosky, Jack Goldthorpe, Char Saper, Flo and Dan Hoffenberg, Lori Gilbert, Paul Sanner, Stewart Baird, Mike Raddie, Peter and Cathy Busch, Steve Murphy, Bob Dugoni, and John Lescroart. Thanks to Gary and Debbie Fields.

Sadly, we recently had to say goodbye to the wonderful Mercedes Crosskill and Marge Gilbert, whose fictional counterparts have been members of Sylvia's mahjongg group for many years. We miss you.

Thanks to Tim and Kandi Durst, and Bob and Cheryl Easter, at the University of Illinois. Thanks to Kathleen

Vanden Heuvel, Bob and Leslie Berring, Jesse Choper, and Mel Eisenberg at Berkeley Law.

Thanks to the incomparable Zvi Danenberg, who motivates me to walk the Larkspur steps.

Thanks as always to Ben, Michelle, and Andy Siegel, Margie and Joe Benak, Joe, Jan, and Julia Garber, Roger and Sharon Fineberg, Scott, Michelle, Kim, and Sophie Harris, Stephanie, Stanley, Will, and Sam Coventry, Cathy, Richard, and Matthew Falco, Sofia Arnell, and Oliver Falco, and Julie Harris and Matthew, Aiden, and Ari Stewart. A huge thanks once again to our mothers, Charlotte Siegel (1928-2016) and Jan Harris (1934-2018), whom we miss every day.

A Note to the Reader

DEAD COIN is a story of San Francisco. It's a tale of hope and greed, innovation and speculation, progress and decline. It's a story that's still being written.

I had been following the crypto boom with fascination, and I was intrigued by the idea of a murder mystery set in the world of cryptocurrency. I had also been following the news of the growing homeless crisis in San Francisco. I wanted to explore how these two worlds might intersect.

I was almost finished with the first draft of **DEAD COIN** when a crypto company called FTX crashed in November of 2022. It was the beginning of what was dubbed the "crypto winter." Thankfully, unlike the plotline in my book, the founder of FTX wasn't killed in Salesforce Park. But I knew that my story was about to become even more timely.

I hope you enjoyed **DEAD COIN**. I enjoy spending time with Mike and Rosie, and I hope that you do, too. If you like my stories, please consider posting an honest review on Amazon or Goodreads. Your words matter and are a great guide to help my stories find future readers.

If you have a chance and would like to chat, please feel free to e-mail me at sheldon@sheldonsiegel.com. We lawyers don't get a lot of fan mail, but it's always nice to hear from my readers. Please bear with me if I don't respond immediately. I answer all of my e-mail myself, so sometimes it takes a little extra time.

Many people have asked to know more about Mike and Rosie's early history. As a thank you to my readers, I wrote **FIRST TRIAL**. It's a short story describing how they met years ago when they were just starting out at the P.D.'s Office. I've included the first chapter below and the full story is available at: www.sheldonsiegel.com.

Also on the website, you can read more about how I came to write my stories, excerpts and behind-the-scenes from the other Mike & Rosie novels and a few other goodies! Let's stay connected. Thanks for reading my story!

Regards,
Sheldon

Excerpt from FIRST TRIAL

Readers have asked to know more about Mike and Rosie's early history. As a thank you to all of you, I wrote this short story about how Mike & Rosie met years ago as they were just starting out at the P.D.'s Office. Here's the first chapter and you can download the full story (for FREE) at: www.sheldonsiegel.com.

1
"DO EXACTLY WHAT I DO"

The woman with the striking cobalt eyes walked up to me and stopped abruptly. "Are you the new file clerk?"

"Uh, no." My lungs filled with the stale air in the musty file room of the San Francisco Public Defender's Office on the third floor of the Stalinesque Hall of Justice on Bryant Street. "I'm the new lawyer."

The corner of her mouth turned up. "The priest?"

"Ex-priest."

"I thought you'd be older."

"I was a priest for only three years."

"You understand that we aren't in the business of saving souls here, right?"

"Right."

Her full lips transformed into a radiant smile as she extended a hand. "Rosie Fernandez."

"Mike Daley."

"You haven't been working here for six months, have you?"

"This is my second day."

"Welcome aboard. You passed the bar, right?"

"Right."

"That's expected."

I met Rosita Carmela Fernandez on the Wednesday after Thanksgiving in 1983. The Summer of Love was a fading memory, and we were five years removed from the Jonestown massacre and the assassinations of Mayor George Moscone and Supervisor Harvey Milk. Dianne Feinstein became the mayor and was governing with a steady hand in Room 200 at City Hall. The biggest movie of the year was *Return of the Jedi*, and the highest-rated TV show was *M*A*S*H*. People still communicated by phone and U.S. mail because e-mail wouldn't become widespread for another decade. We listened to music on LPs and cassettes, but CD players were starting to gain traction. It was still unclear whether VHS or Beta would be the predominant video platform. The Internet was a localized technology used for academic purposes on a few college campuses. Amazon and Google wouldn't be formed for another decade. Mark Zuckerberg hadn't been born.

Rosie's hoop-style earrings sparkled as she leaned against the metal bookcases crammed with dusty case files for long-forgotten defendants. "You local?"

"St. Ignatius, Cal, and Boalt. You?"

"Mercy, State, and Hastings." She tugged at her denim work shirt, which seemed out-of-place in a button-down era where men still wore suits and ties and women wore dresses to the office. "When I was at Mercy, the sisters taught us to beware of boys from S.I."

"When I was at S.I., the brothers taught us to beware of girls from Mercy."

"Did you follow their advice?"

"Most of the time."

The Bay Area was transitioning from the chaos of the sixties and the malaise of the seventies into the early stages of the tech boom. Apple had recently gone public and was still being run by Steve Jobs and Steve Wozniak. George Lucas was making Star Wars movies in a new state-of-the-art facility in Marin County. Construction cranes dotted downtown as new office towers were changing the skyline. Union Square was beginning a makeover after Nieman-Marcus bought out the City of Paris and built a flashy new store at the corner of Geary and Stockton, across from I. Magnin. The upstart 49ers had won their first Super Bowl behind a charismatic quarterback named Joe Montana and an innovative coach named Bill Walsh.

Her straight black hair shimmered as she let out a throaty laugh. "What parish?"

"Originally St. Peter's. We moved to St. Anne's when I was a kid. You?"

"St. Peter's. My parents still live on Garfield Square."

"Mine grew up on the same block."

St. Peter's Catholic Church had been the anchor of the Mission District since 1867. In the fifties and sixties, the working-class Irish and Italian families had relocated to the outer reaches of the City and to the suburbs. When they moved out, the Latino community moved in. St. Peter's was still filled every Sunday morning, but four of the five masses were celebrated in Spanish.

"I was baptized at St. Peter's," I said. "My parents were married there."

"Small world."

"How long have you worked here?" I asked.

"Two years. I was just promoted to the Felony Division."

"Congratulations."

"Thank you. I need to transition about six dozen active misdemeanor cases to somebody else. I trust that you have time?"

"I do."

"Where do you sit?"

"In the corner of the library near the bathrooms."

"I'll find you."

Twenty minutes later, I was sitting in my metal cubicle when I was startled by the voice from the file room. "Ever tried a case?" Rosie asked.

"It's only my second day."

"I'm going to take that as a no. Ever been inside a courtroom?"

"Once or twice."

"To work?"

"To watch."

"You took Criminal Law at Boalt, right?"

"Right."

"And you've watched Perry Mason on TV?"

"Yes."

"Then you know the basics. The courtrooms are upstairs." She handed me a file. "Your first client is Terrence Love."

"The boxer?"

"The retired boxer."

Terrence "The Terminator" Love was a six-foot-six-inch, three-hundred-pound small-time prizefighter who had grown up in the projects near Candlestick Park. His lifetime record was two wins and nine losses. The highlight of his career was when he was hired to be a sparring partner for George Foreman, who was training to fight Muhammad Ali at the time. Foreman knocked out The Terminator with the first punch that he threw—effectively ending The Terminator's careers as a boxer and a sparring partner.

"What's he doing these days?" I asked.

"He takes stuff that doesn't belong to him."

"Last time I checked, stealing was against the law."

"Your Criminal Law professor would be proud."

"What does he do when he isn't stealing?"

"He drinks copious amounts of King Cobra."

It was cheap malt liquor.

She added, "He's one of our most reliable customers."

Got it. "How often does he get arrested?"

"At least once or twice a month."

"How often does he get convicted?"

"Usually once or twice a month." She flashed a knowing smile. "You and Terrence are going to get to know each other very well."

I got the impression that it was a rite of passage for baby P.D.'s to cut their teeth representing The Terminator. "What did he do this time?"

She held up a finger. "Rule number one: a client hasn't 'done' anything unless he admits it as part of a plea bargain, or he's convicted by a jury. Until then, all charges are 'alleged.'"

"What is the D.A. *alleging* that Terrence did?"

"He *allegedly* broke into a car that didn't belong to him."

"Did he *allegedly* take anything?"

"He didn't have time. A police officer was standing next to him when he *allegedly* broke into the car. The cop arrested him on the spot."

"Sounds like Terrence isn't the sharpest instrument in the operating room."

"We don't ask our clients to pass an intelligence test before we represent them. For a guy who used to make a living trying to beat the daylights out of his opponents, Terrence is reasonably intelligent and a nice person who has never hurt anybody. The D.A. charged him with auto burglary."

"Can we plead it out?"

"*We* aren't going to do anything. *You* are going to handle this case. And contrary to what you've seen on TV, our job is to try cases, not to cut quick deals. Understood?"

"Yes."

"I had a brief discussion about a plea bargain with Bill McNulty, who is the Deputy D.A. handling this case. No deal unless Terrence pleads guilty to a felony."

"Seems a bit harsh."

"It is. That's why McNulty's nickname is 'McNasty.' You'll be seeing a lot of him, too. He's a hardass who is trying to impress his boss. He's also very smart and tired of seeing Terrence every couple of weeks. In fairness, I can't blame him."

"So you want me to take this case to trial?"

"That's what we do. Trial starts Monday at nine a.m. before Judge Stumpf." She handed me a manila case file. "Rule number two: know the record. You need to memorize everything inside. Then you should go upstairs to the jail and introduce yourself to your new client."

I could feel my heart pounding. "Could I buy you a cup of coffee and pick your brain about how you think it's best for me to prepare?"

"I haven't decided whether you're coffee-worthy yet."

"Excuse me?"

"I'm dealing with six dozen active cases. By the end of the week, so will you. If you want to be successful, you need to figure stuff out on your own."

I liked her directness. "Any initial hints that you might be willing to pass along?"

"Yes. Watch me. Do exactly what I do."

"Sounds like good advice."

She grinned. "It is."

There's more to this story and it's yours for FREE!

Get the rest of **FIRST TRIAL** at:

www.sheldonsiegel.com/first-trial

About the Author

Sheldon Siegel is the New York Times best-selling author of the critically acclaimed legal thrillers featuring San Francisco criminal defense attorneys Mike Daley and Rosie Fernandez, two of the most beloved characters in contemporary crime fiction. He is also the author of the thriller novel The Terrorist Next Door featuring Chicago homicide detectives David Gold and A.C. Battle. His books have been translated into a dozen languages and sold millions of copies. A native of Chicago, Sheldon earned his undergraduate degree from the University of Illinois in Champaign in 1980, and his law degree from Berkeley Law in 1983. He specialized in corporate law with several large San Francisco law firms for forty years.

Sheldon began writing his first book, Special Circumstances, on a laptop computer during his daily commute on the ferry from Marin County to San Francisco. Sheldon is a San Francisco Library Literary Laureate, a former member of the Board of Directors and former President of the Northern California chapter of the Mystery Writers of America, and an active member of the International Thriller Writers and Sisters in Crime. His work has been displayed at the Bancroft Library at the University of California at Berkeley, and he has been recognized as a Distinguished Alumnus of the University of Illinois and a Northern California Super Lawyer.

Sheldon lives in the San Francisco area with his wife, Linda. Sheldon and Linda are the proud parents of twin sons named Alan and Stephen. Sheldon is a lifelong fan of the Chicago Bears, White Sox, Bulls and Blackhawks. He is currently working on his next novel.

Sheldon welcomes your comments and feedback. Please email him at sheldon@sheldonsiegel.com. For more information on Sheldon, book signings, the "making of" his books, and more, please visit his website at www.sheldonsiegel.com.

Connect with Sheldon

Email: sheldon@sheldonsiegel.com
Website: www.sheldonsiegel.com
Amazon: amazon.com/author/sheldonsiegel
Facebook: www.facebook.com/sheldonsiegelauthor
Goodreads: www.goodreads.com/sheldonsiegel
Bookbub: bookbub.com/authors/sheldon-siegel
Twitter: @SheldonSiegel

Also By Sheldon Siegel

**Mike Daley/Rosie Fernandez
Novels**
Special Circumstances
Incriminating Evidence
Criminal Intent
Final Verdict
The Confession
Judgment Day
Perfect Alibi
Felony Murder Rule
Serve and Protect
Hot Shot
The Dreamer
Final Out
Last Call
Double Jeopardy
Dead Coin

Short Stories
(available at sheldonsiegel.com)
First Trial
The Maltese Pigeon - A Nick "the Dick" Story

David Gold/A.C. Battle Novels
The Terrorist Next Door